# THE LAST TIME I SAW

# RIO

## A Novel

### BY
### DALE BOYD

This book is a work of fiction. Any resemblance of the characters or their names to any person living or dead is purely coincidental. Settings, business names, events,and locales are used fictitiously as part of the storyline.

Copyright @ 2017 by Dale Boyd

All Rights Reserved

No part of this book may be printed or reproduced electronically without express permission from the author. The author has no control over nor does he assume any responsibility for third party websites or their content.

The Last Time I Saw Rio
ISBN: 9781946982780

**Visit the author's website @ daleboyd.net**

# Dedication

*For Celeste —*

*A Knight in Shining Armor*

## Acknowledgements

Whenever I make a list of people who encourage me to write a book, or provide help in some way, however obscure, I'm always afraid that I will unintentionally leave someone's name off the list. So, thanks to everybody out there who cared enough to take an interest in this project. I appreciate your kindness, patience, suggestions, and, most of all, your friendship.

# CHAPTER 1

## July 7  0330 Hours  •  Rio de Janeiro, Brazil

Duncan Ruiz is more than a little peeved when his telephone rings. It is three-thirty in the morning and it is the second time that he has been awakened by an annoying call. The first was from his ex-wife complaining about alimony and child-support. This conversation is different, but no less irritating.

"I'm sorry to disturb you, Duncan, but something has come up and I think you should see it."

The caller can hear the irritation in his boss' voice when he replies, "What's so damn important that you need to call me at this hour?"

The younger voice on the other end of the line is hesitant when it says, "I'm on site at a murder and the victim has a card in his wallet with your telephone number on it. I've kept this from the patrolman who responded to the call and, so far, I'm the only one who knows about it. What do you want me to do?"

Ruiz's mind is racing when he says, "Give me your location. I'll get there as soon as I can. Speak of this to no one."

"You got it, boss, see you soon."

Although his thoughts have shifted into overdrive, Duncan Ruiz takes his time putting on his clothes and combing his hair. He didn't get to be chief of detectives by racing into things without thinking them through. Daniel Montoya, the young policeman who just called him, is his protégé and a fine one at that. The kid had enough political savvy to call him without getting the rest of the unit involved. He'll make an excellent detective someday and Ruiz is grateful for the heads-up.

A few minutes later, he's in his car driving to the scene, a modest hotel near Ipanema Beach. Security is pretty good at the hotel and, while there is crime in this area, a murder inside a guesthouse is highly unusual. Most of the criminal activity in this part of town relates to pickpockets harassing tourists, occasional domestic violence, and some minor gang activity, none of which would readily translate into murder in a hotel room. He thinks this will likely be a crime of passion because most murders fall into that category.

Those are his thoughts when he arrives at the hotel entrance. A squad car is sitting out front with its lights flashing. Ruiz advises the patrolman to kill the flashing lights so as not to draw any more attention to the scene than necessary. His new assignment will be to keep a crowd from gathering in front of the building. Not wishing to offend a high ranking police official, the officer complies immediately. Once inside, Ruiz walks the corridor to a room on the first floor. Daniel Montoya is sitting in a chair blocking the entrance.

Ruiz asks, "What have we got, Danny?"

The younger man snuffs out his cigarette and jumps to his feet, almost standing at attention. Ruiz smiles to himself and places a calming hand on the kid's shoulder.

He says, "Relax, Danny. Take your time and walk me through it — slowly."

Montoya pulls a ragged looking notebook from his pocket and starts his narrative.

"At about eight-thirty, the front desk clerk gets a call from an adjoining room complaining about some sort of ruckus next door. He calls the room and asks what's going on. A man answers and says he and his friend had too much to drink and that things got a little rowdy. He apologizes and says he'll keep it down."

Ruiz asks, "Who found the body?"

"A hotel security guard went up to check on the noise complaint and found the door ajar. He went inside to look around. That's when he found the dead guy in the bathtub and called us. I looked the room over when I got here and the place is pin neat, except for the bathroom. The bed has never been slept in and there is nothing in the drawers or the closet."

Ruiz nods and motions his assistant to continue.

"The room is registered to Richard Hamilton, at least that's the name he gave when he checked in. Normally, they ask for some kind of ID when a guest wants a room, a passport or maybe a driver's license. This guy bypasses the system altogether, pays cash for the room and slips the desk clerk a hundred bucks to let him check in without an ID. He tells him that he may bring a woman to his room later and that he wants to keep it quiet. The clerk takes the money and gives the guy a key, no questions asked. I'm thinking right away that this must be our doer, but you taught me to look at everything before jumping to conclusions."

The more Duncan Ruiz works with this young cop, the more he likes him. He pays attention to details and he knows how to keep his mouth shut.

He asks, "Danny, did you talk to the people who heard the ruckus?"

"I did better than that boss. They're a couple and I kept them waiting in their room until you got here. The guy's pretty nervous, but the woman is cool — you know, like she's been through this before. You want to talk to them?"

"We'll get to that later. What do we have on the victim?"

"The guy's name is Luis Marcos. He's a commercial pilot and the date stamp on his passport says he just got back here from the States. I found some old pay stubs in his wallet. Apparently, he was working for some small charter company on the East Coast called Keystone Airlines. I ran his name through the computer and I was surprised when something popped. The American Feds are looking for him. He skipped out on his bail in some sort of criminal case. I don't have enough information to make a connection between that and what's happened here, but this guy bounced out of there on a two-million dollar bond. Could be whoever put up his bail money is pissed off and came after him."

Ruiz nods and asks, "Did you find anything else that seemed out of place?"

"I haven't had time to give the room a thorough going over, but I did find a syringe in the bathroom wastebasket. At first, I thought it was typical drug paraphernalia, but then, I found a half empty vial of sodium pentothal in there too. The body has a single gunshot wound to the chest. There's also a puncture wound on his left arm and the corpse has a couple of finger nails missing. I'm guessing the guy was tortured and that somebody was looking for information. His passport, wallet, money, and credit cards were all there, nothing was taken. So, it seems to me that robbery is an unlikely motive. Do you recognize him from his passport picture?"

The older detective examines the photo, shakes his head and says, "Nope, I've never seen this guy before. Let me see the card with my number on it."

Montoya hands it to him and says, "It actually has three numbers on it, yours and one that traces back to an apartment here in Rio. The other number is a European exchange and it's encrypted. You have to type in some sort of code to access it. I didn't try either number because I wanted to run it by you first."

Ruiz is upset, but he hides it well. What the hell was this guy doing with his cellphone number? That alone is disconcerting, but what really troubles him is the European telephone number. He has a card in his own wallet with the same number on it, and that is something he can't ignore. It is a number that is only to be called when there is real trouble and he will be obliged to call it within twenty-four hours. He does not like where this is going.

He says, "Danny, let's go talk to the desk clerk and see if he can give us a description of the guy who rented the room."

Montoya asks, "Don't you want to look at the crime scene first?"

Ruiz shakes his head and says, "No, I always like to talk to any potential witnesses and get their information while it's still fresh in their memories. The crime scene is secure and it isn't going anywhere. This way, I'm not biasing what I see with personal opinion or the emotional trauma of seeing the victim for the first time. We cops get to look at some pretty gruesome stuff and most of us don't acknowledge that it can tear us up inside. Doing it this way helps keep the shock of seeing the dead to a minimum and makes it easier to think through the problem."

A few minutes later, they are talking with the desk clerk and he gives them a brief description of their suspect.

He says, "The guy was about six feet tall, mustache, dark-haired, well-dressed with a slightly muscular build. He had bright green eyes, which is something you don't see very often in men. Other than that, he was pretty unremarkable."

Ruiz asks, "Any distinguishing marks — tattoos, scars, or skin discoloration?"

"There weren't any that I could see."

"What language did he speak and did he have an accent of any kind that may give us a clue as to where he's from?"

The clerk pauses a moment to think before saying, "Interesting you should ask that. He spoke to me in English, maybe with an American southern accent, but he spoke to the doorman twice in perfect Portuguese, almost as if he'd lived here all his life."

Ruiz says, "A forensic artist will be here shortly. I want you to tell him what you told me, to see if we can put together a sketch of this guy. Here's my card. Call me if you think of anything else and thanks for your help."

The clerk nods and Ruiz and Danny Montoya walk down the hallway to interview the couple in the room adjacent to where the murder took place.

# CHAPTER 2

## July 7 0030 hours • Brooks Falls, Pennsylvania

My name is Devin Ross and I wake abruptly from a deep sleep startling my girlfriend, Harley, who is sleeping peacefully next to me. I glance at the clock. It's half past midnight.

She sits up, places a hand gently on my shoulder and asks, "What's wrong, babe? You look like you've just seen a ghost."

"Bad dream," I say hastily.

She snuggles closer and says, "You want to talk about it?"

I am reluctant to discuss the cause of my sudden wakefulness, because I am not certain that she will be comfortable with my explanation. I occasionally have prescient dreams and they are sometimes disturbing. When I was in college, I dreamed of meeting a beautiful woman and walking the beach with her in Portugal. I also dreamt that the relationship ended abruptly with great disappointment and it came to pass shortly after our romance had started. I woke on another occasion after having a terrible vision of a close friend perishing in an automobile accident. She died a day later, almost exactly as I had envisioned it. This dream was different.

I could see a faceless man standing in the shadows watching, or possibly even following me. He was unassuming and of modest stature, maybe six feet tall. Yet, I knew that he was capable of great violence. An even stranger thought was that

I had the sense that I was looking for this man and that we were connected to each other in some way, but I couldn't say how. There is one other curious element from my dream that I'm able to recall. The setting for this vision seems to be somewhere in South America, possibly Rio de Janeiro. I lived in that city from time to time and I am wondering if my imagination is conjuring these images to help me make sense of the rest of the dream. It is all quite unsettling and Harley is keenly aware of my discomfort.

She makes another inquiry asking, "Are you worried about losing your job? I know you chewed out the owner's nephew today and his uncle didn't take it kindly. You don't rile easily, what'd the kid do to get your dander up?"

"He was hung over, Harley, and I could smell the booze on his breath. The weather was bad and I didn't want him flying one of my airplanes into a raging rainstorm while he was still half in the bag. I wanted to give him a breathalyzer test, but he refused. If I got the FAA involved, they'd probably yank his license for six months and that would kill his career. So, I grounded him and docked his pay, which kept the whole business in-house. I figured he'd go to the old man and cry foul, but I'm not worried about it."

She says, "I saw him in Bruno's office singing his greatest hits after you left today and that didn't do you any favors. If it makes you feel any better, I would have done the same thing if I'd seen him first, but this situation is a political time bomb and you know it. Bruno is quietly looking for someone to replace you."

I smile back at her and say, "I'm pretty sure he's going to offer you the job."

She's a bit taken aback and says, "How'd you know? He talked to me about it a couple of days ago."

"Harley, outside of me, you're the most qualified person in the company for the position."

She laughs and says, "He's only offering me the job because he likes looking at my butt whenever I walk past his office."

"Can't say that I blame him for that, Harley, I like watching your butt when it walks by, too!"

She says, "You don't seem to be too concerned about losing your job."

"This was an interim position when the company was sold a few months ago. New owners like to put their personal stamp on everything and I knew I'd be a goner when Bruno bought the company."

"What are you going to do if he lets you go?"

"I don't know, but I'm in no hurry to look for work. Money's not a problem and it might be nice to have a little time off. Maybe, I'll visit some friends for a few days."

She muses for a moment and asks, "If that's not on your mind, what woke you up?"

I love Harley and, although we've only known each other a year or so, I trust her completely. So, I tell her about my dream and my prescient experiences with dreams in the past. I can see from her expression that she's skeptical and she dismisses the matter with a marvelous suggestion.

She jumps on top of me and says, "Why don't we make the problem go away with some wild and raucous sex?"

I smile back and say, "I thought you'd never ask."

A moment later, the room fills with laughter.

# CHAPTER 3

## July 7  0445 Hours  •  Rio de Janeiro

Duncan Ruiz enters the hotel room next to the one where the murder victim was found. Detective Montoya introduces him to the man who heard the ruckus through the wall. He hands Ruiz the man's passport and the detective compares the picture to the man in front of him.

Montoya says, "Duncan, this is Mr. Stewart, he's an American traveling here on business."

Ruiz extends his hand and says, "Thank you for taking the time to talk with us, Mr. Stewart. What brings you to Rio?"

Stewart is a balding man of indeterminate age who is sweating profusely, and he is unable to look at Ruiz directly. The detective tries to put him at ease. He pours a glass of water and hands it to him.

"Sir, you're not in any trouble here. We're just trying to find out what happened. Try to relax and tell me a little about yourself."

The man hesitates ever so slightly and says, "I'm a software engineer from St. Louis. My company sent me here to get one of our systems up and running for an insurance company."

"Are you traveling alone?" he asks.

"No, my wife came with me. She's staying at a hotel across town."

Ruiz gestures toward the bathroom, where he can hear water running.

"Then," he asks, "Who's the lady in the lavatory?"

The man is literally squirming in his seat when a very attractive woman emerges from the bathroom. She speaks directly to the detective.

"Hello, Duncan," she says, "Long time - no see."

He smiles back at her and says, "Hello, Belle. It's been awhile."

Ruiz now has the answer to his question. Belle is a call girl working for a high-class escort service in downtown Rio. They met several years ago when he was working vice. Mr. Stewart is one of her clients.

She says, "Let him go, Duncan. He doesn't know anything and I can fill you in on the details later."

The detective winks at Belle and nods to his assistant, "Danny, why don't you take Belle down to the hotel bar and buy her a drink on me. I'll meet you there in a few minutes."

After they leave, he turns his attention to Mr. Stewart and asks, "What can you tell me about the guy in the room next door?"

"I really don't remember anything. Belle was the one who saw the guy. I just want to go home."

Ruiz knows instinctively that Stewart is lying and he is suddenly very angry. He reaches over and grabs the front of his shirt and shouts at him.

"Listen, you little weasel! I've got a dead body next door and you're going to tell me everything or I'm going to arrest you for soliciting a prostitute and then I'm going to call your wife. So, what's it going to be?"

Stewart is shaking badly when he says, "I didn't see much. I was on my way down the hall to get some ice so Belle and I could have a drink. I'm headed back to the room when two guys come stumbling by me. One is really drunk and the other man is holding him up. The sober one says his friend had too much to drink and that he's helping him back to his room. I didn't think much about it, until I heard the ruckus in the bathroom a little later. Belle heard it too."

"Anything else?" he asks.

"We heard what sounded like a muffled gunshot, you know, like the kind you hear in the movies when the guy uses a silencer. Belle says let's get the hell out of here and find another hotel. We got dressed and started to leave. When we opened the door, we ran smack into a different guy leaving the other room."

"What did he look like and what was he wearing?"

"You know, he looked almost like the first guy. They could have been brothers, except this guy doesn't have green eyes. I'm five foot eleven and he was maybe an inch or two taller than me, six feet or so. He had on a blue T-shirt and jeans and he was carrying a briefcase. I'm guessing he was in his late forties, possibly fifty. He was clean-shaven, mostly ordinary looking. It would be hard to pick him out of a crowd back in the States. except that he looked very fit, military fit, just like the other fellow. He was wearing a Rolex watch, a Submariner model I think. It was hard not to notice a forty thousand-dollar wristwatch, because I've always wanted one. He also had on a pair of rubber gloves, the kind doctors wear."

Ruiz stops him and asks, "Are you sure the guy was clean-shaven?"

Stewart says, "Yeah, I'm sure, because he looked right at me."

"Anything else?"

"Yeah, his eyes were a little strange, almost like he was wearing grey contacts, but I'm not sure."

"What'd he do when he saw you and Belle?"

"He didn't do anything. He just smiled at us, nodded, glanced at his watch, and walked down the hall to the exit."

"You mean he ran down the hall, don't you?"

"No sir, he walked very casually."

"Why didn't you and Belle leave?"

"A hotel security guard was making the rounds and Belle thought he might recognize her. So we ducked back into the room. Things were quiet again and we decided to stay. The next thing we hear is detective Montoya knocking at our door. He calls you and here we are."

Ruiz says, "We've got a sketch artist coming to the hotel and I'd like you to spend a few minutes with him and describe what you saw. You'll need to stay in town a day or so until we wrap up this part of the investigation. I'll need to keep your passport temporarily."

Stewart panics and grabs the detective's arm.

"I can't do that," he says. "My wife will divorce me if she finds out that I was with another woman. I'll pay you whatever you want to make this go away."

Ruiz can feel the anger rising in his body. His own wife, whom he loved dearly, left him after she had an affair with another man and he's never gotten over it.

He snaps at Stewart and says, "Take your hands off me!"

Stewart backs away and thrusts some money at Ruiz.

"Look, here's five hundred. Just let me go."

Ruiz starts to walk away when Stewart grabs his arm again. The detective explodes and punches him squarely in the face, knocking the man to the ground. Stewart is in shock.

"What'd you do that for?"

"That's for trying to bribe a police officer and cheating on your wife. Clean yourself up and then we'll go talk to Belle."

A short time later, they enter the hotel bar. Montoya is shocked, but hardly surprised when he sees the bruise on Stewart's face. He knows that Duncan Ruiz has a short fuse when people try to lie to him or cover things up. This guy must have done something really stupid to aggravate his boss.

Ruiz says, "Danny, take Mr. Stewart back to the lobby and then call his wife. If she asks what happened, tell her somebody mugged him and tried to take his wallet. Mr. Stewart fought back gallantly, but the perp got away. He's going to give a description of the guy to the sketch artist when he gets here. Afterwards, drive him back to his hotel to meet his wife. If she has any questions, she can call me."

Ruiz turns to Stewart and says, "Isn't that right, sir?"

Stewart nods gratefully and Montoya escorts the man from the room. Duncan takes a seat across from Belle and has a sip of her scotch.

"Talk to me," he says.

She responds with, "The guy you're looking for was bald with a bushy beard and ---."

Ruiz raises a hand and speaks emphatically, "Stop right there, Belle. Mr. Stewart tried to lie to me and things didn't go well. We've been friends a long time and I'd hate to see you do anything to change that."

She sighs and says, "I've seen your suspect a couple of times and I slept with him once. I met him during a party at the American Embassy here in Rio. The Embassy calls me now and then to take care of some of their high-profile visitors. I'm over there doing the deed for a Saudi Arabian dignitary in one of the back offices. When I finish, he wants to hand me off to his security guard. I say no way and get up to leave. The guard pulls out a knife and threatens to cut my throat if I don't take care of him."

"What happened next?"

"The man you're interested in shows up out of nowhere and gets between me and the fellow with the knife. The security guard lunges at him with the blade and your guy takes him out instantly. I've never seen anyone move that fast. He hit him three or four times before I could blink and the guy crumbles to the floor, out cold."

"You think our man works at the American Embassy?"

"I don't know, but it's possible. After the excitement, he drove me home and walked me to my door. I wanted to thank him, so I gave him my card and told him to look me up if he ever wanted to have a good time. He dropped by my condo a couple of months later. He took me out to the best restaurant in town and we went dancing. The guy was a perfect gentleman and damn good in bed, too. After that, I didn't see him again until tonight."

"Your guy got a name?"

"He calls himself Richard Hamilton. That's everything I know. Can I go home now?"

Ruiz sighs and says, "Yeah, get the hell out of here."

Belle leans across the table, kisses the detective on the

cheek, and says, "You're a good man. Your wife was a fool to leave you."

She pauses a moment before leaving and says, "Be careful, Duncan. This guy's dangerous. He took out that Arab security guard in a couple of seconds and he wasn't even breathing hard when the guy hit the floor. He's armed, too, and he wears a pistol like it's part of his body. I saw it that time he spent the night at my place."

Detective Ruiz is alone with his thoughts, and although he's worried, he's beginning to develop a game plan. When Danny Montoya gets back, they'll give the dead man's room a thorough going over, looking for anything that might help them track down the killer. Next, they will follow up on the telephone numbers found in the dead man's wallet. In the morning, he'll make a call to the States and talk to the FBI to see what they have on the dead guy and see why he left the country. Then, and only then, will he call the European number printed on the business card and update the voice on the other end about the status of his investigation. He finishes the last of Belle's drink, lights a cigarette, and waits for his younger assistant to return. It is going to be a long night.

# CHAPTER 4

## July 7 1145 Hours • Erie Airport

## Keystone Airline Offices

I'M SITTING AT MY DESK FINISHING UP SOME FAA paperwork for our little charter airline as the company owner steps into my office and closes the door. He looks stressed and I'm pretty sure he's dropped by to fire me. I decide to launch the first volley.

"Morning. Bruno. I assume you're here to tell me that I'm out of a job."

My boss is completely bewildered, something, that at least for the moment, pleases me to no end. He recovers quickly and comes directly to the point.

"Devin, I've decided to move the company in a different direction and put my own management team in place. It's nothing personal, just a business decision that had to be made. You haven't done anything wrong and I'd be happy to keep you on as a line pilot until you find something else. But, I've decided to promote Harley Jensen from chief pilot to director of operations."

I smile back at him and say, "Getting fired is always personal, Bruno, but I knew this position wouldn't last when Walter Paris sold you the company. I've already typed my resignation and all that's left for me to do is to date and sign it. When would you like me to leave?"

He hesitates slightly before he says, "I hate to ask, but would you mind sticking around a couple of days to break Harley in?"

"No problem, I've been anticipating this and I've already put together some material for my replacement. Is there anything else on your mind?"

He stares at me incredulously and asks, "How is it that you're so calm about all of this?"

"It was a pretty easy call, Bruno. During the last year, some people associated with the company were arrested for money laundering, an employee was murdered, there was an FBI investigation, we had an airplane crash, killing the pilot, and another airplane heavily damaged when it struck a flock of seagulls. On top of everything else, the FAA is watching us like a hawk, hoping we'll screw up so they can yank our operating certificate. Some of that happened on my watch and it seemed likely that I'd catch the heat for it."

He says, "Yeah, but I heard through the grapevine that when you found out what was happening that you worked behind the scenes with the police to catch the people responsible. None of it was your fault."

"It's all about perception, boss. People don't like digging for the truth because it's easier to read the headline or catch the sound bite on the six o'clock news. If you fire me, the public and private perception will be that you got rid of the problem."

He nods and stands to leave the room, but not before taking a parting shot.

"I think you were pretty hard on my nephew yesterday. Basically, he's a good kid. He just needs to get a handle on his wild side. You were young once and I'm surprised that you can't see that he only needs a little guidance."

I don't even try to hide my contempt when I say, "Bruno, you're the only reason I didn't fire the little snot. I checked his driving record and he's got a DUI, two speeding tickets, and a citation for disorderly conduct, all in the last year. The kid's a mess and you need to get rid of him before he crashes an airplane and takes you and the company down with him."

He snarls back at me and says, "Well, that's my call now, isn't it?"

My phone rings almost immediately after he leaves my office. It's my friend Sam Dorsey and he wants to get together for lunch. Sam was the FBI agent I helped when our company was under investigation a few months ago.

He says, "I got a couple of things to run by you that might be of interest. You want to meet at Eddie's Place at about twelve-thirty and down a couple of chili dogs?"

"Sounds like a plan, Sam, I'll meet you there in about twenty minutes."

A short time later, my friend and I are munching away on a couple of Eddie's famous Chicago Dogs with mustard, jalapenos, kraut, and pickles. Sam interrupts my reverie with some sobering news from his side of the tracks.

He says, "Got a call from a cop in Rio de Janeiro this morning about a man they found murdered in his hotel room last night."

I ask casually, "Why'd he call you?"

"The guy was a pilot who used to work for Keystone Airlines. His name was Luis Marcos, remember him?"

I stop eating immediately because Sam has my undivided attention. Luis Marcos was one of three pilots hired by my airline's former owner, Walter Paris, to work out of our company's satellite operation in Cleveland. Paris used those men and some of the company airplanes to move laundered drug money to a series of small town banks across Indiana and Ohio. Paris promoted me to director of operations and transferred me to the Erie office, effectively locking me out of their activities. His plan was to make it look like I was running the show if things went sideways and leave me holding the bag. I got suspicious and started quietly nosing around their activities. When I finally figured out what was going on, I went to the authorities who, unbeknownst to me, were already investigating Walter Paris and his cronies. There was a plethora of government agencies involved, DEA, CIA, FBI, Treasury Department, Secret Service, along with state and local police. There was a lot of jurisdictional infighting and I was caught in the middle of it, because they all wondered if I might have been involved in some of the shenanigans. Sam Dorsey was the only one who trusted me enough to act on the information that I had. Over time, we became friends.

"Sam, I assume that you wanted to talk to me because you think the trouble down south might be getting too close to home."

"That's about the size of it, Devin. Altogether, there have been four murders associated with this case, most of them potential witnesses against Walter Paris."

"I thought you arrested some of those people and offered them witness protection."

"That's exactly what we did. There were six potential witnesses and three were murdered before we could go to trial. The other three, all of whom were pilots, skipped town against multi-million-dollar bails and left the country. Even if we could find them, extradition would be nearly impossible. Without them, we have no case against Walter Paris."

I say, "So, you think Paris is cleaning house, making sure there is absolutely no possibility of proving his involvement?"

"I can't prove it, but yeah, that's exactly what I think. I also think your friend Tommy Rollins should tread lightly. He had ties to Paris' operation and Mr. Paris doesn't like loose ends. We tried to keep your name out of the investigation, but I'm afraid Paris may think you had something to do with shutting him down. So, watch your back, buddy."

I've completely lost my appetite as I think through what I've just been told.

I ask, "Anybody on your end have any idea who might be doing the shooting?"

"Haven't got a clue, Devin, but this guy is damn good and very well informed, too. We think he blew up Raul Silva's car when he was on his way to testify. A month earlier, he clipped another witness in Panama from more than three hundred yards away. Last night was number three. The only possible description I got is a sketchy take from the Brazilian cop who called me this morning. Said the guy was white, nondescript, about six feet tall, maybe late forties, possibly fifty. That's it, not much else to go on."

I can feel the hair on the back of my neck going up because my friend's cursory description of the killer correlates with the images from my previous night's dream. Sam notices right away.

He asks, "You alright, Devin, or did I say something that triggered a thought?"

I elect not to tell Sam about my dream, but I do share another observation with him.

"Yeah, something does come to mind, Sam. This guy, if it is in fact just one guy, has killed people in two different countries and three different locations, all within three to four months of each other. In all three cases, he would not only have to know where they were, but when they would be in the best possible position for him to shoot them. My question is: where does he get his Intel? Stuff like that doesn't grow on trees."

Sam says, "You should have been a cop, Devin, because I was thinking exactly the same thing. Do you think someone leaked information to this guy about the victims' whereabouts?"

"It seems likely, but right now, I'm not thinking about much of anything except finding another job. The company owner fired me this morning. You know anybody who needs a pilot?"

"Jesus, Devin, you can't catch a break. You come to us, do the right thing, save the guy's company and he throws you under the bus. What are you going to do?"

"I'm not going to do anything for the next three or four weeks except take a little vacation and do some fun stuff."

Sam grins mischievously and says, "You gonna take that hot redhead, Harley, with you? She's got half the guys back at the office drooling, including me."

"I doubt she'll be able to get the time off, Sam. The boss gave her my old job this morning."

"Damn Devin, the boss fires you and then gives your girlfriend your old job. If it weren't for bad luck, you wouldn't have any luck at all."

Now, we're both laughing and I'm finally able to finish my hotdog. Five thousand miles away, in Rio de Janeiro, there are two cops who can't find anything at all to laugh about.

# CHAPTER 5

## July 7 1435 Hours • Rio de Janeiro

## Police Headquarters

Duncan Ruiz turns to his assistant and says, "Danny, let's take ride."

The younger man says, "Where are we going, boss?"

He holds up the business card they retrieved from the murder scene the previous evening.

"The telephone company just called me with an address for the third number on this card. Let's go over there and find out who lives on the other end of the line. You're driving."

Detective Ruiz is tired and operating on very little sleep. He's using the drive time to think through where they are with the investigation. They still don't have much to go on, but there are a couple of things that are encouraging. First, Belle's story about meeting the killer at the American Embassy may be of some help. People don't usually get into the embassy without some form of ID and there may be security cameras to help identify their mystery man. Second, even though they didn't find much to help them in the murdered man's hotel room, there were two things worthy of note. Danny Montoya found a fake mustache in the toilet. The killer tried to flush it, but it resurfaced. His assistant also fished the syringe and sodium pentothal bottle out of the waste basket next to the toilet. Hopefully, they will be able to get a fingerprint from the syringe or the sodium pentothal vial. They also found a single green contact lens that the killer may have dropped in his haste to leave the scene. That may indicate that their man likes to use disguises when he's on the job. It'll make him harder to recognize, but it's still an important piece of information.

The contact lens may be the single most useful piece of evidence. Earlier in the day, Ruiz talked with an FBI agent named Sam Dorsey. Since his department does not have the equipment to do DNA sampling, Dorsey agreed to have it done at his office and send him the results. Ruiz was surprised by the gesture because most of the America Feds he's worked with in the past play things close to the vest and they don't give out much information. Dorsey seemed like a nice guy and he wanted to help right away. Since the killer was probably from the United States, Ruiz is hoping something will pop from the FBI's DNA database. Those are his thoughts when they arrive at a nice apartment building in an upscale section of the city. Ruiz and Danny Montoya enter the structure and flash their credentials to the building manager. They ask who lives in apartment four-twenty-one.

The man says, "His name is Ruben Clemente. He's one of my best tenants --- quiet fellow, pays his rent on time, and I almost never hear from him. Is he in some sort of trouble?"

Ruiz lies and says, "There is no trouble, we'd just like to talk to him about a friend of his who died across town last night. Do you know if he's home?"

"Yeah, I saw him come in a few minutes ago."

Ruiz turns up the empathy in his voice when he asks, "Do you mind if we go up and talk to him for a minute and let him know what happened?"

The man is instantly cooperative saying, "He's on the fourth floor. You can take the elevator at the end of the hall."

A few minutes later, they are knocking on the entrance to the apartment. The door opens slightly with the chain latch still attached. A man, perhaps in his late twenties or early thirties, peers through the opening.

"Yeah," he says, "What do you want?"

The detective shows the man his ID and says, "I'm Duncan Ruiz and this is my partner Danny Montoya. We'd like to talk to you about Luis Marcos."

The young man is nervous and reluctant to open the door.

"Luis is my friend, but I haven't seen him in a couple of days. What's the problem?"

"Somebody murdered him last night and we'd like to talk to you about it. Can we come in?"

All of the color goes out of the young man's face and he's shaking badly when he opens the door and escorts the policemen into the room. They take a seat on the sofa and Ruben Clemente sits across from them. Detective Ruiz lets his assistant begin the questioning so he can observe Clemente's behavior dispassionately. Sometimes, body language speaks louder than words.

Danny Montoya asks, "How did you meet Luis Marcos?"

Clemente removes a picture from a nearby shelf and hands it to him.

He says, "The three of us went to flight school together in the States. We're all commercial pilots. I've known Luis about five years."

Montoya asks, "Did you know that the American FBI was looking for your friend because he skipped on his bail in a criminal case?"

The young man shakes his head nervously and says, "I had no idea."

Duncan Ruiz immediately senses that this kid is lying to them, but he lets the conversation continue.

Montoya hands him the police sketch of the murder suspect and asks, "Have you ever seen this man?"

Clemente studies the sketch carefully and answers truthfully, "Nope, I've never seen this guy before."

The two policemen question him for another twenty minutes before leaving. On the way out, Duncan Ruiz makes one last inquiry.

"Who is the other man in the photograph you showed us earlier?"

"That's my friend, Jorge Alda."

"Do you think he can help us with Luis' murder?"

Clemente is deceitful when he says, "I doubt it, Jorge lives in Sao Paulo now and I haven't seen him in a couple of years."

Ruiz hands him his business card and says, "I'm sorry about your friend. If you think of anything that can help us, give me a call."

The moment the policemen are gone, Ruben Clemente is on the telephone.

"Jorge," he says, "A couple of cops were just here asking about Luis. Somebody killed him last night. They asked me about you, but I told them you lived in Sao Paulo. I'm pretty sure they're going to follow up on what I told them, but I think I bought you a little time."

Jorge looks at his watch and says without hesitation, "I'm already packing. You'd better get out of town, too. When they find out that you lied to them, they'll come looking for you. Call me about eight o'clock this evening on my cellphone. We'll set up a meet somewhere and put together a game plan. I gotta run."

Ruben Clemente hangs up quickly because he knows he doesn't have much time. He and Jorge always have an exit strategy because of the work they do. They fly drugs for the cartels, and sometimes they move money around for them. He never knows when the cops or some angry cartel member will come looking for him. He's more worried about the cartel than he is about the cops. Sometimes, drug traffickers will kill a pilot if they think there's any chance of them talking to the police. So, he always keeps a suitcase ready with plenty of cash, clothes for a week and a couple of fake passports. He steps onto the outside balcony to call a cab. Half a block away, two detectives are watching the entrance to his condominium.

Detective Montoya asks, "Why are we doing this Duncan?"

Ruiz pops a stick of gum into his mouth and says, "Ten bucks says our guy is going to run and I also think he knows where his other friend is located. We're going to follow him and maybe get two for one."

Montoya trains a pair of binoculars on Clemente's balcony.

"Well, now he's on the balcony talking on the phone."

Ruiz says, "I'm betting he's speaking to Jorge Alda or he's calling someone to pick him up."

Half a mile away, another eye is trained on Ruben Clemente through the scope on a sniper's rifle. A nondescript man has been patiently sitting in a high-rise apartment building all morning waiting for a good shot. He got Clemente's address from the man that he tortured last night. It usually takes days to find a target and set up a shot like this. Today, he got lucky. He takes a deep breath, exhales very slowly, and squeezes the trigger. Ruben Clemente's chest explodes and he falls to the floor of the balcony.

Danny Montoya screams, "Jesus, somebody just hit our guy!"

He jumps from the car and starts running toward the building. Duncan Ruiz yells at his partner to stop. Across town, a nondescript man picks up a spent shell casing, disassembles his rifle, packs it into a small suitcase, and calmly walks from the apartment. The apartment's occupant lies unconscious, bound and gagged in the bathroom.

# CHAPTER 6

## July 7 1345 Hours • Brooks Falls, Pennsylvania

## The Jogging Path at Cambridge Lake

AFTER BEING FIRED THIS MORNING, I decided to take the afternoon off and get some exercise. I've run just over three miles and I've slowed to a walk heading toward my cabin. It's a beautiful day, but the weather inside my head is partly cloudy to overcast with rain showers. I'm not worried about losing my job. It's today's earlier conversation with my FBI friend that has me concerned. Although I don't think I'm in any immediate danger, my former associate, Tommy Rollins, may be in for some trouble. I'm debating whether or not to contact him and let him know what's going on. By my choice, we are currently not on speaking terms, because he's the one who got me into this mess in the first place.

Tommy used to own Keystone Airlines and he was using it as a tax dodge. He hired me to play undercover boss to investigate the company's problems, report back to him, and develop a plan to whip the business into shape so he could sell it. At the last minute, he sold the company to Walter Paris, who used the airplanes in our Cleveland office to move millions in laundered drug money. Tommy didn't tell me what was going on or about his involvement. He had purchased a number of banks in Ohio and Indiana and sold them to Walter Paris, who used them to launder money before he bailed out and moved to Europe. When the police finished their investigation, nearly thirty people went to jail. Tommy only escaped a prison term by the skin of his teeth. Although there were no criminal charges, the IRS came after Tommy's millions with a vengeance. When it was all over, he was nearly broke. He got to keep his car, his house, and a few thousand dollars in cash. To my mind, that sure as hell beats going to jail, but he doesn't see it that way. He's angry at me for going to the police and I'm pissed at him for putting me in the middle of it.

I've known Tommy since we were ten years old and we've been through a lot together. Despite my anger, there is still no one that I'd rather have standing next to me when there's real trouble. That is why I've decided to call his ex-wife, Kathrine Holloway. The two of us are close. In fact, so close, that Tommy once accused me of having a fling with her. It never happened, but it very easily could have, because she's my dearest friend. If Tommy hadn't met her first, I would love to have had her in my life. I'm reluctant to call because they've only been divorced a few months. I have no wish to open old wounds, but this is important and it's why I now find myself dialing her number.

"Hello, Kate. It's me Devin."

I can feel her warm smile through the telephone line.

She says, "I was wondering when you'd get around to calling me. It's been a few weeks. I thought it was Tommy that you're mad at, not me."

"I didn't want to stir the pot, kiddo. I figured everybody's nerves were still raw and it seemed best to give it some time."

She jokes with me and says, "I'm a free woman now, and if you weren't with Harley, I'd drop by and jump your bones. When are you going to marry that girl, anyway?"

"That would suit me just fine, Kate, but Harley's a free spirit, and a conventional relationship is probably not in the cards. I think she loves me, but she's keeping her options open. I'm okay with that for now, but if things change, your house will be my first stop."

She pauses a moment and says, "You always seem to get a little shot of weird with your women, Devin. I suppose that Harley's no exception."

"I wouldn't argue that point with you, Kate. Life with Harley is never dull."

She says, "I've known you a long time, Devin, I'm guessing this isn't a social call."

I don't want to alarm Kate, but I don't like keeping secrets either.

"No, it's not. There may be some trouble brewing from the Keystone Airline fiasco a few months ago. There was a murder last night in Rio de Janeiro and the guy was a known associate of Walter Paris. Somebody's bumping off anyone who can tie him to the airline money laundering scheme or our murdered employee."

She says, "You mean Susan Parks, the pilot who once worked for you?"

"Yeah, that's it. My FBI friend dropped by today and let me know that not counting Susan, there have been three murders in the last three months, all of them tied to Walter Paris in some way."

"Have you heard anything over at the airline?"

"No, they fired me this morning, so I won't be able to get any information on that end."

"Do you plan to let Tommy know what's going on?"

"I'd like to talk to him, but I don't have a current telephone number."

She says, "I'll give you his number, but I doubt that you'll be able to reach him today. He's on his way back from Europe and his flight doesn't get in until later this afternoon. The good news is that he'll be in Pittsburgh on business tomorrow. That's just down the road from where you are now and you may be able to catch up with him there for a face-to-face meeting."

"Is this your way of telling me it's time to kiss and make up?"

"I think so. You guys haven't spoken to each other in months. I know you're still sore at him for dragging you into this mess, but it's time to let it go."

Katherine is right and the information that I have may be a way to rekindle a childhood friendship. She gives me the number along with an admonishment.

She says, "What about you, Devin? You weren't exactly on Walter's top-ten friend's list."

I say, "This may be nothing, but Tommy and I may want to look over our shoulders for a while until the dust settles. I'm taking an extended vacation to look for another job. As for the rest of it, I'll cross that bridge when I get to it."

"If you're really taking a vacation, why don't you drop by and visit me and the kids. I'll fix you a genuine New England lobster dinner."

I laugh and say, "You're a terrible cook, Kate."

"Yeah, but you and I could have a hell of a lot a fun watching the water boil."

I can't help but smile when I say, "I have to go now. Harley just got home."

She says, "Party pooper. I love you. Call me sometime. Bye, Devin."

"I love you too, kid. See you soon."

When I hang up the phone, Harley asks, "Who was that?"

"That was Kate."

She says, "I'm sorry I missed her, she's always a lot of fun. Does she still have the "hots" for you?"

"One can only hope."

Harley slides her arms around my waist and kisses me for a long time.

She says, "I know you've had a rough day, baby. You got fired and the bastard gave your girlfriend your old job. That had to rattle your cage."

"Not really, I was looking for a change anyway."

"Then, why the long face?"

I fill Harley in on my conversation with the FBI, the murder in Rio, and my concerns about Walter Paris.

"So, you think there might be trouble headed our way?"

"I don't think there is anything headed your way, Harley. Paris has no axe to grind with you because you weren't involved in any of his troubles."

"I know that, but you were partly the cause of his problems with the police. I'm your girlfriend and some of that could rub off on me."

I say, "That's why I've made arrangements for you to stay in a cabin on the other side of the lake. We probably shouldn't be seen together for a while. I'll come visit you after dark and we can go skinny dipping in the moonlight."

"You're scaring me Devin. I don't like this."

"It's just a precaution until I can figure out what's going on or get an all-clear from my FBI friend."

She says, "I'll do it, but only under protest."

"Harley," I say, "After I clean up, let's take the boat out and have dinner at that little restaurant at the north end of the lake. We'll have a glass of wine and worry about today's problems some other time."

She gives me a peck on the cheek and says, "You've got a deal."

# CHAPTER 7

### July 7 1610 Hours • Rio de Janeiro

### Ruben Clemente's Apartment

Duncan Ruiz and Danny Montoya have gone more than twenty-four hours without sleep and the younger man is out of breath when he reaches the elevator in Ruben Clemente's apartment building. His boss urges him not to enter the victim's apartment.

"The shooter may still be active, Danny. If you go rushing in there without thinking, you could get your head blown off. Call for backup and then we'll go in together."

The young detective makes the call and they enter the apartment when the swat team arrives. A short time later, they are on the balcony examining the crime scene and the body. There is not much to salvage except Ruben Clemente's cellphone, which they bag and log into evidence. Duncan Ruiz receives a call from his office indicating that an apartment owner across town has been mugged and sedated. Apparently, the shooter used his place as a sniper's roost. That apartment is nearly three quarters of a mile away from the victim.

Ruiz mutters to himself, "Damn, this guy can shoot and I'm not even close to catching him."

He turns to his assistant and says, "Danny, I want you to go back to the station and call an American FBI agent. His name is Sam Dorsey and the number is on my desk. Tell him what's happened and ask him if he'll run Luis Clemente's and Jorge Alda's names through their database. There's a connection here and we need to know what it is right now."

"I'm on it, boss, but where are you going?"

"If you need me, you can reach me on my cellphone. I'm headed to the American Embassy to follow up on what Belle told me. Get moving, I want you talk to that FBI agent before he goes home today."

Thirty minutes later, the detective is sitting in a very business-like embassy office. A man enters and introduces himself as Bill Marston. Duncan Ruiz hands him his police credentials.

"What can I do for you, detective? My secretary said it was urgent."

"I'm sorry to barge in like this, Mr. Marston, but I've got two murders in the last twenty-four hours and at least some of it traces back here to the embassy."

There is no hesitation in Marston's response when he says, "What can I do to help?"

Ruiz gives him the police sketch of the killer and asks, "Do you recognize this man and is it possible that he is an embassy employee?"

Marston studies the sketch for a moment and shakes his head.

"No, I've never seen him before, but that doesn't mean he's never been here. People visit this embassy from all over the world every day. It's entirely possible that he's been in and out of the building many times without us tracking him."

Ruiz asks, "How about camera footage? I noticed one at the front entrance when I came into the building. Is it possible to get a look at that surveillance footage?"

"That would be a problem. Many of the people, especially any American citizens in the footage, are protected by diplomatic immunity when they walk through that door. I want to help you, but legally, I can't. I can be sent to jail if I release any information that might compromise the protections offered by the United States government."

Duncan Ruiz is exhausted. Marston notices and he offers him a cup of coffee.

"I'll tell you what, detective, I just happened to pull up a file with a picture of every embassy employee here on my laptop. Just be sure not to look at them while I'm out of the room getting your coffee."

He winks at Ruiz and leaves to retrieve the coffee. The detective immediately flips the laptop around and begins perusing the files and pictures. There are only twenty-four embassy employees, not counting Marston, and none of them looks like his suspect. It's disappointing, but at least he knows the guy is not an embassy employee. Marston returns with the coffee minutes later.

He nods toward the laptop screen and asks, "Is there anyone else on the embassy staff that you'd like to speak with besides me?"

Ruiz has a sip of coffee and says, "No sir, but thank you for your help – official and otherwise."

The two men chat casually for a few more minutes. Just before Ruiz leaves to return to the police station, he shows Marston a picture of Belle, the beautiful call girl he knows worked at the embassy in the past.

Marston says, "I've seen her at embassy functions once or twice, but she's not an employee."

The detective thinks Marston knows more than that. He decides not to pursue it, because he can't force anyone at the embassy to help him. The good news is that he now knows the killer definitely has some connection to the embassy. He politely excuses himself and thanks Marston for the coffee. As soon as he's gone, Bill Marston is on a secure embassy telephone. A gravelly voice answers on the other end. Marston is angry.

"Who the hell was that guy you sent me a couple of months ago? I just had a Rio cop in here asking about him. He says that he's somehow connected to at least two murders in the last twenty-four hours. If you're running some sort of black ops down here, you need to keep us out of it."

The voice on the other end of the line asks, "How did the cop tie our man to the embassy?"

"Your guy ruffed up a dignitary's security guard when he tried to manhandle a call girl that sometimes entertains embassy guests. Somehow, the cop traced him back to the embassy through her."

"What did you tell the cop?"

"I showed him some innocuous pictures of embassy personnel to throw him off the track, but I don't think he bought it. I think the guy's pretty sharp and I'm betting he's not going to let this go."

There is a pause on the other end of the line and Marston is growing impatient.

"You still there?" he asks.

"Yeah, I'm here, I was just thinking. Is the girl the only one who can tie our man to the embassy?"

"I think so, what'd you have in mind?"

"Let me worry about that, just get me her name, address, and telephone number. I'm also going to need one of your embassy cars. I have another man in Rio and he can take care of it."

Marston panics and says, "What the hell are you going to do, Bob?"

He is unprepared for the vehemence in the man's voice when it says, "Damn it, Bill, get me that address and stay the hell out of it. It's my problem now and the less you know the better it is for both of us."

Marston provides the man with the information and hangs up. He's worried that things are going to get out of hand and that detective Ruiz is going to keep nosing around. He's right, because at that very moment, Duncan Ruiz is on the phone talking to his assistant.

He says, "Danny, were you able to talk to that FBI agent I asked you to call earlier?"

"Yeah, Duncan, we got lucky, because he was just leaving the office when I called. Your hunch was right about Luis Marcos, Ruben Clemente, and Jorge Alda. They were all wanted by the FBI for skipping bail in a criminal case. It seems they were supposed to testify against some guy named Walter Paris, because they allegedly heard him plotting to murder an airline employee in Ohio. It was all part of some big drug and money laundering deal."

"Did he say anything else?"

"No, but I sent him the contact lens, the syringe, and the sodium pentothal vial we found in the dead man's hotel room last night. FedEx said he should have it tomorrow. Agent

Dorsey indicated that it would take a few days for their lab to run a DNA test on it, but that he would get back to us as soon as it was done."

"Okay, Danny, go home and get some sleep."

"What are you going to do, Duncan?"

"Right now, I'm all out of ideas and I'm headed home. I'm going to have a drink and take a nap. If you come up with anything else, give me a call."

Detective Ruiz is completely exhausted when he stumbles into his condominium. He has a few clues, but he's still no closer to catching his man. There is also the matter of calling the mysterious number on the card in his wallet. He's never had to call it before, but he knows it's something that he should do soon. Right now, he's just too tired. He pours himself a scotch and stretches out on the living room sofa. The drink he has prepared goes untouched and he immediately drifts into a restless sleep.

# CHAPTER 8

July 8 1830 Hours • Brooks Falls, Pennsylvania

The Anchor Restaurant, Cambridge Lake

HARLEY AND I ARE SITTING at a window table, where I'm enjoying a glass of Chianti and the view across the lake as the sun drops low on the horizon. A female pianist is playing and singing a jazz tune called "Gentle Rain," and it's exquisite. She's being accompanied by a dark-skinned bass player, who's been staring at Harley for the last half hour. He grins and gives me a thumbs-up. I've known the man all my life. He was my father's bass player, among other things, and I brought Harley here to meet him. That will have to wait because our entrees have arrived and the sixty-five year old restaurant owner has served us personally.

She says, "Medium New York strip for the lady and spaghetti with clam sauce for the gentleman. Can I get you anything else. Devin? More wine maybe?"

"No thanks, Della, but Harley may want something."

Harley waves her off and says, "Thank you, Mrs. Greco, but I'm flying first thing in the morning and I'll just stick with water."

Our waitress takes Harley's hand and says, "Honey, I still have a hard time believing that you fly airplanes. You just don't fit the stereotypical image of a commercial pilot. With legs like that, you should be in a Broadway chorus line."

Harley is dressed casually in a tasteful blouse, shorts, and deck shoes, perfect summer attire. She's beaming from the compliment as our host returns to the kitchen.

I reach over and pat her on the knee to say, "She's right about those gams, you know. I'm a very fortunate man."

She grins and says, "I've been telling you that for months."

I begin to eat, but Harley interrupts me.

"Earlier you said that you brought me here to meet some people. Where are they?"

I gesture toward the musicians playing in the corner and say, "They'll come over and talk to us when they finish this set."

She says, "I hope not, that old guy on the bass has been ogling me all evening."

"He's been that way for years and he's harmless. Finish your dinner so we can talk to them when they stop by."

Harley always eats with great gusto and it is fun to watch. It doesn't matter what it is, she savors every bite. Somehow, she never seems to gain weight and I'm terribly envious. I jog, meditate, swim, practice Tai Chi and it's still the battle of the bulge. She does almost nothing and somehow manages to look terrific. We finish eating just about the same time that the pianist and bassist finish their first set. They wander over to our table to say hello. I greet them both with a hug.

"Harley, this is Paul, better known as Rocky. The lovely vision on his arm is Emma, who sometimes pretends to be his wife, but only when the cops aren't looking for him."

She says, "It's always a pleasure to meet Devin's friends. He says he's known you all of his life. You must be really close."

Harley's comments are greeted with quizzical looks from both parties.

"Did I say something wrong?" she asks.

Emma puts her arm around Harley and says, "Child, didn't this little imp tell you that Rocky and I are his aunt and uncle? Rocky and Devin's dad were brothers."

Harley punches me squarely in the shoulder and says, "No, Emma, he neglected to mention that."

Rocky smiles and says, "I think you should hit him again, Harley, only this time with a baseball bat."

I say, "Pull up a chair and join us for a few minutes before you have to play your next set."

We all settle in for some fun conversation, during which my aunt and uncle tell some raucous childhood stories about me and provide Harley with a little family history.

"Did Devin tell you about the time his dad robbed a bank and got away on his bicycle?"

Rocky says, "Straight up truth, Harley, my brother used Devin's bike to rob a bank and he got away clean."

Harley's head is spinning as she stares at me in disbelief.

Emma squeezes her husband's arm and says, "This old fart isn't innocent either. He and Jimmy ran an illegal floating card game for years. I always worried that one of their schemes would land Rocky in jail like his brother, but, fortunately, it didn't happen. We were able to make enough money as musicians to buy a hardware store and get out of the scam game. That's how we pay the bills. We do a few jazz gigs now and then because we enjoy playing music so much. Harley, did you know that Devin is a pretty fair jazz pianist?"

"No, Emma, he never told me that either. He keeps his dad's piano back at the cabin, but I've never heard him play it."

Rocky says, "Harley, maybe you can talk him into playing a couple of tunes with me and give Emma a short break on the next set?"

Harley is staring daggers at me. It's clear that there is no getting out of this and I decide to acquiesce.

"Okay guys, I'll do a couple of tunes with Rocky, but I need to visit the men's room and take a short stretch. Why don't you play something until I get back?"

I excuse myself, not because I need to use the restroom, but because my cellphone has been on vibrate and I've received a couple of calls while we were eating. Once I'm alone, I play back the messages from my voicemail. The first one is from an old friend offering some contract work ferrying an airplane from California to the East Coast. After losing my job today, it's nice to know I'm still in demand. The next message is somewhat less satisfying. It's from FBI agent Dorsey and there's been a second murder in Rio de Janeiro. The victim was another pilot who used to work for me. When I return to the dining room, I choose not to tell Harley what has happened. I don't want to spoil her evening or have her worry about it when she goes flying tomorrow.

She says, "Okay, piano man, show me your stuff."

Alright, but I have to warn you, I'm a little rusty."

I haven't told Harley that I've been practicing a couple of times a week at Rocky's house so that I could surprise her tonight. I open with a jazzy version of a tune that she sometimes sings in the shower, Paul Simon's "59th Street Bridge Song." She seems quite pleased. My second piece is Horace Silver's "Song for My Father," the significance of which is not lost on Rocky and Emma, because my Dad taught me to play it. I close the evening with a Bossa Nova tune from Brazil called "Wave."

I thank Rocky and Emma for a lovely evening and explain that we must leave now because Harley has an early morning flight. We say our goodbyes and we're soon motoring back across the lake in my Boston Whaler. It's a beautiful summer night, but I'm having trouble enjoying it because of the telephone message I received earlier. Harley is exhausted and she goes to bed almost immediately after we return to the cabin. I slide beneath the covers next to her. My only thoughts are of finding ways to protect her from what may be coming our way. In another part of the world, the faceless man from my dream is also trying to protect someone that he cares about.

## Chapter 9

### July 8 2130 Hours • Rio de Janeiro

### Belle's Apartment

A BLACK MERCEDES is parked outside a very expensive condominium complex. A nondescript, athletic-looking fellow is sitting inside the car dressed in a chauffeur's uniform. He is screwing a silencer onto his weapon. He re-examines the photo of the beautiful woman he is to kill this evening and it troubles him. His targets are normally really bad people and he can see no reason why this woman should die. They don't pay him to ask questions, but this is really bothering him.

Earlier in the day, he received a coded message from his "handler," a gravelly-voiced man who calls him with assignments from time to time. This evening, he is to pick up a prostitute who sometimes entertains guests at the American Embassy and make her disappear. As a cover, a call has been placed to her apartment indicating that the embassy has need of her services and that one of their limousines will pick her up at eight-thirty this evening. The man looks at his watch. The woman is five minutes late. If she doesn't show soon, he will be forced to enter her apartment and conclude his business there, something he does not wish to do. There may be security cameras or possible witnesses, which would complicate his task.

A block away, another nondescript man is watching the Mercedes through a pair of infrared field glasses.

He smiles and says to himself, "Sullivan, I figured they'd send you, you're our only other operative here in Rio."

He punches a number into an encrypted cellphone and watches the man in the Mercedes touch the headset attached to his ear.

"Yeah," he says.

A familiar voice speaks almost mischievously, "Hello, Sully. Leave the girl alone and don't make me kill you."

The man in the Mercedes shakes his head and says, "Well, well, Ricky, I haven't heard that voice since that last job we did together a few months ago. We were friends once and you know that I can't let this go."

"You have exactly five seconds to get out of the car or you're dead. Leave your weapon behind."

Sully drops the gun on the seat and exits the car immediately. He's worried that someone will see him, but he looks around and there is no one else on the block.

The voice in his earpiece says, "Now, walk away from the car, quickly."

Sullivan begins a slow jog away from the apartment complex. He's traveled perhaps twenty yards when an enormous explosion rocks the entire neighborhood. He is nearly knocked to the ground from the force of the blast and some light debris falls on top of him. The Mercedes is completely demolished and engulfed in flames. Sullivan ditches the chauffer's hat and jacket in a nearby trash can and disappears into the darkness. A short distance away, the man who detonated the bomb starts his car and drives off. He can hear sirens in the background, no doubt racing to the scene of the explosion. That does not concern him because someone he cares about is safe as a result of his handiwork. Belle is an innocent caught in the middle of events that have nothing to do with her. For her own safety, he moved her out of the apartment earlier in the day.

That was yet another act out of character for a man in his line of work, but recently, he has been doing a lot of things out of character. He's been rethinking his profession and the choices he's made. He might never have chosen this life were it not for his parents. They both served in the U.S. Army and he traveled the world with them. He was a military brat growing up in three different countries and more than a half dozen cities before he was a teenager. Unlike most kids who are reared in military families, he loved moving around with mom and dad making friends all over the world. Dad taught him hand-to-hand combat as a kid and later encouraged him to join the ranks and serve his country. Mom spent nearly all of her free time with him, attending his competitive swimming events and sharing her love of books and languages. His was a happy childhood, but it all came to a screeching halt during his last year of high school when pancreatic cancer took his mom. His dad was terribly despondent over the loss of his wife. He didn't know it, but his father, then a military vet, was also suffering silently with PTSD. He took his own life a year and a half later during his son's second year of college. When he graduated from Yale, majoring in science and languages, he joined the military as a way to honor his parents, who had instilled in him a strong sense of patriotism.

He got his commercial pilot license right after he graduated from college and he entered the Navy thinking it would give him a leg up to become a naval aviator. At the time, there were no pilot openings and he became an intelligence officer. He helped plan covert missions, direct air strikes, and coordinate communications. Occasionally, he traveled with SEAL units as an onsite tactical observer. Working with these men stirred his adrenalin and a yen for action. He applied for SEAL training three times before he was accepted. Sullivan, the man sent to kill Belle, was often his partner during the grueling training program. They both emerged at the top of their class and they were sent to sniper training where he again excelled. Shortly after graduation, he married a young accountant and they had a daughter a year later.

He was happy until he was sent to the Gulf War and the killing started. He spent a lot of his time on rooftops providing cover for soldiers doing house-to-house sweeps, looking for weapons and enemy combatants. He and Sully often spotted for each other, ranging targets from hidden positions in the blazing desert heat. They saw themselves as protectors for the men on the ground and that lent a kind of credence to the killing. It kept good men from dying at the hands of enemy snipers or those planting roadside bombs. He had twelve kills and in his mind, they were all justified, until he had to shoot a teenager. The youngster was a suicide bomber wearing a vest packed with explosives as he walked toward some American soldiers who were storming a house in Bagdad. He couldn't sleep after the shooting and over the course of the next few months, he started drinking. When his tour was up, he left the Navy and returned home to a family that hardly knew him. His story was not unlike that of a lot of men who return from combat thinking their lives will suddenly return to normal.

Killing had changed something fundamental in his nature making him edgy and suspicious of his surroundings. The learned behaviors that kept him alive in war were a serious hindrance to his re-acclimation to civilian life. His wife and daughter sensed it right away and it drove a wedge between them. He sought counseling from a psychologist and it helped, but the damage was done. His family left him a year after he returned home. He was alone and unemployed because, despite his formal education, there was no equivalent civilian occupation for an assassin. That's when the CIA came knocking with promises of a spy-like existence and a much needed paycheck. It seemed like a good idea at the time.

The CIA, sometimes known as the "Company" or the "Agency," taught him Tradecraft, which is another name for the art of deception, secrecy, and espionage. He was issued several different passports using a variety of disguises and identities. His current identity, Richard Hamilton, was just one of a half dozen monikers he's used on a variety of assignments. He'd been posted in Brazil and Venezuela for the last three years because of his fluency with Portuguese and Spanish. Most of that time was spent chasing drug dealers while working closely with the DEA. The work had been mostly undercover observing the traffickers and gathering intelligence about their operations. He sent the information he gathered to headquarters in Langley, Virginia for analysis. He'd been on aerial surveillance missions as an observer in western Venezuela and in Columbia several times. Later, he and Sullivan led a couple of search and destroy missions in the jungle, blowing up drug labs and running down the bad guys.

They liked putting criminals away, but it all changed on a questionable mission. They were supposed to shoot a drug kingpin living in a lavish compound twenty miles outside of the city. Their target was a man responsible for several murders and he ran a narcotics empire worth nearly a billion dollars. The Company provided them with the man's location. He and Sullivan were sent as a team with one man backing up the other in case something went wrong. He was setting up, ranging the target, and checking the wind as he prepped for the shot.

The intended victim was having a dinner party with his relatives and they were waiting for the man to be alone, so as not to hurt anyone else. That's when the entire building erupted in a massive explosion, killing nearly twenty innocent people, many of whom were women and children. Sullivan had secretly been given orders to destroy the entire compound. Hamilton was appalled because the rules of engagement for this assignment clearly stated that the family and friends of that target were not to be harmed. He'd been lied to about the mission and he swore he'd never be a part of anything like this. It was on that day, that he started planning his exit strategy from the Company.

Belle, the lovely woman whose life he had just saved, was part of his plan for leaving. She was standing in the doorway of the ocean-side bungalow that he had rented earlier, waiting nervously for his return. He was going to ask her to go with him. He wasn't sure she'd accept his offer, especially since it meant that they'd be on the run for some time. All of his doubts vanished when his car stopped in front of the house and she came running out to greet him.

# CHAPTER 10

July 9 1145 Hours  •  Rio de Janeiro

Police Headquarters

Duncan Ruiz is staring at the messages his secretary handed him when he entered the building moments ago. He walks into his office and yawns as he pours himself a cup of coffee. He's slept nearly twelve hours, but he is still tired. He smiles when his assistant, detective Montoya, walks into his office.

He says, "Morning Danny, did you get any rest last night?"

"Not much, because a couple of things came up. Not to worry though, I took care of it. I would have called you last evening, but I thought I should let you sleep late today. There wasn't much you could have done anyway. I left you a cellphone message about an hour ago, but you didn't pick up."

Ruiz removes the phone from his briefcase and examines the call log. There are three messages. He was so tired that he didn't hear the phone ring.

He waves the younger man to a seat and says, "Okay, buddy, let's have it."

Montoya says, "Someone blew up a car on Belle's block last night, but no one was hurt."

"Do we have any idea who owned the car?"

Montoya says, "We do. I just ran what was left of a license plate through the DMV database and you're not going to like it. It was a limousine registered to the American Embassy. By strange coincidence, they called it in as stolen yesterday."

Ruiz can feel the anger rising inside him, but he takes a deep breath and gently places his coffee cup on the desk. His immediate thought is to revisit the embassy and grill Bill Marston, but he knows he won't get much out of him. He's sure the embassy official knows something, but the guy is a pro and he's covering his tracks pretty well. He and Danny will have to find another way to get what they need.

Ruiz says, "Anything else?"

"Yeah, we found a gun with a silencer on it inside the car. I sent it to the forensics lab for testing. What do you want to do, Duncan?"

He sighs and says, "For now, we do nothing. Give me a few minutes to return some calls. Afterwards, I'll take you to lunch and we'll talk it over."

As soon as Montoya leaves his office, Ruiz punches a button on his phone and listens to his voice mail. The first call is from Montoya and the second call is from a woman. "Duncan, it's me, Belle. Things are really crazy and I'm leaving town for a while. You won't be able to find me, but I just wanted you to know that I'm okay, so you wouldn't worry. Someone is helping me and I'll be fine."

He is relieved that Belle has not been harmed, but her call raises questions. Who is the friend and is it the same fellow who protected her at the embassy? If so, why would he help someone who could potentially identify him as a murder suspect?

He pushes the voicemail prompt again and a male voice says, "Detective Ruiz, you have a telephone number on a business card in your wallet. I expect to hear from you soon."

The number that the voicemail is referring to is the same one that Danny Montoya found on the first murder victim. He's been dreading making the call. His former supervisor, who is now effectively the police commissioner, gave him the card when he was working vice. He was new on the job and it was right after his wife left him. He made a mistake and had a fling with a beautiful hooker named Belle. His boss found out and threatened to fire him if he didn't take the card. The only other instructions he'd received were to update the person at that number on any investigation he might be involved in --- no questions asked. So far, he'd never been asked to call the number and it seemed a small price to pay to keep his job. It also earned him a promotion to chief of detectives. He dials the European exchange and the call connects to a man who has a slightly British accent. The voice is almost cheery, but it gets directly to the point.

"Detective, would you be kind enough to give me the salient details of your current investigation and, please, leave nothing out."

Ruiz is reluctant, but he gives the man everything that he requests. The mystery man thanks him politely and tells him to check the bottom drawer of his office desk. The line goes dead instantly. Ruiz unlocks the drawer and finds an envelope filled with cash along with a note from his boss, which reads: "This should cover your alimony and child support payments for a couple of years."

He quickly stuffs the envelope back in the drawer and pauses a moment to catch his breath. What has he gotten himself into? Now is not the time to ask that question because Danny Montoya is walking toward his office expecting to join him for lunch. As they leave for the restaurant, a man in Switzerland places a call to the United States.

A gravelly voice answers on the other end, "Yeah?"

"Good afternoon, Bob, I just got off the phone with my contact in Rio de Janeiro. He passed on a few things that may be of interest to you. He thinks the man you're looking for may be traveling with a prostitute named Belle. Apparently, she used to provide services for your embassy in Brazil. Those two people and Jorge Alda are the only ones left who may be able to tie us to any of this. I need you to make the problem go away and soon. I know you have the resources to track them down. Call me when it's done."

Robert Davenport pockets his personal cellphone and thinks about his next move. He's a government employee in the upper echelons of the CIA. His job is to coordinate intelligence with the DEA when they run drug interdiction operations in Central and South America. This whole business has gone sideways because a CIA operative, currently known as Richard Hamilton, has suddenly developed a conscience. Hamilton used to work for him, and one day he stopped returning his calls. The man in question is one of the best in the business and he and the woman will be difficult to find. Jorge Alda, on the other hand, is a much easier target because he is currently in a safe house just outside of Rio. He places a call to the DEA office across town and speaks with Gil Pepperdine.

"Gil, this is Bob Davenport. I want you to pull Jorge Alda out of Rio because his cover is blown. You're his handler and he trusts you. It appears that the agent, you know as Richard Hamilton, has gone rogue, killing two of Alda's associates in the last two days. We think he's planning to go after Alda as well. Use the standard pickup protocol and I want you to get on it right away. Call me when you've made the necessary arrangements. I want this guy on a plane back to the States tonight. I'll authorize any resources that you may need. Call me back when you have something mapped out and we'll go over it together."

Pepperdine asks, "What do you want me to do about Hamilton?"

"Don't worry about him. I'll take care of that on this end. Now, get rolling."

Gil Pepperdine is in deep thought. Jorge Alda is a confidential informant who was part of the Keystone Airline drug money laundering bust that happened a few months ago. The FBI had arrested him and two others pilots for flying drug money across Indiana and Ohio using Keystone's airplanes. They didn't know that Alda was a DEA informant when he and his buddies skipped bail and fled to Rio to escape prosecution. He'd been quietly feeding the DEA dirt on Walter Paris' operation for months, but he dropped off the grid when he thought someone was trying to kill him. Pepperdine wanted to share this information with the FBI, but his boss refused. It complicated his relationship with the Bureau and generated a lot of interagency friction, particularly with Sam Dorsey, who was the FBI's lead investigator on the case. Without Alda's testimony, they had no case. Bob Davenport argued that the

DEA should close out the case, which would be a huge feather in his cap. Davenport would also get a lot of credit for his efforts when he retires in a couple of months.

Pepperdine and Davenport have an unusual relationship. They work for different agencies, but Davenport is effectively his boss. The CIA is, by law, not permitted to run operations inside the United States. But, some of the drug money in this current operation was used to fund terrorist activities overseas. That's how the CIA and Bob Davenport got involved in this case. Pepperdine privately wonders if Davenport has other motives which are driving his decision to pull Jorge Alda out of Rio. Davenport has intentionally not been very cooperative with the FBI, who also has a stake in the investigation. It's almost as if he's trying to keep the Bureau from looking at things too closely. Lately, he's been very secretive about calls on his cellphone whenever he's in the room with him. In recent months, he has visited Europe twice for extended stays, and he bought a fancy condo in Switzerland along with a new sports car. Where is the money coming from? He respects Bob Davenport, but he's worried that this Alda business might blow up on them because of the pressure to get it done so quickly.

Alda has been holding up somewhere in Rio, waiting for a call from the Agency to bring him in. News of the death of another pilot-friend has spooked him. This situation will require some delicacy. Those murders sent him into hiding and Pepperdine is the only one he trusts to bring him in. Jorge Alda is not the only one concerned about the death of the two pilots. I'm uneasy, too, and it means that there is a conversation that I need to have with my girlfriend.

# CHAPTER 11

July 11 1400 Hours • Brooks Falls, Pennsylvania

Cambridge Lake

I'M SITTING ON THE DOCK next to my cabin when I hear Harley's jeep pull up. I've just reeled in a couple of lake trout, which will be dinner this evening. She gives me a quick wave and scurries into the cabin. Instinctively, I know that something is wrong. When I enter the kitchen, she's already munching on a sandwich that she's assembled with lightning speed. Harley eats wildly when she's upset and the wine she's chosen to imbibe with the sandwich is another indication of trouble because she never drinks during the day. Rather than pry into something she might be reluctant to talk about, I decide to wait her out. I put my arms around her and give her a kiss on the cheek. Without speaking, I retire to the living room and begin to doodle on the piano. I choose a song made famous by Ray Charles and Kenny Loggins, "You Don't Know Me." When I finish, I notice Harley standing in the doorway.

She says, "It's ironic that you should play that tune, because, even after all these months, I really don't think I know you. I enjoyed meeting your uncle and aunt last night and I've enjoyed meeting some of your friends, but even they don't seem to know who you are sometimes. There is always something a little mysterious in your nature. It's fascinating, and it's in part what keeps our relationship so interesting. Every time I think I've got you figured out, you take a detour in a completely unexpected direction."

"Well, all you have to do is ask, Harley, I'm not hiding anything."

"Is that so? Then, when were you going to tell me about the second murder? Ruben Clemente is dead and I found out about it today at work. You knew yesterday, but you never said anything."

"We were having a good time last night and I didn't want to spoil the evening. I was planning to tell you this morning, but you left to go flying while I was in the shower."

She asks, "What else are you not telling me?"

"You know as much as I do, Harley. There's nothing left to tell. What's really bothering you?"

She joins me on the piano bench and says, "I quit my job this morning or maybe I got fired, I'm not really sure."

"What happened?"

"When I got back from my trip this morning, the boss dropped by my office to talk about my promotion to director of operations. On his way out, he grabbed my ass and insisted that I have dinner with him."

I know that Harley has absolutely no tolerance for that sort of thing and I have to suppress a smirk when I ask, "What did you do?"

She's very matter-of-fact when she says, "I drop-kicked the bastard in the groin and punched him in the face. I think I broke his nose."

I raise my hand for a quick high-five and say, "You go girl!"

Now, we're both laughing and I say, "I'm pretty sure you got fired, babe."

There is a momentary lull in the conversation. We are both contemplating what's next. I know that Harley has an invitation to return to her old job at a major airline. It was a source of friction between us a few months ago because she moved to Denver and became involved with her ex-husband. She's always been an adventurous soul and I suspect that losing her job has stirred the wanderlust. The nagging question is: "Will I be a part of whatever change she's planning?" At the moment, it's clear that she's not quite ready to talk about it.

"Let's change the subject," she says. "I want to go back to this business of me living on the other side of the lake. I was in this mess when it started a few months ago and I'd like to see it through with you, wherever it goes."

"I appreciate your willingness to hang with me on this Harley, but I really do think you should stay in the other cabin, at least until things cool down a bit. Nobody knows where this thing is going. Right now, most of the action seems to be happening in South America, but my gut sense of things is telling me that it's not over yet and that trouble may be moving our way."

"Is that why you keep the pistol taped to the bottom of the bed or didn't you think I'd notice?"

I hesitate slightly before saying, "I think it's better to be prepared, even if nothing happens. I don't want to get caught wanting if things get ugly."

"May I also assume that's why you've been going to the shooting range to practice on the weekends?"

"Yes, it is. A weapon is only as good as the person using

it. I'm a little rusty and knocking the cobwebs out seemed prudent."

"Devin, I don't like guns, they make me very uncomfortable."

"I don't like them either, but I had to carry one as part of my job once and I was trained how to use it."

"You could teach me to shoot," she says.

I sigh audibly and say, "Yes, I could teach you to handle a gun, but shooting paper targets is not the same as pointing the gun at another human being and pulling the trigger."

"I know that you had to shoot someone once, Devin. Your friend Katherine told me it was self-defense and that it saved you and Tommy Rollins. I love you and I know that you would never have done something like that unless there were no other options. You are by all accounts, and by my own experience, a decent, kind, and loving person. How were you able to do that and how in the world did you ever get over it?"

I walk to the window and stare out at the lake before speaking.

"You never get over it, Harley. That was nearly five years ago and I still think about it sometimes. It all happened so quickly that there was no time to think. It was an instinctive act, driven mostly by the formal firearms training I'd received and from a martial arts teacher I once had in high school."

She says, "You mean Mr. Nakamura, the little fellow that I take Tai Chi from at the gym? That guy wouldn't hurt a flea."

"One and the same, but don't let his size or demeanor fool you, Harley. He was a battle-tested soldier in World War II and he knows about death and killing. He passed the lesson of combat on to me and I never forgot it."

"What do you mean?"

"We were in a boxing ring sparring together one day and I was finally getting the hang of some karate moves he was teaching me. I'd never seen anyone's hands and feet move as fast as his and he was getting the better of me for most of the match. I was actually a little afraid of him. Then my adrenalin kicked in and I realized that I was taller, stronger and that I had a longer reach than he did. It triggered something very primal in my nature and I began swinging and kicking in a way that I'd never done before, knocking him down. He fell to the floor and didn't get up. I thought I'd hurt him and I knelt down to help him, only to feel a swift kick to my legs that sent me tumbling to the floor."

"A split second later, he was on top of me. He had me in a choke-hold and I couldn't get free. When he released me, he said, "There are only two kinds of people in a real fight — the quick and the dead. When you get your man down, finish him and don't give him another chance to kill you. Twenty years later, that advice saved my life, but I had to take another life to do it."

"Are you telling me that's why you were able to shoot that guy in the jungle?"

"Yes, that's part of it, but off and on, when Tommy Rollins and I were working in South America, we flew missions for the DEA and probably the CIA. I never really knew for sure. Mostly, we did aerial photography, but sometimes we picked up soldiers in remote jungle locations who were doing black ops work, blowing up drug labs and shooting drug traffickers. When you're exposed to stuff like that, it rubs off on you. I quit after a few missions because I didn't like hanging around people who did that kind of work."

"Weren't they supposed to be the good guys?"

"Most of them were good men Harley, especially the Navy Seals. But, killing changes a person, even very good people. I think that's especially true if you're a sniper and its part of your job description. People who kill professionally become something different — harder, more callous, and far less responsive to human emotion. It's almost as if empathy and emotion somehow get switched off in their DNA. Personally, I think it's a coping mechanism. They have to turn off their feelings or they can't do the work."

"And you think some of these people may be coming our way?"

"I don't know for sure, but it's possible and I think we should take every precaution."

She says, "Still, I find it hard to believe that an American soldier would come after us. We haven't done anything wrong. We did the right thing when we saw something bad happening and we went to the police. I would think they'd be on our side."

"Look," I say, "Every once in a while one of these guys goes off the rails. They come home from a war and there is no civilian equivalent for the job of assassin. They get restless and hire themselves out as soldiers of fortune, doing dirty work for whoever pays the best. People who kill for money have no allegiances. I don't have any idea who the person or persons doing the killing in Rio are, but they have long since lost any semblance of right or wrong. Someone is trying to tie up loose ends and they don't care how it gets done."

She hugs me and says, "Okay, I'll stay at the other cabin, but not tonight. Right now, I don't want to be alone."

There is someone else who does not want to be alone, either. He's sitting in a Rio de Janeiro hotel room waiting for a phone call and a way out of trouble.

# CHAPTER 12

July 11 1730 Hours • Rio de Janeiro

Windsor Copa Hotel, Ipanema Beach

Jorge Alda asked the hotel desk clerk for a room overlooking the street. He peers out and checks the main road every few minutes with a pair of binoculars. He doesn't really expect to see anything. If they send a real pro to kill him, he knows he'd never see it coming. Still, there is some comfort to his sleep-deprived mind when he doesn't see any obvious signs of trouble. He stretches out on the bed and stares at the ceiling. He's worried because he was supposed to meet his friend Ruben Clemente last night and he didn't show. He knows something is wrong, but they agreed not to call each other unless there was an emergency. It's unlikely that anyone will be able to trace his phone in Rio, but he's not taking any chances. He has removed the battery making it impossible to track its GPS signal. He will turn it back on soon because he's expecting a call from Gil Pepperdine, his handler, who is working on a game plan to get him out of the country.

They'll make contact on the next quarter hour at 1745 hours. He'll put the battery back in ten minutes before that to allow for any minor time discrepancies between Pepperdine's watch and his own. His hands are shaking slightly as he replaces the battery and turns on the phone. He's shocked when it rings almost immediately, but he's also relieved, because caller ID shows the incoming call to be from Ruben Clemente. He answers quickly.

"Hey, Ruben, where the hell have you been, I was really worried about you?"

A stranger's voice says, "Mr. Alda, please don't hang up. I have some important information for you. This is detective Ruiz with the Rio police. Your friend, Ruben Clemente, was killed yesterday and we think the same people are after you. You need to come to police headquarters so we can protect you."

Click. As fast as that, the call ends and Jorge Alda is in the wind. Duncan Ruiz is frustrated because he may have just lost his last lead in his murder case. A few minutes later, a frantic Jorge Alda disappears into the crowd on a busy Rio street. He knows that Gil Pepperdine will call him again with an escape plan, but it will have to wait until he has found another place to hide. Later, when he's sitting in a local pub, he turns on his phone. At forty-five minutes before the hour it rings again. Gil Pepperdine is clearly agitated.

"Jorge, where the hell have you been? I tried to reach you an hour ago."

"The cops are looking for me now. I got a call from one of them telling me that my friend Ruben is dead and that the killer is searching for me, too. Why didn't you tell me what happened when we talked earlier today?"

"Jorge, I just found out about it a little while ago myself. That's why I need you to go to a safe house, so we can get you the hell out of there."

"Alright, I'm listening."

Pepperdine gives him directions to a secure location and tells him that he should be there promptly at eight o'clock this evening. There will be cash waiting and a new passport. He'll be flown back to the United States in a private jet. Alda hangs up and immediately hails a taxi. Gil Pepperdine makes another call to Bob Davenport to give him the details.

He says, "Bob, it's all set. Alda will be at our safe house at eight o'clock. One of our agents will take him to the airport. We have an airplane standing by and he'll be airborne shortly after we pick him up. Two of our men will meet his flight when it lands in Miami."

A gravelly voice says, "That's good work, Gil. I knew that I could count on you to make it happen. Why don't you meet me after work for a drink? I'm buying."

Davenport hangs up the phone and makes an overseas call on a secure line. A man named Sullivan answers on the other end.

"Sully, I've got an assignment for you. It's a follow-up to the business that you handled with Ruben Clemente yesterday. The job needs to be done quietly with no trace evidence. You'll get a text message with the details shortly."

Sullivan looks at his watch and says, "You're not giving me a lot of time to pull this together. The last time you sent me out on a job, somebody blew up my car. How do I know there won't be trouble tonight?"

"I'm sending you a couple of other guys from your old crew as backup just in case. They've worked with you in the past and you can pay them when they get into town. They're on a flight from Sao Paulo and you can pick them up at the airport in about an hour. Weapons and anything else you need to do the job are at the usual location. Payment has already been wired to your offshore account."

Sullivan hangs up and quickly goes online to check his bank account. He doesn't like this assignment. It has been hastily conceived and he senses panic in Davenport's voice, which makes him uneasy. This is high stakes gambling and the essence of successful gambling is to know when to quit and turn down a job when the risk is too high. He has killed two people in as many days and they were both rush jobs. His preference is to take his time and plan things carefully, but he's been paid three times his usual fee to get this done. He reluctantly gets into his car and drives to the airport.

The international airport in Rio is named after Antonio Carlos Jobim, the famed Brazilian composer who wrote "The Girl from Ipanema." The song is playing in the background when Sullivan enters the terminal to pick up the other two mercenaries. He's surprised when he sees that their commuter flight from Sao Paulo is running nearly an hour late. This will seriously alter their timeline for going after Alda, who has already arrived at the safe house. Sullivan is considering aborting the mission.

Jorge Alda isn't considering anything except getting out of Rio as fast as possible. He quickly finds his new passport and the cash that Gil Pepperdine promised would be waiting at the safe house. Two of his friends are dead and he doesn't want to join them. He has no intention of staying here any longer than absolutely necessary. He has his own escape plan. A fellow pilot has offered to sneak him aboard a freighter that he's flying to Manaus, Brazil tomorrow evening. He has an apartment there that no one else knows about. He'll hide there and plan his next move. He's on his way out the door when someone grabs him from behind and covers his mouth and nose with a cloth laced with chloroform. He collapses to the floor moments later. A nondescript man, about six feet tall, injects something into his arm and carries him to a waiting van and drives off.

# CHAPTER 13

## July 11 2055 Hours • Rio de Janeiro

## CIA/DEA Safe House

SULLIVAN AND TWO OTHER MEN arrive at the safe house and exit their vehicles with weapons drawn. They've come in separate cars. That way, they will have a second escape vehicle in the event one of the automobiles has a mechanical problem. Sullivan leaves nothing to chance and he's planned three different escape routes for himself and his men after they finish here. Killing is the easy part, but getting away with it is a lot harder. He had his companions drive an extra vehicle because he only very narrowly escaped after doing a job in the past when his car quit running.

He nods to one of his men and the man approaches a side window and peers inside. He signals to the others that the place appears to be empty. Moments later, they enter the house to conduct a room-to-room search and find nothing. Jorge Alda is not there and Sullivan is angry because his men will have to be paid either way. His associates leave in a separate car, but Sullivan lingers a few minutes to make a phone call. A gravelly voice answers on the other end.

Bob Davenport says, "I assume you're calling to let me know the job is done."

Sullivan is angry and it shows in his response.

"Alda wasn't there and you're not getting your money back. That's twice in two days that you've sent me out to do a job and something's gone wrong. I think you and I are done, because working for you is either going to get me caught or killed."

"Sully, you've been doing this long enough to know that stuff like this happens. Nothing ever goes exactly the way it's planned and you're very well paid to compensate for any trouble along the way. Tonight, you got a pretty big paycheck and you and your men didn't have to do a damn thing."

Sullivan knows he's right. He's prepared to call it a night when Davenport throws him a curve. There's a chance to make even more money.

"Sully, I have another deal for you. You can name your price if you decide to do it and this should be pretty easy."

"I've never been averse to making lots of money. What have you got?"

"We've been tracking Belle's cell phone, the hooker you were supposed to take out the other night. She's made a couple of calls to her sister and we've almost triangulated her general location. We should have the exact address by morning. I'll text you the details as soon as we get them, if you're interested?"

Sullivan asks, "What about Hamilton, he was protecting her last time and it nearly got me killed?"

"No pain, no gain, Sully. Do you want the job or should I call one of the other guys to do it?"

"I'll do it, but I'm not jumping into anything else tonight."

Davenport says, "Fair enough, but keep me posted on your progress."

Sullivan hangs up and checks the text message that is already coming in on his secure phone. Belle's exact location is unclear, but the general area is just a few miles from where he is currently living.

He laughs out loud and mutters to himself, "You're one cool customer, Ricky. You stashed the girl right under my nose thinking I wouldn't look for her so close to home and you were right. I made the mistake of rushing into things last time and underestimating you, but that won't happen again."

As he drives away, Sullivan realizes that a part of him admires the man he knows as Richard Hamilton. Of course, that isn't his real name and Sullivan isn't his birth name either. When they went to work in the field for the Company, they were both given new identities. It was mostly to protect their families from any backlash that might result from something they might do while on the job. If the cartels ever found out their real names, the people close to them would be in jeopardy. A job which sometimes included undercover assignments, illegal phone tapping, blowing up drug labs or working as a sniper wasn't something to share with friends.

Sullivan and Hamilton graduated together from the CIA training program and they'd become close friends. Shortly afterwards, Bob Davenport recruited Sullivan to work for him directly on special assignments. Davenport liked Sullivan because he didn't ask a lot of questions and did what he was told. Most of his assignments seemed quite legitimate, at least at first. Over drinks one evening, Davenport asked him if he was interested in doing some "off book" contract work when he wasn't working for the Agency. Sullivan wanted the extra money and he said yes. He did a couple of jobs that involved surveilling two known drug dealers who had a reputation for violence and murder. Based on Sullivan's surveillance, a hit squad was sent to take the traffickers out. Sullivan went with the men on their third mission and participated in the shooting. It was a mistake, because he was now implicated in a killing that was not government sanctioned. Davenport later used it as leverage to get him to do his bidding.

It wasn't long before Sullivan realized that Davenport was working with another party who was supplying information about drug traffickers that could only have come from a person on the inside. For months, Sullivan wondered who this mystery man was until he overheard Davenport mention the name, Walter Paris, during a private telephone conversation. That's when he was able to put the pieces together. Without Davenport's knowledge, Sullivan used his CIA resources to do some digging into Walter Paris' background. With that information, he knew who was really running the show.

Paris was a multi-billionaire (once on the cover of *Forbes Magazine*) who quietly made his fortune serving as banker to the drug cartels, not just one, but at least a dozen big time players. Every day, he funnels millions of their money into legitimate businesses making it almost impossible for the authorities to track the funds. Normally, Sullivan got his assignments from Davenport, but one day, Walter Paris contacted him directly and asked if he would do a job for him. He was paid half a million dollars to take out a drug dealer and told not to tell Davenport about it. The target's name was Raul Silva, a drug dealer in Caracas, who'd been business partners with Paris. Paris had him blow up the man's car because he was about to testify against him in court. Working for Paris, in effect, meant that he now had two bosses, one paying a lot better than the other.

After Sullivan had been working off-book for a few months, Paris allowed him to form his own team comprised of two other Special Forces soldiers turned mercenaries. They were not on the Agency payroll and it turned out that they had worked for Paris on and off for years. On paper, Sullivan was still with the Agency, which allowed his team access to agency resources like weapons, surveillance gear, intelligence reports etc. Sullivan was trapped and he decided to make the best of a bad situation by continuing to do side jobs for Davenport and Paris. What surprised him was how well the work paid. In just a few months, he'd become a millionaire.

That's when he approached Rick Hamilton to see if he was interested in helping on the jobs that required more than one person. Walter Paris and Bob Davenport insisted they set up some kind of test to see if they could trust him. The test came the day Sullivan blew up a drug dealer's house, killing his family and friends. Hamilton thought the operation was a normal operation sanctioned by the Agency. He was furious after the explosion and wanted no part of it. Davenport immediately transferred him to the American Embassy in Rio until they could figure out what to do with him.

Things were quiet for several months, until a few days ago, when Hamilton ran off with Luis Marcos, one of the guys Sullivan was supposed to kill. Sullivan had been following Marcos, looking for an opportunity to make his move when his target stopped at a bar for a couple of drinks. He was shocked when Hamilton followed the man in and slipped something into his drink. His first thought was that Hamilton had a change of heart and had joined the program. He mistakenly believed that Hamilton had been assigned to take care of Marcos, but when he called Davenport to confirm it, he learned that was not the case. He was ordered to kill Hamilton and Marcos.

Sullivan was conflicted because he'd been ordered to kill a friend. He followed them to a hotel and watched Hamilton help Marcos into a room. Hamilton was in there with Marcos for maybe an hour and then he left the hotel. Sullivan should have killed Hamilton in the hotel hallway, but there were people coming down the hall at the same time. He was worried about witnesses so, he stayed in the shadows. He waited until Hamilton left and he jimmied the lock on the hotel room, where he found Marcos semi-conscious, dosed with sodium pentothal. He slapped Marcos around and later yanked a couple of his fingernails off. The man gave him Ruben Clemente's address, a stroke of luck, which enabled him to set up the hit the following day. He tried to get some more information from Marcos to see what Hamilton was up to. That's when Marcos tried to wrestle his gun away and Sullivan shot him in the chest.

Sullivan was puzzled by Rick Hamilton's behavior. Apparently, he was looking for some kind of information from Marcos because he'd dosed him with sodium pentothal. What was he looking for? Sullivan had no idea, but that was the least of his worries. His biggest concern now was that his former friend had gotten away. In a moment of weakness, he had spared his life. He might live to regret it because Rick Hamilton was one of the best operatives he'd ever worked with. The man was absolutely brilliant and highly skilled in subterfuge and disguise. He was an excellent marksman and a wiz at electronics and languages. It would be a near impossible task to find him if he didn't want to be found.

# CHAPTER 14

July 12  0130 Hours  •  Brooks Falls, Pennsylvania

Devin's Cabin, Cambridge Lake

ONCE AGAIN, I AM AWAKENED by a disturbing dream. I'm fairly certain that the setting for it is Rio de Janeiro, some place near the water. The same faceless man from my previous dream is center stage. This time, he is accompanied by a beautiful woman. The vision was a hodgepodge of scrambled images, but I could also see Jorge Alda, the pilot who used to work for me. He appeared to be having a conversation with the faceless man. There were other armed men in the dream, but I have no idea who they are. I have very few facts to help me harmonize the images from my sleepy musings into something useful. I don't know if it is my intuition trying to tell me something or if it's my imagination simply chasing its own tail because it has nothing better to do.

I ease out of bed slowly so as not to wake Harley. I get a glass of water from the kitchen and stare out across the lake. It's raining lightly and I open the sliding door looking out on the deck at the rear of the cabin. Fresh air whooshes in and rustles the curtains with just a hint of pine from the large spruce tree growing a short distance away. It's very soothing and the quiet in this moment lends itself to thinking. I grab a legal pad, and sit at the kitchen table, where I begin to write. Perhaps, I can make some sense of recent events if I set my thoughts to paper. Sometimes, one needs to look at the players to bring things into focus. So, who are the players? I'm not a cop and I don't have access to all of the relevant facts surrounding these individuals, but maybe I can make some educated guesses.

To begin with, there are the three pilots who used to work for me, Luis Marcos, Ruben Clemente, and Jorge Alda. The first two men are dead and the truth is that I really know very little about either of those fellows. I was chief pilot when I first met them. I had an FAA mandated training flight with each man, but that was more or less the extent of my contact with them. They weren't particularly friendly and Walter Paris went to a lot of trouble to keep them away from me. I spent more time with Jorge Alda. We had lunch together occasionally and we talked about the women and the beaches in Rio de Janeiro, a city we both loved.

Walter Paris seemed to show Jorge more deference than he did the two other men. He was a few years younger than Marcos and Clemente, and he hadn't worked for Paris as long as they had either. It was almost as if Alda was some sort of protégé being groomed for other things. He was Paris' personal pilot even though the other men had more flying experience. He flew the billionaire all over the eastern seaboard whenever his boss was stateside. Their relationship was most curious, because, from what I could see, Paris never really let anyone get close to him. My guess is that Jorge probably knows more of Walter Paris' secrets than the other two men.

One of those secrets is the name of the person or persons who killed Susan Parks, another young pilot who used to work with me. She dated Jorge Alda briefly and it may have been the reason she was killed. I don't think Jorge is the killer because he just doesn't seem the type. Apparently, Susan knew something about Walter Paris' money laundering operation. She got drunk one night and told Jorge Alda about it. The authorities' working theory is that Jorge said something to Paris and that he ordered a hit on Parks. The police think that Alda may have overheard the other two pilots planning the murder and they were counting on his testimony to go after Paris. All three men were arrested initially, but they all made bail and skipped town before that could happen.

The other players in this mess are the various government agencies involved in the investigation. There are a lot of them including the DEA, CIA, FBI, Treasury, and state and local police. The DEA and the FBI did most of the heavy lifting. The DEA would normally have handled the case, but the CIA got involved because some of the drug money had been traced to terrorist groups overseas, where the DEA had almost no resources. The CIA has eyes and ears all over the world and they agreed to supply any pertinent information they had to the DEA, but only when it suited them. My previous relationship with a DEA agent named Gil Pepperdine was how I got dragged into the investigation. Gil and I used to work together on DEA's drug interdiction task force in South America, primarily in Venezuela.

I didn't work for the Agency as an employee. I was a contract pilot, mostly doing aerial photography taking pictures of marijuana groves and poppy fields. Based on that reconnaissance, the government would send a DC-3 into the area and dust the illegal drug crops with Agent Orange, which killed them before they could be harvested. On two or three other occasions, I was asked to fly out into the jungle and pick up special ops soldiers who were blowing up drug labs and popping drug traffickers. We did this quietly, mostly without the approval of the local and national governments of the respective countries. Gil Pepperdine was the DEA section chief and he gave me nearly all of my assignments, swearing me to secrecy. I served as his translator and I also helped him plan some of the missions. Pepperdine liked me and he offered me a position with the DEA, but after nearly getting killed on one of the missions, I quit and left South America.

When I discovered the money laundering operation at my airline, I went to Gil and told him what I'd found. He went to some higher-ups at the Agency and he was told they didn't want my help and to keep me out of it. I was worried that I might be implicated in the investigation. So, I illegally planted listening apparatuses in Walter Paris's car and a few other places. Since I wasn't with the police and had no court order for the devices, the information I collected could not be used against anyone in court. Never the less, I took the information to the FBI, but they, unbeknownst to me, were already conducting their own investigation independent of the DEA. At first, I got the same story and I was told to butt out, except for Sam Dorsey, who chose to believe me. He was FBI lead on the case. He couldn't use any of the information I'd collected to go after anyone officially, but it was more than enough to jump start his stalled investigation. The stuff I gave him showed him where to look and helped him catch a lot of the bad guys. We became friends, which is why he called and briefed me on the murders in Rio.

There was, and still is from what I can see, a jurisdictional turf war going on between the DEA and the FBI. I don't think it's between Gil Pepperdine and FBI agent Dorsey. My guess is that the in-fighting is happening at a higher level. The fact that the killer or killers knew exactly where their targets were located also suggests a possible information leak from someone well-placed in the DEA or FBI hierarchy.

Finally, there is Walter Paris, an enigma wrapped inside a conundrum. No one knows much about him other than his educational background and his investment prowess. He's a Harvard business grad and lawyer who made millions as one of Wall Street's rising stars. He later turned those millions into billions, quietly moving money around for drug traffickers. He's reclusive with homes in Switzerland, South America, Asia and Block Island off the New England Coast. The man is never in one place more than a couple of months at a time. Jorge Alda told me that Paris once took an around-the-world cruise spending an entire year aboard a ship, all the while running his business operations from his luxury stateroom. On the surface, he is a modern-day aristocrat with friends in high places all over the world. I believe that beneath it all lies a devious psychopath who'd slit your throat for looking sideways at him. Jorge Alda seems to know more about Walter Paris than anybody else. The question is, how did that happen? It is all quite troubling.

I am, by instinct and training, not a worrier. Pilots are trained to make rational decisions based solely on the available facts. At the moment, the available facts in this case don't provide much to go on, which leaves me in a quandary. Should I trust my intuition or base any future decisions that I may have to make exclusively on the facts and cold hard logic? Past experience has taught me that relying solely on facts and logic can sometimes be a way of going wrong with complete confidence.

All of this thinking is suddenly very draining and I realize that, for now, there is nothing I can do about any of it. I'm very tired and ready to go back to bed. I gently crawl beneath the sheets next to Harley and close my eyes, but I cannot drive the image of Jorge Alda from my mind.

# CHAPTER 15

July 12  0445 Hours  •  Rio de Janeiro

Location: An Empty Warehouse

Jorge Alda is groggy and he has a slight headache. He can't see because there is a hood covering his head and he is strapped to a chair. He feels a slight pinch on his left arm as someone injects something into one of his veins. Moments later, the headache is gone and he's feeling euphoric. The hood is suddenly removed from his head and he's staring at a man wearing a ski mask who's pointing a pistol directly at his forehead. A slightly baritone voice speaks calmly from behind the mask.

"Good morning, Mr. Alda. You are here to answer my questions truthfully or I'm going to blow your head off. Please nod if you understand me."

Alda nods in agreement, but he is on the verge of passing out. There is something wet on his chin and it takes a moment to realize that it is drivel oozing from the corner of his mouth. The masked man gently dabs it away with a handkerchief and switches on a tiny tape recorder hidden in his shirt pocket. He asks a series of test questions first.

"What is your given name?"

"I am Jorge Alda."

"What country are we in right now?"

"I think we are still in Brazil, but I'm not sure."

"What do you do for a living?"

"I'm an airplane pilot."

"Okay, do you know Luis Marcos?"

"Yes, he was my friend, but somebody killed him."

It is only now that Jorge realizes that there are electrodes attached to various locations on his body. He's being given a lie detector test and he has some questions of his own.

He asks, "Why are you doing this to me?"

The masked voice says, "I'll ask the questions. While you were sleeping, I found a business card in your wallet with several telephone numbers on it. Your friend, Luis Marcos, had a card just like it in his wallet. The digits on the top of the card are a European exchange. Whose number is it?"

"It's for Walter Paris, but we only call it if there's an emergency."

"The second number on the card is a Rio de Janeiro exchange. Who does that number belong to?"

"It's for the police commissioner. We're supposed to call him if we get into trouble here in the city."

"Does Walter Paris know the police commissioner?"

"Yes, they're friends."

"Are they real friends or does Walter bribe him?"

"Walter pays him for favors and information."

"Tell me what you know about Keystone Airlines."

"Walter Paris owned the company and I worked there as a pilot."

"Why did you leave the company?"

"I heard Luis and Ruben plotting a murder and the FBI wanted me to testify against Walter Paris, who was behind the whole thing. I was afraid that somebody would kill me and I came back here to Brazil to hide."

"Who did Ruben and Luis kill?"

"It was a woman named Susan Parks. She was mouthing off about Walter's money laundering operation and he wanted to shut her up."

"Did you know the woman?"

"Yeah, she was a friend and we went out on a couple of dates."

The hooded man nodded and asked, "Do you know where Walter Paris lives?"

"He moves around a lot and he has homes in New England, Switzerland, Venezuela, Hong Kong, Italy, and one here in Rio."

The masked man quizzes him for another hour asking dozens of questions. Jorge Alda's throat is dry and he wants a glass of water. The man hands him the water and pulls out a syringe.

Jorge yells, "Please don't kill me!"

The man angrily injects a clear liquid into his arm, and a few seconds later, Alda is unconscious. The stranger removes his ski mask and takes a deep breath. He got a lot of information that might be useful to the cops, but it wasn't exactly what he was looking for. He did get three names that might be useful, Bob Davenport, Tommy Rollins and Devin Ross. They would have to wait because his immediate plans were to leave Brazil as soon as possible. There are people looking for him now, the local police and probably a mercenary hit team. The cops think he killed Luis Marcos and Ruben Clemente. His former friend, Sullivan, and his hit team are after him because he's getting too close to the truth. He can't think about that too much right now because he's physically and emotionally exhausted.

There is still a lot to do before he leaves the country, especially if he is to keep Belle safe. He can feel his muscles relax just mouthing her name. What is it that has drawn him to an aging prostitute? In another place and time, he would have written her off as just another roll in the sack.

He thinks, "Maybe it's just two lost souls offering each other a few moments of comfort. Or, was it because she made him really feel something for the first time in years?"

He really couldn't think about that too much right now. Belle's friend, Detective Ruiz, wasn't likely to let this go. If he was as good at his job as Hamilton expected, Ruiz would have men posted at the airport, bus terminals and the train station. Sullivan and his cronies would also be looking for him in the obvious places, but they didn't have the same resources as the police. He could slip by them without too much trouble. The cops were a different matter. He had a plan to bypass the usual modes of transportation, but perhaps it was time to pay the detective a visit and provide him with an incentive to look the other way.

# CHAPTER 16

July 12 0745 • Rio de Janeiro

Location: Detective Ruiz's Apartment

Duncan Ruiz rolls over and shuts off the alarm on his clock radio. He usually likes waking up to music, but he didn't sleep well last night. He had a lot on his mind and it kept him awake. Two murders in as many days and Jorge Alda's disappearance are very troubling. His friend, Belle, has vanished after an explosion in front of her condominium and she is apparently traveling with a man who may have been responsible for all of it. He can't make sense of any of it. What he needs is a good strong cup of coffee to clear his head. He slips into his bathrobe and walks to the kitchen to brew a fresh pot. He is in the room for several minutes before he notices the package sitting on the kitchen table.

He thinks it odd at first because he doesn't remember putting it there the previous day. It is only now that he realizes someone has been in his apartment while he was sleeping. He quickly moves to a nearby cupboard where he keeps his service weapon when he's at home. He removes a pistol from its holster and does a quick sweep of the apartment to make sure his visitor isn't still on the premises. Satisfied, he returns to the kitchen, still visibly shaken, and opens the package. It contains a note attached to a small digital recorder.

The note reads: "Good morning detective. My apologies for breaking into your apartment last night, but there are a few things you should know. First, I did not kill Luis Marcos or Ruben Clemente. I'm pretty sure that was the work of some mercenaries working for a former associate of mine. You've no reason to believe me, but they are trying to make it look as though I'm responsible for the killings.

"First, I should say a few words about these men. They are former military and extremely dangerous. They often work in teams or in pairs with expertise in explosives, electronic surveillance, and espionage. They've all had sniper training and they can easily take out targets from nearly a mile away. One of these men was assigned to kill your friend, Belle. Fortunately, I was there to keep that from happening. You and detective Montoya will have to watch each other's backs, because the men in question may be working for a billionaire named Walter Paris. I found his telephone number along with yours in Jorge Alda's wallet. The information I have is a little sketchy at the moment, but your boss, the police commissioner, seems to have some connection to Walter Paris as well. It all seems to be tied to a company called Keystone Airlines located in the United States. There was money laundering and a murder, the details of which are still unclear to me.

"You're probably wondering how I came by this information. Early this morning, I had a conversation with Jorge Alda, a man you've been chasing for two days. Alda used to work for Keystone Airlines and he knew quite a lot about Walter Paris and his friends. I recorded the conversation and I've left a tape with you as proof that I'm telling the truth. My suggestion is that you keep this material to yourself. Asking too many questions right away, especially around your boss, might get you both killed.

"Finally, I want you to know that your friend, Belle, is in a safe place where no one will harm her. She says you're a good man and that you deserve to know that she's okay. One last thing. I'd keep my weapon a lot closer than the kitchen cupboard, especially when you're at home. If these guys come for you, the gun won't be of much help if it's in the other room. I'll be in touch if I learn anything else useful."

There is no name or signature at the bottom of the note and Ruiz's head is spinning as he asks himself, "Who the hell is this guy?"

He pours a cup of coffee and takes a seat at the table to play the tape. He is completely mesmerized. Although Alda sounds as though he's been drugged, the information he's providing is frightening. Ruiz learns that his boss might somehow be connected to multiple murders. As a cop, he's seen lots of gray areas where right and wrong bump up against each other. He's even looked the other way a few times himself. He's let people out of parking tickets and other minor offenses. He once let an attractive prostitute go when he walked in on her with a high-dollar businessman. That was how he met Belle. He thought that what she did with another consenting adult didn't seem like much of a crime to him. But, this is murder and Ruiz realizes that he may have given Paris information that led to the deaths of Marcos and Clemente. Worse yet, it is evidence which could be used to implicate him in this awful business. He is wondering what to do next when it occurs to him to call his father. His dad is police chief for a small town about one hundred fifty miles from Rio.

"Hello, Pop, it's your son calling to say hi and get some advice."

"Hi Duncan, it's good to hear your voice, it's been awhile."

"It's been too long, Dad. I should drop by and visit more often because I always enjoy our conversations. That's why I called. I could use a break from the city for a couple of days and maybe some advice. I'm working a really tough multiple murder case and I was wondering if I might drive up to your place and talk to you about it."

"You don't want to do this on the phone and maybe save a long drive?"

"No, Dad, I don't. Some of this stuff is hitting pretty close to home and we should probably discuss it in private. I've got a couple of things to take care of this morning, but I'd like to drive up and see you later today if that's ok."

"Enough said, I'll tell your mother to set an extra place for supper."

"Thanks, Dad, I'll see you later."

That was what Duncan loved about his father. There were never any wasted words. It was always, "Tell me what you need and let's get to it." He knew that he could lay it all out for his father and probably get some shrewd advice as to how to handle things. He was also wondering if he should discuss his personal involvement or the money his boss left him to keep it all under wraps.

"No matter," he thought, "Dad and I will work it out over a cold beer."

He throws a few clothes in an overnight bag, showers, and begins to run his morning errands. He still can't help thinking about Jorge Alda. Where is he? Did this mystery man kill him after he got what he wanted? There was so much that he didn't know and it was frustrating.

# CHAPTER 17

## July 12 1045 hours • Rio de Janeiro

## Location: Abandoned Cargo Van

Jorge Alda begins to wake slowly while lying on the floor of the vehicle. The powerful drugs in his system are making the journey to full consciousness extremely difficult. After a time, he is able to sit up and lean against the inside of the van. Even more time will lapse before he is able to fully grasp what has happened to him. He can hear faint indistinguishable noises outside the van, but he has no idea as to his location. A few more moments pass and he is able to open the door at the rear of the van. It is parked in some trees on a hillside. He attempts to stand and walk, but he quickly drops to one knee because his legs are not yet ready to fully support him. There is a sturdy-looking piece of wood lying just a few feet away and he uses it to prop himself up so he can examine his surroundings in more detail. At first glance, nothing is immediately recognizable, but then he sees Rodrigo Lagoon down below. The van is parked in a stand of trees overlooking a prominent Rio landmark. He can see the statue of Christ the Redeemer, the city's most recognizable attraction. But, this is not a time for sightseeing. The police are looking for him and this is a public area. He is, in fact, surprised that a parked van hasn't already caught someone's eye.

He stumbles back to the driver's side of the vehicle. To his great surprise, the keys are still in the ignition. Moments later, he finds his wallet, passport, cellphone and suitcase. Nothing has been taken. His head is pounding as he tries to make sense of what has happened to him. The first order of business should be to get the hell out of here, but he is not certain if he is well enough to drive any distance. Besides, someone might be tracking the van. Even if he could drive, where should he go? The police will be watching all of the obvious places and returning to the safe house is out of the question. His original plan was to spend a couple of days in a hotel and have his friend and fellow pilot, Lucas Vega, smuggle him out of the country on a cargo flight tonight. He's not even sure if that is still an option.

He hastily decides that he's stable enough to drive a short distance and he steers himself to a side street near the lagoon. Still woozy, he exits the van with his suitcase and makes his way to a nearby street corner, where he hails a taxi. He tells the driver to take him to a friend's address in an upscale part of the city. A short time later, they arrive at a gorgeous condominium complex and the driver whistles aloud as he pulls up to the entrance.

"Your friend must be a very wealthy fellow if he lives here."

Jorge is in no mood for conversation. He quickly pays the fare and tips the driver handsomely. Alda knows that he's taking a terrible chance coming here, but at the moment, there is no place else to go. This is one of Walter Paris' getaway homes. The security guard recognizes him almost immediately.

"Good morning, Mr. Alda. It's nice to see you again. Will you be staying long?"

"Hello, Federico. It's been a few weeks since I've seen you. The boss will be in town in a couple of days and I'll be flying him around the country for about a week. Does he have any other guests staying in the villa?"

"No sir, it's just you."

"Good. There's no need to buzz me in, I have a key. And oh, by the way, if anyone comes by the villa looking around, give me a call and let me know will you? There were a couple of guys following me yesterday and I'd appreciate a heads-up."

"Certainly, sir."

Alda hesitates a moment, then he smiles at the guard and tips him fifty bucks.

"Thank you sir, that's really not necessary."

"You're a good man, Federico, and I always look after my friends. Stop by when you get off shift and we'll have a beer together."

"Thanks for the offer, but I'm working a double today. My replacement called in sick. I'll be on until later this evening. I'll call you if I see anything unusual."

Jorge nods and takes the elevator to the top floor of the villa overlooking the city. His head is beginning to clear now and he knows he'll only be able to linger for a short time before the people who killed his friends will come here looking for him. He takes a quick shower and changes clothes before calling his friend. He's still toweling off when he places the call.

"Hey, Lucas, it's me, Jorge. Are we still on for tonight? I really need to get out of town because some guys are trying to kill me."

He is less than enthused by his friend's response.

"Yeah, and I heard the cops are looking for you, too! I don't know if I want to get involved in this, buddy. I was lucky enough to get out of the drug running business and I don't want to get dragged back into something nasty again."

Jorge pleads with him and says, "Look man, I bailed you out of trouble a couple of times and you owe me one. I just need this one last favor and you'll never hear from me again."

His friend hesitates momentarily before saying, "Alright, I'll help, but after today, I don't know you. You got someplace to stay until we fly out tonight?"

He says, "No, I'm on the move and I plan to stay that way. The guys chasing me are pros and I can't take a chance of staying in one place too long. Where do you want me to meet you?"

"I'll be home in a couple of hours, so how about coming by my place? You can hang out there until it's time to go to the airport. When we hook up, I want you to get into your pilot's uniform. Security at the air freight dock is pretty laid-back. You'll look like part of our crew when we walk through the screening area. It should be a piece of cake."

He sighs gratefully and says, "Thanks, Lucas, I'll see you later this afternoon."

Jorge's immediate plan is to linger here at the villa until it's time to meet his friend and leave the city. At that moment, the telephone is ringing at the security post in front of the villa and the call will force him to alter his plans.

The guard answers the telephone, "Good morning, security, this is Federico."

"Good morning, Federico, this is Walter Paris, how are you?"

"I'm fine sir, thank you for asking. It's been a few weeks since I've seen you. If you're in town, I'd be happy to send the limousine to pick you up."

"Thank you, but that won't be necessary. I'm calling to ask if you've seen my associate, Jorge Alda. I've been trying to reach him, but he isn't picking up his phone."

"He's here at the villa, sir. He just checked in a short time ago. I'd be happy to go up to the residence and let him know you've called."

Paris responds cheerfully, "Actually, I gave him a promotion last week and we're having a little celebration for him tonight. I'm going to send a couple of my people by to pick him up. I'd like this to be a surprise, so let's keep this between the two of us."

Federico nods and says, "My lips are sealed, sir."

Paris says, "Thank you Federico. If you'd like to join us for the party, I can have a car pick you up later and bring you into town."

"That's very generous of you, sir, but I'm working a double shift today and someone needs to keep an eye on the place."

"Fair enough, maybe we can do it next time. I've got to make another call, but I'll be sure to stop and say hello the next time I'm in town. Goodbye."

Walter Paris' next call is to the hit team that killed Ruben Clemente and Luis Marcos.

## CHAPTER 18

### July 12 1400 hours

### Location: Fifteen Miles North of Pittsburgh, 3000 Feet

EVERY AIRPLANE HAS its own unique flying characteristics, some good and others that are less than good. These are the engineering design compromises that people who fly professionally learn to live with. Pilots generally try to operate an airplane in such a way to take advantage of the machine's good qualities and avoid those areas that are less than perfect.

For example, the single-engine V-tail Beechcraft Bonanza, that I'm currently flying, is one of the faster airplanes in its class. It's expensive and it looks terrific, which often makes it the weapon of choice for well-to-do doctors, lawyers and other high-dollar professionals looking for a weekend toy. That's the good news. The less than good news is that in exchange for the speed and good looks, the airplane requires the pilot to be more attentive to the flight controls in turbulence than would be necessary in some other models. Also, the aircraft demands that passengers or cargo be loaded more carefully than similar airplanes in its class. If it is burdened by too much weight or if that weight is improperly positioned inside the cabin, the airplane's less than desirable characteristics are amplified. Under these circumstances, particularly in the hands of a really careless or inexperienced pilot, the airplane's flight characteristics can be downright dangerous. This is an apt metaphor for my friendship with Thomas Samuel Rollins, aka, Tommy.

I'm thinking about this as I begin a slow descent into Pittsburgh's Allegheny County Airport. I've borrowed a friend's airplane to turn a nearly four-hour roundtrip drive into a fifty-minute two-way flight. Tommy has agreed to meet with me to talk about the fallout from the unsavory events at the airline he once owned. I am conflicted about meeting with him. He put me in an awkward position when he allowed the airline I was managing to be involved in money laundering and making illegal flights for some underworld thugs. He made millions on the deal and I was nearly left holding the bag for all of it when the police started their investigation. We haven't spoken in months because I was furious with him when I found out what was happening. I am not at all sure this will go well.

Another part of me is looking forward to this shabby little reunion. I've known Tommy since we were kids and there is something about childhood friendships that you just can't replace. We grew up together and I've always considered him part of my family. Over the years, we have shared the good, the bad, and the ugly. We've been business partners; we've flown together, gotten drunk together, been shot at, even lusted after the same women and none of it ever came between us. We had frequent disagreements, which sometimes led to heated and extended arguments. But, in the end, we were always able to work it out and stand together whenever there was serious trouble. There was never a moment of jealousy, suspicion or distrust until recently.

The tower clears me to land, and a few minutes later, I'm taxiing to the terminal. I secure the airplane and walk inside to meet Tommy. As I enter the building, I can see him standing in the corner admiring a photograph of an old DC-3 airliner, an aircraft that we used to fly together. Always the clothes-horse, Tommy is dressed like a Wall Street banker top to bottom with an expensive haircut, navy blue pin-stripe suit, silk tie, Rolex watch, and black, highly polished, wing-tip shoes. He appears to be exactly what he is, a bright, educated, and elegant professional.

By any measure, Tommy Rollins is a genius and it's been that way since we were kids. He was my father's best piano student, and, even as a teenager, he could hold his own with some of the finest jazz pianists in the country. He graduated at the top of his high school and college classes, all the while becoming a commercial pilot in record time. His shrewd business acumen made him a millionaire before he was thirty. We are both six feet three inches tall, but Tommy caps it all off with graceful athleticism, James Bond good looks, and a line of BS that routinely charms women right out of their socks. Men like him too. He has a vast reservoir of off-color jokes, which, over the years, he has shared with the guys in boardrooms and back street bars all over the world. He is what some would call a complete package and that is the problem.

The trouble with being dubbed a genius at an early age is that the afflicted individual isn't always self-reflective. There is no need if you've repeatedly been told that you're perfect, especially if most of your actions bear it out. That was Tommy's trouble --- he was good at everything and he rarely failed in any of his endeavors. He takes chances and he frequently shoots from the hip. I used to jokingly say that his motto was, "Ready-Fire-Aim!" This methodology afforded him great success in the business world, but it has cost him dearly in other ways, including a failed marriage, estrangement from friends, a run-in with the IRS, and very nearly a trip to jail when a money laundering scheme was discovered by the authorities. Yet, for me, he is still a valued friend, which is why I've asked him to meet with me.

"Hello, Tommy. Thanks for coming."

He grins, gives me a bear-hug and slaps me on the back saying, "I'm glad you're not still pissed off at me."

I grin back at him and say, "Oh, I'm still pissed, but I missed you. You always make me laugh."

Tommy laughs amiably and takes off his jacket. He hangs it on the back of a chair and waves me to a seat at a table in the lobby.

He says, "I've been traveling in Europe and I've been out of touch for a couple of weeks. Kate said you needed to talk with me, but she didn't give me any details. What's up?"

"I don't mean to bring up a sore subject, Tommy, but how are things going with you and the Keystone Airlines business?"

I can see his mood shift when he says, "Well, thanks to you, I'm broke and I almost went to jail."

I am equally irritated when I say, "You mean 'we' almost went to jail. You hung me out to dry on that little adventure, too! As I remember it, I kept us both out of prison."

Tommy suddenly looks very tired, and he raises his hand to say, "Look, I didn't come here to fight. I was hoping we could bury the hatchet and get on with our lives."

I relax and say, "Me, too!"

He says, "Besides, I just cut a deal for a million-dollar loan and I'll use the money to get back on top in no time. What'd you want to talk to me about?"

"Walter Paris."

"It's odd that you should bring up his name, Devin. He's going to arrange the loan to help me jumpstart my life. He's really not such a bad person."

I'm frustrated when I say, "You just love to play with fire, don't you? You're doing business with a man who apparently had a former associate of yours killed. Remember Raul Silva?"

"Walter told me he had nothing to do with that. He thinks it was the other cartel members that bumped him off because he was going to rat them out. I don't condone murder, but Silva's death kept him from testifying against Walter and that, coincidently, kept me out of jail."

"What about Susan Parks?" I ask.

Tommy says, "The police never charged him with that and as far as I know, they closed their investigation."

"Listen to yourself, you're making a deal with the devil."

He sighs and says, "Kate used to tell me the same thing."

"She's your conscience, Tommy, maybe mine too."

"Look, I know it's risky, but I'm dead broke. My creditors are hounding me and I could lose my home. I only have enough money to live for a couple months. I got my old flying job back at the airline, but I don't go to training for another six weeks and money's tight until I start getting paid. I have to do something or I'll lose my house. Besides, I'll set up the loan so nobody will know where the money came from."

I ask, "How much cash do you really need to tide you over, if you don't take Walter's money?"

He says, "About twenty grand."

"I've got that much, why don't you let me write you a check so you can stay away from Paris."

"Why are you so down on Walter Paris?"

"I take it you haven't heard the latest?"

"I've been traveling, what's going on?"

"There were two more killings and they were both pilots who used to work for me at Keystone Airlines, Ruben Clemente and Luis Marcos. They were supposed to testify against Paris about Susan Parks' murder. The FBI is pretty sure that Paris ordered the hits. Do you still want to hook up with this guy?"

Tommy is visibly shaken. I give him a few moments to regroup before speaking again.

"Look," I say, "I have plenty of money and I can give you whatever you need. The upside is that you won't have to worry about me shooting you in the back. Plus, it'll reduce the chances of getting your family involved in this again. Remember how Raul Silva threatened them to get you to launder money for him? Paris might do the same thing, or worse."

He says, "Kate and I are divorced. She was never involved in any of this and Paris has no reason to go after her or the kids."

This is vintage Tommy Rollins, making grand assumptions without fully thinking through the consequences of his actions. I remain silent for a time and it's not long before I can see that he's reconsidering his options.

He finally says, "You're right. I'll unwind the deal with Walter and take you up on your offer. Thank you."

I write out a check and hand it to Tommy.

He asks, "Is there anything else that I should know about this Rio de Janeiro business?"

I quickly bring him up to speed on everything I know concerning the shootings and Jorge Alda's disappearance. I explain that Alda is probably on the run because he thinks Walter Paris is worried about his potential court testimony. Tommy provides some additional information that leaves me reeling.

He says, "I don't think Walter is worried about Jorge because the kid will never testify against him."

"Why is that?" I ask.

Tommy smiles and says, "I thought you knew, Devin. Jorge is Paris' kid. Walter hooked up with a Brazilian gal named Lara years ago and he couldn't keep it in his pants. Jorge was the end result. Walter is 'Mr. Ivy-League Proper.' Although he likes to keep his public image squeaky clean, he let that little tidbit slip one day when we were having drinks. Jorge is not going to send his dad to jail and Walter is not going to put a hit out on his own son."

We don't know it yet, but at this very moment, events are taking shape that will blow Tommy's theory right out the window.

# CHAPTER 19

## July 12 2015 Hours Local Time

## Location: A Beautiful Chalet
## Zurich, Switzerland

WALTER PARIS HANGS UP his encrypted phone and stares out the window for a moment. His view of Lake Zurich and the Alps is spectacular. He can't enjoy it because there is some terrible business that must be handled first. He has just sent Sullivan's war dogs after his son. He doesn't want to kill Jorge, but he hasn't taken his calls for several days. If he could only talk to the boy, he would reassure him that everything would be fine as long as he refuses to cooperate with the authorities. He's a good kid and Walter has enjoyed showing him how the family business works. The problem is that if he talks, his old man will be staring at the death penalty.

Jorge was an accident from a youthful indiscretion in his distant past. Walter grew up in a wealthy neighborhood just outside London. His father was a successful English businessman. When he was in college, he visited his dad, who was then running a company in Brazil. He met a beautiful young Brazilian woman during Carnival and they had a torrid affair which produced a child. Walter's father knew nothing of this until the baby was born nearly a year later. By then, his son was nearing the end of his last year of college with plans for law school and possibly an MBA. When Paris senior found out about the child, he bought the mother off, who had already contacted Walter and let him know that he had a son. Walter pleaded with his father to disclose the location of the woman and his child, but the older man refused. After graduating, Walter spent nearly a year looking for his Brazilian family to no avail. He honestly believed that he loved the young woman. He wanted to continue his search, but he was broke and his father refused to help him. At about the same time, a job opportunity and a chance to make a lot of money presented itself. Walter accepted vowing to resume his search when he was better off financially, but life intervened.

It would be nearly twelve years before he would resume his search and even that was a fluke. Walter's dad died and left him a sizeable inheritance. While closing out his late father's affairs, he discovered that the old man had been secretly sending checks to Rio de Janeiro, supporting the woman and her child the entire time. At first, Walter was furious, but another part of him was happy that his dad had taken care of the boy and the mother. The situation raised any number of questions because twelve years is a long time. Had the woman married? Did the boy know that he was his father? Were they both healthy and what would be her feelings toward him after all of this time?

He had always been a cautious man and rushing back into this woman's life hardly seemed prudent. Walter was now a millionaire several times over and he hired a top notch detective agency to find his family, monitor their activities, and report back to him. After two months of surveillance, he flew to

Brazil to have a look for himself, but at a discrete distance. The woman was married and the boy believed that her husband was his father. The family lived modestly. The man was a burly construction worker and she worked a few days a week as a waitress. Neither of them made much money and the monthly stipend from Walter's father was all that kept them from drifting into wretched poverty. Walter's initial thoughts were to move on and let them live out their lives, but an incident in a park one day changed his mind.

The family was having lunch together chatting away amiably. There was some sort of disagreement and the man suddenly stood and slapped the boy, giving him a bloody nose. The mother tried to intervene and the man struck her, too. Walter, who was observing this through a pair of binoculars on the other side of the park, was livid. By this time, he was involved in money laundering for the drug cartels and he knew people who could take care of this sort of thing. He had the husband beaten to within an inch of his life and he was told that if anything like this ever happened again, he would be killed. He was also warned not to speak of the beating to his wife or the boy. Walter waited six months and then he reached out to the mother.

He sent her a note pretending to be his father, saying that he needed to make an adjustment in the monthly stipend. He asked the woman to have lunch with him at one of Rio's finest restaurants. Their reunion was bittersweet. Her name was Lara, which loosely translated from Portuguese means "elegant lady." Although she was modestly dressed, her physical presence and demeanor lit up the room. She looked older, but to Walter, she was just as lovely as he remembered. He stood as she approached his table and they embraced immediately. They both burst into tears.

Walter said, "My father tried to hide you from me, but I never stopped looking."

"I know," she said, "My friends told me that you tried to find me."

They talked for more than two hours, leaving their meals nearly untouched. The conversation was problematic, because time and distance had changed everything and they both knew it.

She said, "Walter, when we first met, I was a young uneducated woman looking to get out of poverty. I'm embarrassed to say this now, but I saw you as a way to do that. Your father offered me the money and he told me that you never wanted to see me again. I accepted because our child would have died in the favelas without it. I could not let that happen."

"I don't care about any of that, Lara," he said, "The only question now is what happens next?"

She smiled a sad smile and said, "Look at me, nothing has changed. I'm still an uneducated woman from the slums. You are a wealthy, sophisticated man of the world and I would no more fit into your life than you would into mine."

He shrugged and said, "I know, but what about the boy. I can give him a life beyond this place. I can make him a rich man."

Lara frowned and said, "Giving a kid too much too early is not necessarily a good thing. He needs to grow and figure life out for himself. Sometimes, there is value in struggle. Instant wealth would interfere with that."

He nodded in agreement and said, "There must be something that I can do?"

They reached a compromise. Walter would pay for Jorge's education. He also quadrupled Lara's monthly income by having it appear as though she was working for one of his companies. This enabled her to move the family into a nicer home and a better neighborhood. They also agreed not to tell Jorge that Walter was his father until he was older. This arrangement worked well for a couple of years until Jorge's adoptive father was injured in a construction accident and was unable to work for several months. He resented the fact that Lara was now the primary breadwinner in the family. His male ego was badly bruised. They argued about it frequently and, as soon as he was able to work again, he divorced Lara and married another woman. Without local fatherly guidance, Jorge drifted into friendships with members of a local street gang and had a couple of run-ins with the police. He was eighteen years old when Walter decided to intervene.

He had Lara introduce him to the young man as her employer who was offering him an educational scholarship as one of the company benefits afforded his mother. Jorge wasn't interested until Walter pulled him aside and made him an offer that he couldn't refuse.

"Look," he said, "I don't care how you want to live out your life. If you wish to spend it hanging out with your buddies from the favelas, that's fine with me. All I ask is that you give me a few minutes and listen to what I have to say. If you don't like what you hear, you can walk away and you'll never have to see me again. I'm a man of my word and to prove it, here's five grand in cash that is yours to keep, whether you say yes or no to my deal. If you say yes, I'll show you how to make five times that money every month. Here's my number, and you have exactly twenty-four hours to think it over. After that, the deal is off and you and I are done, period. One last thing — this conversation is just between us. You are not to speak to your mother or anyone else about it. Do I have your word on that?"

Jorge agreed and shook his hand. Walter nodded politely and walked away. His son's head was spinning because he'd never seen so much money. His first inclination was to simply take the money and run, but after a restless night with no sleep, he decided to talk to Walter Paris.

Walter said, "Here's the deal, kid. I'll give you another five grand to spend a few weeks traveling with me to see how my business works. If you like what you see, I'll make sure you get a good education, and, after that, I'll find you a job with one of my companies making a lot of money. That's it in a nutshell. Take it or leave it."

Jorge had nothing to lose. He accepted the offer and his life immediately shifted into high gear. They boarded Walter's private jet and his education began with a whirlwind tour of European cities, Prague, Paris, Rome, Madrid and London. Then it was on to the trading floor at the New York Stock Exchange and a brief explanation of commodities trading. He was introduced to some of Walter's business associates and the world of pin-striped suits and three martini lunches. Walter purposely kept him away from the illegal side of his business. The young man was overwhelmed, something that Walter didn't understand until Jorge told him.

He said, "This is what you want for me, not what I want."

Walter thought for a moment and said, "You know, you're right. My father forced this life on me and it wasn't what I wanted either. I owe you an apology Jorge, I was being selfish and I'm sorry. What do you want to do?"

Jorge wasn't expecting an apology and he was reluctant to tell Walter about his childhood dream until the older man smiled and told him that it was ok.

"I want to be a commercial pilot, but the best schools are in the United States and my parents could never afford to send me there."

Walter said, "Well, I think we can take care of that. Did you have someplace in mind?"

He was intrigued when Jorge immediately pulled out a brochure for Ohio State University, which had one of the oldest and most prestigious aviation programs in the country. Walter made arrangements for him to enter the school that fall and Jorge graduated five years later with a degree in aviation management and his commercial pilot license. After graduation, Walter used his influence to get him a job as a copilot for a commuter airline, which Jorge enjoyed for nearly three years. He was bored looking for a bigger paycheck and a little excitement. He'd met Ruben Clemente and Luis Marcos in flight school and they were friends. They were already flying drugs and money for the cartels and they made Jorge an offer, who was soon working with them on his days off.

Walter always kept tabs on Jorge and when he first found out what he was doing, he was angry. Then he had an epiphany, what better way to introduce him to the seamy side of the family business? He concocted an elaborate scheme buying several small banks in Ohio and Indiana. He bought a small charter airline to quietly move laundered drug money between the cities where the banks were located. Then he cut a deal with his cartel friends that would let him hire Luis Marcos and Ruben Clemente to fly for him along with Jorge. It worked perfectly, and, in just a few weeks, they were moving nearly a billion dollars a month for the cartels with plans to expand. Walter was so enthusiastic that he became involved personally with the operation so that he could be near his son. It was a mistake that would cost him dearly.

Walter usually took great care to distance himself from the front lines of all of his businesses so he could maintain what he liked to call "plausible deniability" if things went sideways. One of the airline's employees, Susan Parks, had a pilot boyfriend who accidently leaked some information to her about his money laundering flights. She got drunk and started spouting off to a few people about it. She had to go or they would all be in jail. Walter was going to have a couple of pros do it, but Luis Marcos and Ruben Clemente overheard him talking about it on the phone. They were so worried that they jumped the gun, deciding to take her out on their own. They were sloppy and the police quickly found the body bringing a lot of unwanted scrutiny to Walter's airline operation. Worse yet, Jorge had a few dates with the woman and he liked her. When he learned of her death, he began to distance himself from Walter and his business.

What most people didn't know, including Walter, was that Jorge had been previously arrested by the American authorities, who were using that as leverage to get him to feed them information about Paris' operation in exchange for not being prosecuted. When the police raided Keystone Airlines, they arrested Luis and Ruben immediately. They also took Jorge into custody to maintain his cover as a police informant. They set very high bail amounts for all three men. What the authorities hadn't anticipated was that Walter would pay those bails and get them out of the country using fake passports. Once they settled in Brazil, he had Luis and Ruben killed. So far, Jorge had managed to elude Walter's men, but now he knew that Jorge was hiding in his villa in Rio. He'd just dispatched a team of mercenaries to take care of the problem.

It troubled him at first, but in his mind, this was business and he'd given Jorge several opportunities to resolve the matter peacefully. What really bothered him was Lara. He is going take the one good thing left in her life and kill it. He knows that his actions will crush the very soul of the only woman he has ever truly loved and he can feel a large tear running down his cheek.

He ponders the situation for a few more moments and pours himself a double Scotch before saying aloud, "This too shall pass."

# CHAPTER 20

## July 12  1130 Hours

## Location: Rio de Janeiro

Federico Garcia is sitting in the guard shack enjoying a pulled-pork sandwich when the black Mercedes slowly drives past the front entrance of the very expensive condominium he is watching. There are two men in the car with military-style haircuts. Normally, he'd let it go, but the car rounded the block again and that got his attention. As a retired cop, he'd learned to spot trouble long ago and Jorge Alda told him that there might be some people following him. He picks up the phone and calls upstairs.

"Jorge, this is Federico. There are a couple of guys cruising around here in a black Mercedes and they don't look friendly."

"Thanks for the call, Federico. You just saved my life. I'll be out of here in a couple of minutes. Do you still have a key to this place?"

"I do, why?"

"After those guys leave, check under the cushion of the sofa in the living area. I'd like to leave something for you. And listen, don't hassle those men because they're trained killers. I don't want you to get hurt. I'm out of here, thanks again."

The line goes dead just as the car pulls up to the entrance of the complex. Federico waves them to a stop and the window rolls down on the driver's side of the vehicle.

He greets them politely, "Yes sir, can I help you?"

The driver holds up a cardkey for the gate and says, "Walter Paris sent us by to pick up one of his employees. Have you seen Jorge Alda?"

Federico lies and says, "I don't know for sure, but he was here earlier with a couple of policemen. I went on break for a few minutes and I don't know if they are still in the residence. Would you like me to call upstairs to see if he's in?"

Federico works to suppress a smile when the man in the passenger seat mutters under his breath, "Shit."

The driver is cool when he says, "We'll come back after Mr. Alda finishes his business with the police. Thank you."

The Mercedes backs away from the entry gate and disappears down the main street. After waiting a decent interval, Federico uses his key to enter the residence. Jorge is gone, but the young man left him five hundred dollars for his trouble. Federico can only hope that his little diversion has bought the kid enough time to get away. Those men in the car were comfortable with violence and he could see it in their eyes. Upon reaching a discrete distance from the condominium, the black Mercedes rolls to a stop and the man in the passenger seat makes a call to Walter Paris.

He says, "Sir, we've pursued Mr. Alda as directed, but the security guard at your residence says that he is in there with some policemen. We can still complete the mission, but we thought we should check with you before proceeding. Are we still a go?"

Walter almost panics when he says, "No, I don't want the police involved in any of this. Cancel the operation. I'll contact you later with further instructions."

He promptly hangs up, actually relieved that he won't have to kill his son. The men in the Mercedes drive back to their hotel. Jorge Alda is twelve blocks away hailing a cab as part of his hastily conceived getaway plan to leave the city.

Across town, the man known as Richard Hamilton is also leaving Rio de Janeiro, but in the lap of luxury. He and Belle have boarded a cruise ship bound for Miami. He chose this method of travel because it is doubtful that the police will be looking for him on a twenty-eight-day cruise. More likely, they'll be searching the bus terminals, the airport, or the train stations. He and Belle are traveling in disguise as Mr. and Mrs. Robert Johnston on forged passports. They had no trouble clearing customs and the big ocean liner is already powering itself away from the dock. Once they are clear of the harbor and underway, he can feel his shoulders relax. Belle is taking a nap in their stateroom. He is standing on the stern of the big ship watching the shoreline fade in the distance as he plans his next move.

Now, it's time to be patient and let things settle. Experience has taught him that life is often a dance between making things happen and letting them happen. There is no hurry because he has the names of the key management people at Keystone Airlines. He got them during his early morning interrogation of Jorge Alda. He removes a sheet of paper from his shirt pocket with a list of the men in question. There are two at the very top of the page and he can feel the anger coursing through his veins as he reads their names aloud, "Devin Ross and Tommy Rollins."

He'll be paying them both a visit.

# CHAPTER 21

## July 12 1430 hours Local Time

## Location: Pittsburgh, Allegheny County Airport

TOMMY AND I are wrapping up our conversation about Walter Paris and Keystone Airlines.

I say, "I would never have guessed that Jorge was Walter's kid. They don't look anything like each other."

Tommy says, "The story gets even more bizarre. Jorge doesn't know that Walter is his father. The kid is in his late twenties now and somehow Paris has managed to keep it a secret all this time."

I'm perplexed and completely worn out from all of this talking, but Tommy is not yet finished when he says, "I don't know about you Devin, but I'm going to invest in a Kevlar flak vest and renew my carry permit for the nine millimeter pistol you gave me years ago."

"I've taken some precautions too, Tommy. I moved Harley across the lake to another cabin and I've been to the shooting range a few times to dust off the cobwebs."

"How is that feisty redhead anyway? She has great gams and you're a lucky man, Devin."

"She called me this morning and she said that she's taking her old job back at the big airline in Denver. It's just a guess, but I'm betting she'll try and get in touch with her ex-husband."

Tommy laughs and says, "Sounds like another wild ride on the male-female merry-go-round to me. As I recall, she's done this before. Why do you stay with her?"

"I don't know for sure. Sometimes, I like it when romance is a little topsy-turvy. I think the uncertainty and the wild passionate interludes are what attract me to her. If there wasn't any mystery or a little excitement, we both might lose interest. It's probably the same way between you and Astrid."

Tommy is suddenly very quiet and some time passes before he speaks.

"What made you think about Astrid?"

I point to the airline boarding passes in his shirt pocket. "Those tickets are to Montreal and you and I both know that she is the only one you know living there. How long have you two been seeing each other?"

He sighs and says, "It's been almost a year. You don't miss much, do you?"

"Does Kate know?" I ask.

"Yeah, Astrid told her a few months ago. I wanted to keep it quiet, but Astrid didn't want to play games and she told her straight away. I'm amazed, because somehow they've managed to remain close. It's got to be tough when your best friend hooks up with your husband, divorced or not."

"Kate's always been a class act, Tommy. That's why you married her."

He grins and says, "That may be true, but if I hadn't met her first, she would have married you. The two of you finish each other's sentences and she's loved you for as long as I can remember. We're divorced now. So, here's your big chance to snag my ex-wife."

"Let's not go there, Tommy. I've got enough on my plate without digging up the past."

"You mean past, present, and maybe future," he says.

He's right, I do love Kate and I always have, but there are a myriad of sticking points in that equation. One of them is the fact that Tommy and Kate will always be tied together through their children. Even though I'm very close to the kids, an untimely romance with their mother wouldn't sit well with either of them right now. My relationship with Harley, the errant girlfriend, is also unclear. Romance is the farthest thing from my mind and I want to end this conversation.

"Tommy, I haven't got time for this. I'm unemployed, my girlfriend is probably leaving me, and there may be some really nasty people looking for both of us. Let's move on."

Before he can respond, my cellphone rings. It's my friend, Sam Dorsey.

"Hi, Sam, what's up?"

"Devin, we need to get together and talk and I don't want to do it over the phone. I'm in Erie, where are you now?"

"I'm in Pittsburgh, but if I leave now, I can meet you in less than an hour."

Sam says, "Jesus, that's almost a hundred and twenty miles by car on the Interstate. What are you going to do, fly?"

I glance at my watch and say, "Exactly, pick me up at the Erie airport in about forty-five minutes."

"Okay, see you soon."

Tommy asks, "Who was that?"

"That was Sam Dorsey over at the FBI. He wants to meet with me away from his office and I'm guessing that it's important. I've got to run, but I'll keep you in the loop if there's anything that affects you. Also, let me know what happens when you unwind that deal with Walter Paris."

I shake Tommy's hand to say goodbye and he says, "Watch your back, brother!"

"You too, Tommy!"

Ten minutes later, I'm airborne in a near cloudless sky on my way to Erie.

# CHAPTER 22

## July 12 1430 Hours • Rio de Janeiro

## Location: Lucas Cruz's Apartment

"Thanks for letting me hang out here, Lucas, I have no place else to go."

"Jorge, how the hell did you get into this mess in the first place?"

"I overheard a couple of guys planning to murder a woman. The police want me to testify against my boss and he wants to kill me because he thinks I'll rat him out. I don't want to go against him because he's done everything for me. He paid for college and all of my flight training. He's always looked out for me. On top of everything else, he takes care of my mom. I can't burn him for that."

"So, what are you going to do?"

"If you can get me to Manaus tonight, I'll hang out there for a while and work up some kind of game plan. I've been on the run since this business started and I haven't really had time to do any serious thinking."

"Does your mom know what's happening?"

"No, and I want to keep her out of this."

"You have to tell her something, Jorge. I know your mom, she's cool. She can handle this if you tell her, but she'll be worried sick if she doesn't know where you are."

"You're right. I'll call her before we leave and let her know that I'll be gone for a few weeks."

"That's good. Why don't you change into your uniform so we can head over to the airport? We'll grab something to eat on the way over there."

Jorge nods and goes to the other room to change clothes. He's worried because he has no idea what he's going to say to his mom. Walter Paris is already on the telephone telling her his side of the story.

"Hello, Lara, this is Walter. I'm glad I caught you because I'm trying to reach Jorge and it's urgent that I contact him. I've tried to reach him several times, but he's not answering his phone."

He can hear the panic in her voice when she says, "I haven't heard from him in a couple of days and he hasn't been picking up my calls either. You're scaring me, Walter. What's going on?"

"He's in trouble with the police. I'm trying help him, but he won't talk to me."

Lara says, "He's been in trouble with the cops before, but nothing too serious. He always tells me what's going on, but not this time. What's really happening, Walter? It must be something awful if you're calling me."

"It's really bad, Lara, but I can't go into the details with you."

"Walter, I grew up in the favelas with murderers, prostitutes, and drug dealers and I lived in the middle of gang wars. There's not a damn thing you can tell me that I haven't experienced firsthand. On top of that, I work for one of your companies and I hear things. I know that a lot of your money comes from the cartels. Is there a connection between Jorge's trouble and your underworld buddies?"

Walter is shaken to the core. He's gone out of his way to hide his "side business" from Lara and he can't imagine how she found out about it. There's nothing he can do now, so it's time for some half-truths.

"Do you really want to know?" he asks.

"You're damn right I do, and don't you dare leave anything out."

He only hesitates a few moments before laying it all out for her.

"Alright, here it is," he says. "The American and Brazilian authorities are looking for him in conjunction with a murder investigation. They want him to testify against me because they think I had something to do with it."

"Did you?"

"No, I didn't, but the woman who was killed worked for one of my companies and she was Jorge's friend."

"Is there anything else?"

"Yes, there are some professional hit men from the cartels looking for Jorge. They'll kill him if they get the chance. I can use my money and influence to stop it, but I need to talk to our son in order to make that happen. Will you help me?"

"What do you want me to do?"

"Just have him call me if he contacts you. I can take it from there."

"Alright, I'll try and get him to call you, if I hear from him. But I'm not making any promises. Our son is his own man and this is his decision, not mine."

Walter says, "Fair enough, Lara. In the meantime, I'll do what I can to slow things down. I'll call you if I hear anything."

Lara puts down the phone. She's crying and her hands won't stop shaking.

# CHAPTER 23

## July 12  1610 Hours

## Location: Erie, Pennsylvania

As I taxi into the General Aviation parking area, I can see Sam Dorsey on the other side of a chain-link fence standing next to a government issued black sedan. I give him a quick wave and park the airplane. He greets me with a wry smile.

"I don't think I'll ever understand airplane people," he says. "Were you really in Pittsburgh forty-five minutes ago?"

"Yes, I was, but you beckoned and I came a running with bells on, boss."

"Well, I hope it's worth the trip. Is there some place close where we can talk and maybe get a drink and something to eat?"

"Hayfields Restaurant is in the airline terminal on the other side of the field. They even have a well-stocked bar."

"Good, because I could use a libation and you may want one, too."

"That sounds ominous."

"Let's just say there is some material that has crossed my desk which may be of interest."

"I'm afraid to ask how you come by your information, Sam."

He grins and says, "I'm the freaking FBI and I know damn near everything."

Once we are seated, Sam begins his narrative.

"For the last couple of days, I've been chasing down a few things. Item number one: I ran DNA and fingerprint checks on some stuff the Rio cops found near one of your murdered pilots and I got two hits."

"So, you have a lead on who's doing the killing?"

"Well, yes and no. We have a positive ID on both individuals, but the files are classified under the heading of national security and no one will give me access to them."

"Sam, that suggests to me that we've got a couple of former American military pros pulling the trigger for the bad guys."

"I'm right with you, buddy, which brings me to item number two: The cops found the weapon that killed one of your pilots in a burned out American Embassy vehicle in Rio de Janeiro. You worked at that embassy doing missing persons work, did you not?"

"How did you know I used to work there, Sam?"

He smiles and says, "Like I said before, I'm the freaking FBI and I know everything. Let's move on to item number three: The weapon found in the burned-out car was also American military issue."

Sam raises a finger saying, "Item number four: Someone above my boss' paygrade told him to drop the investigation and move on."

"What did your supervisor say?"

"He's the freaking FBI, too, and he said to keep digging, but to do it quietly and on my own time. I have no budget for this, and, if I get caught, my career with the Bureau is over. Which brings me to item number five: Will you help me?"

"Sam, you trusted me with this stuff when no one else would. The least I can do is give you a hand. What do you need?"

"I honestly don't know where to start. I was hoping you had some ideas. I'd like to get more information from the cop running the investigation in Rio, but I don't speak Portuguese and his English isn't the best, either. So far, we've just been sharing bits and pieces of information and I don't think either of us has the whole story. Would you be willing to talk to him?"

"Do you think he knows more that he's letting on?"

"Could be, but I don't know if this guy is the real deal or part of the problem. I'd have to see him face-to-face to make a decent guess about that. It's hard to tell about that kind of thing without getting a read on his body language. You got any ideas?"

"I used to work with a couple of cops when I was based in Rio. I don't know if they are still on the job, but I could try and look them up to see what they think of your guy. I still have a few friends at the embassy and I may be able to get some help from them, too."

"I do see one fly in the ointment, Sam. I don't have your credentials and some of these people won't talk to me without them. But, I have a suggestion in that regard."

"What'd you have in mind?"

"I'll buy us some tickets and we'll go down there, stir the pot a little, and maybe do a little horse trading for more information. You can flash your badge and tell them I'm consulting with you on the case. Can you get a few days off?"

"Getting the time off is no problem, but I can't let you do that, Devin. You're unemployed. How would you pay for it?"

I give him a wink saying, "This won't even put a dent in my budget and I was planning a little vacation anyway. I can visit some old friends and we can both check out the bikinis on a Brazilian beach, when we're not asking questions."

"Alright, I'll touch base with my boss, but let's not tell my wife about the bikini watch. What are you going to tell Harley?"

"There's nothing to tell, Sam. She got her old flying job back with an airline in Denver and I think she's reconnecting with her ex-husband. She hasn't made it official yet, but I'm expecting a call any day now."

"I'm sorry to hear that, buddy. I'll miss dropping by your place and checking out those fabulous legs of hers."

"I'll miss it too, Sam. Tomorrow, I'll get some airline tickets and set up our hotel rooms. My truck is parked on the other side of the airport. Would you mind dropping me by there?"

"Sure."

As I get out of Sam's car, he says, "I've been so busy talking that I didn't give you a chance to say much. Did you hear anything that might have any bearing on the case?"

I've been waiting all day for this and I flash him my best Cheshire cat smile before speaking.

"There is one thing, Sam, but it's probably not important. Jorge Alda is Walter Paris' son and Jorge doesn't know that he's his dad."

"Why the hell didn't you say something? If he refuses to testify against Paris, it will throw our whole case out the window."

I laugh out loud and say, "You're the freaking FBI. You already know everything!"

He flips me the bird and says, "You really enjoyed dropping that bomb didn't you?"

"Yes, I did. See tomorrow Sam."

It begins to rain as I leave the airport. My cabin is on a lake about twenty miles away and by the time I get there, the sky has opened into a roaring downpour. I'm soaked to the bone during the short walk from the driveway to the front porch. It's getting dark and the lights are on inside the house. I can see Harley standing in the living room holding a glass of wine. She does not look happy when I enter the room.

I greet her with a wave, "Hi babe, I wasn't expecting you back so soon."

She says, "We have to talk because I won't be staying long."

"Do I need to be sitting down for this?"

"That might not be a bad idea," she says.

I pour myself a glass of wine and take a seat on the sofa. Harley eases into the rocking chair across from me. She's upset and it shows. Her hands are shaking and her eyes are darting about the room nervously. It is several minutes before she's able to speak.

"I've decided to move back to Denver," she says. "This Keystone Airline stuff is making me really uncomfortable. In fact, it's downright scary."

"I can't say as I blame you there. I'm none too happy with the situation either. But, I don't think that's the whole story is it?"

"No, it isn't. I'm going back to Mike."

"It sounds like that's what we should really be talking about."

She says, "If you'd like, we don't have to talk about anything. This happened once before and you didn't want to talk about it then. Why go into it now?"

"Humor me. You owe me that much. Are you leaving because you don't think I love you? I sure as hell tell you that often enough."

"No, that's not it. It's just that —."

In complete frustration, I blurt out, "What is it, Harley? Is the sex bad, do I snore, have I been mean-spirited in some way, what?"

She leans forward and gently places a hand on my knee saying, "You've never once said an unkind thing to me and I don't believe for one second that you ever would. You are a gentle and generous man and nasty is simply not part of your character. It's just that, sometimes, I don't connect with you because you're always so damned self-contained. You never seem to need anything and I want to feel needed."

I let out a sigh and say, "So, you'd feel better if I was needy?"

"You have secrets Devin and you don't share them."

"Harley, I've said this many times before, if you want to know something, all you have to do is ask. I'm not hiding anything."

She raises her hand and says quietly, "Let's not argue that point. There is something else that would have come between us eventually — Kate Holloway. She's in love with you and I suspect it's been that way for a long time."

"She's my closest friend Harley, but there has never been anything physical between us. Besides, she is married to Tommy."

Harley lets out a chortle saying, "They're divorced, Devin, and you're just kidding yourself. I know you love me, but sooner or later your relationship with Kate will get in the way. It's better for both of us if I leave now. There's really nothing else to say. It's better if I just go."

She stands and extends her hand. "Will you walk me to my car?"

A couple of minutes later, I open the door to her Jeep and she slides in under the wheel. I lean in to say goodbye and she kisses me. A moment later, she is gone. I return to the house and stare quietly out the window at the rain, which seems to increase its intensity. It is also raining hard outside of a restaurant in Rio de Janeiro.

# CHAPTER 24

## July 12 1730 Hours • Rio de Janeiro

### Location: Eduardo's Cafe

THE RAIN IS HAMMERING the neighborhood bistro's windows as Jorge Alda watches his friend Lucas wolf down part of a double order of paella they are sharing. At the moment, he has no appetite.

Lucas chides him playfully, "This is really good stuff, man. You should have some."

"I've got a lot on my mind and I'm not very hungry."

Lucas asks, "Did you call your mom and let her know what's going on?"

"No, I really don't want to get her involved in this."

Lucas points a nagging finger at him saying, "Look, your mom grew up in the favelas just like us. She can handle anything you throw at her. You should give her a call so she doesn't worry about you."

"Here," he says, "You can use my phone. This way, you won't have to worry about anybody tracing your call."

Jorge takes the phone and reluctantly dials the number.

A voice says, "This is Lara."

"Hi mom, it's your bad boy son."

"Where the hell have you been," she asks? "I've been trying to reach you for three days."

"I'm in a little bit of a jam with the police and I didn't want to bother you with it."

She's angry when she says, "From what I'm told, it's really serious trouble. There was a murder and there are some people trying to kill you. Have I left anything out?"

"Where'd you hear that?" he asks hastily.

"Walter called earlier today and he told me what was going on."

Jorge explodes, "He's the son-of-a-bitch who's trying to murder me!"

"What?"

"Yeah, he thinks I'm going to rat him out to the cops and he sent some mercenaries to blow me away. They've already killed two of my friends. I'm not sticking around to be their next victim."

"Walter told me it was the cartels that are after you."

"That's a load of BS, Mom. I know those guys and they work for Walter."

"Listen to me, son. I've known Walter Paris since before you were born and he would never do anything to hurt you. I'd stake my life on it."

"It's my life that's hanging by a thread here. What would make you say something like that anyway?"

Lara is desperate when she says, "A long time ago, Walter and I had an affair."

"So what? That doesn't mean squat to him. He'll kill me anyway."

She is adamant when she says, "No, he won't."

"What makes you so damn sure he won't?"

"I should have told you this a long time ago, Jorge, and I'm ashamed because of it."

"You don't have anything to be ashamed of, Mom. You were young and you had a fling with the guy. It's no big deal."

Lara is crying when she blurts out, "That's not it, son. Walter is your father and I never told you."

Suddenly, Jorge is gulping for air. He's hyperventilating and he's having trouble breathing. He is unable to speak and he drops the cellphone. Lucas sees what's happening and immediately tries to help, but Jorge vomits on the floor.

Lucas grabs his friend and says, "Take it easy, brother, I've got you."

He escorts Jorge to the restroom and helps him clean up. Once his friend has recovered enough to speak, Lucas begins to question him.

"What was that all about, Jorge? Your mom must have laid out some really heavy stuff for you to blow lunch like that."

Jorge looks at his watch and says, "You have no idea how messed up that conversation was, man. Right now, we'd better pay our bill and get over to the airport. I'll tell you about it later."

As soon as they get into the car, Lucas' cellphone rings. He glances at the caller ID and says, "It's your mom dude. You'd better take this."

Lucas can see the rage in his friend's face when he says, "I don't want to talk to her right now. Let it ring."

He nods in agreement and they continue their drive to the airport. Fifteen minutes later, they arrive at the employee parking lot. They both flash their pilot IDs at the security guard and he waves them through. Lucas drops by the flight operations office to pick up his flight plan, the cargo manifest, and a weather briefing. He'll be flying a load of machine parts to Manaus in northern Brazil, a distance of fifteen hundred nautical miles, which translates into about three and a half hours in the air for the ancient 737 freighter they're flying tonight.

"I've already briefed my copilot," he says, "You can ride up front with us in the cockpit or there is a little cot in the cargo bay if you'd prefer that. I'd suggest the cot because it's a lot more comfortable than the cockpit jump seat."

"If it's alright with you, Lucas, I'll ride in the back with the boxes. I wouldn't be very good company right now."

"Okay, let's get going."

They are airborne at seven-thirty. Two hours into the flight, Lucas waves the controls to his copilot and wanders back to the cargo bay to use the toilet and check on his friend.

"How are you doing, buddy?" he asks.

"I'm okay now, Lucas. Thanks for giving me some time to sort things out."

"So, what's going on?"

"My mom just told me that Walter Paris is my father. For twenty-eight years, I thought it was somebody else. I'm having a tough time getting my head around that."

Lucas says, "I'm having a tough time getting over the fact that your own father is the guy trying to kill you. You have to be a really cold bastard to do something like that."

Jorge says, "I never saw the dark side of his personality until the last few months. Walter has always been kind to me and supportive of anything that I've ever wanted to do. Then, two of my friends murdered a woman for him. Until that happened, I'd never heard him utter an unkind word. The woman that was killed was a friend and we dated a couple of times."

"I knew Walter was connected to the cartels, but I thought all he did was move money around for them. He seemed to keep his hands clean of everything else. This is all a big shock to me. When my friends were killed, I hit the ground running and I haven't looked back since."

"You've got a lot on your plate, Jorge. What are you planning to do?"

"I'm not going to do anything for a couple of weeks. I've got a place where I can hide out for a while to think things through. I'll give it some time and then maybe call Walter to see if I can cut some sort of deal with him."

"What about your mom? Are you going to call her back or just leave her hanging?"

"I don't know yet. I'm still pretty pissed about the whole thing. Everything I thought was true about my life has just been turned upside down. I'll send a message to let her know that I'm okay, but right now, I'm in no mood for conversation."

Two hours later, the aging 737 touches down at the Manaus Airport. Jorge thanks his friend and hails a cab. Moments later, he disappears into the city. Manaus is located at the confluence of the Negro and Solimoes Rivers in northern Brazil's Amazon Region. It is literally in the middle of the jungle and in the early part of the century it was called "The City in the Forest." It is an industrial center now with a population of a little over two million. Jorge chose it as a safe haven because it would be easy for him to blend in with the population and because there are lots of escape routes. It has an international airport, heavy river traffic, and officials who are more than willing to accept a little cash to look the other way.

He bought a condo here when he first started flying money and drugs for the cartels. One of the hazards of this kind of work is that you never know when the cops or some angry drug trafficker will come looking for you. Ironically, it was Walter Paris who suggested that he create such a place for himself. No one knows its location, including Walter. Still, he can't be too careful. He has the cabby drop him off several blocks from the condo and he walks the rest of the way using the back streets.

He arrives a little after one in the morning and quickly checks that all of the pertinent items are immediately available. There is a handgun with a hundred rounds of ammunition. He checks a floor safe in his closet and verifies that there is nearly one hundred thousand dollars of cash in there along with debit cards for two offshore bank accounts containing even more money, if he should ever need it. There is a "go-bag" in the closet with a change of clothes, toiletries, fake IDs and a map identifying the safest escape routes. The refrigerator is empty, but he can restock it later. Next, he moves to the garage where he has a car and a motor scooter. He starts them both and checks the fuel level on each vehicle. Satisfied that he has everything he might need for an emergency bugout, he climbs into bed and immediately drifts into a restless sleep. Walter Paris is just waking up in Switzerland and he's looking forward to his morning coffee.

# CHAPTER 25

July 13 0900 Hours • Zurich, Switzerland

Location: Walter Paris' Home

WALTER IS DROOLING over a breakfast consisting of eggs benedict, fresh fruit, orange juice, a French pastry, and expensive Columbian coffee when his manservant asks, "Will there be anything else, sir?"

"No thank you, Andre, this will do quite nicely. In fact, I want you to take the rest of the week off and spend it with that lovely wife of yours. It's your anniversary and you should celebrate. I'll be traveling the rest of the week and it would be good for you to get away from this place for a few days."

The manservant smiles and nods politely, but before leaving he says, "Thank you for sending the flowers to my wife, she loved them."

Paris gives him a casual wave saying, "It was my pleasure, a woman like that deserves the very best. Just be sure to take good care of her."

After the man leaves, Walter slowly savors every morsel. One should not rush a meal that has been so graciously served. It takes him nearly forty-five minutes to ingest the morning repast. Unlike so many of his business associates, he does not mix business with pleasure. He consumes his meal in complete silence, no telephone calls, no television or radio, and no newspaper bringing the world's gloomy anecdotes to his table.

When he has finished dining, he pushes a button on a remote and Stan Getz's saxophone fills the room with soothing jazz. He spends the entire morning luxuriating in the music, all the while enjoying a magnificent view of Lake Zurich and the surrounding landscape. At eleven-thirty, it's time to go to work. He retreats to the desk in his home office and removes a legal pad from the drawer. He makes an orderly list of the day's tasks and problems. Then, he begins to noodle out their probable solutions. The first item on the list: Jorge Alda.

From his perspective, there are four players in this particular drama, Jorge, the police, the cartels, and himself. The first issue is whether or not Jorge will talk to the police. Since he is currently on the run, it seems doubtful. Even if he were to go to the authorities, it would be several months before any case could be brought to trial. That would likely give him enough time to contact Jorge and reach some sort of compromise that would be beneficial to them both. Either way, there is no point in worrying about something that he can't control.

The police are the second set of players in the game and it is also very doubtful that they will find Jorge. Walter knows that his son has an escape plan and his own safe house. He doesn't know its location, but no one else does either. So, no need to worry about the police for now.

The trickiest part of this equation will be the cartels. They encouraged and sanctioned the killing of Ruben Clemente and Luis Marcos because they botched the Susan Parks murder. They were angry because they did it without Walter's or the cartel's consent. The cartel leaders are currently unaware of Jorge's potential involvement in any legal action against Walter, but they don't like leaving things to chance. If they knew about his connection with Jorge, they would almost certainly send teams to kill them both. Walter ordered the hit on his son so that none of this would get back to the group's leadership. He is fond of Jorge, but he isn't willing to die for him. He thinks there may still be a way to salvage this thing if he can just talk to Jorge. If not, he may have to employ an emergency exit strategy.

He has been planning his own departure from the cartel's influence for months. After the Keystone Airlines debacle, he thought it best to have a surefire way to extricate himself from all of it. It is a very difficult thing to do. Normally, when one gets into the upper levels of the drug trafficking business, you're in for life. The only way out is through a pine box in the cemetery. If you are a billionaire like Walter, you have resources at your disposal that lesser men couldn't even consider.

The first step in his plan was to quietly move most of his financial assets to offshore banks and shell corporations, something he has been doing for months. In the interim, he conducted business as usual, moving vast sums of money and making other business arrangements for the cartels as if nothing had changed. He faithfully attends the cartel's quarterly business meetings and gives them regular status reports. He has had an exceptionally good year investing their cash in the stock market. Instead of taking his usual fifteen percent fees, he only took ten percent, making the cartel's bottom line look even better. He correctly reasoned that if they were happy financially, they would be more likely to leave him alone. In an effort to further build trust, he has cultivated friendships with the cartel leadership and their families, or at least as much as one can have trust and friendship with violent men. So far, this strategy has worked perfectly and he is well regarded by his unsavory associates.

He scored a major coup when he gave the cartels Raul Silva. Walter and Silva were long-time friends. It was, in fact, Silva who had first introduced him to the drug business and money laundering. Initially, Silva was a relatively minor player in the cartel structure. He was running a small distribution network in Caracas, Venezuela when he came to Walter looking for financial advice. Using Walter's investment prowess and lots of laundered drug money, Silva became a billionaire. Walter quickly saw the enormous financial potential in the drug business. He combined his financial resources with Silva's and, in a relatively short period of time, he too became a billionaire.

After he became wealthy, Silva wanted out of the drug business. He made a behind-the-scenes deal with the authorities, feeding them information on the cartels in exchange for one day going into the witness protection program and taking all of his money with him. Silva shared this information with Walter over drinks one night, and out of friendship, he asked Walter if he wanted in on it.

Walter was afraid the cartel leadership would find out and kill them both. He met with them privately and it was decided that Silva should be killed. They blew up his car before he could testify against any of them. As a result, Walter has become something of a hero within the organization. What they didn't know was that he was willing to cut his own deal with the authorities, just as Silva had done. It is an inelegant solution to his troubles, but it is certainly a possibility if things get out of hand. If push comes to shove, he will go into witness protection and never be seen again. He also has a Plan B, which is an alternative to witness protection.

He has a small army of mercenaries like Sullivan already working for him. They will do whatever he tells them to do if he pays them enough. If need be, he will unleash the hounds and have them kill some key cartel players and fake an attack on his own home making it look as if he had nothing to do with it. It is a messy solution, but it is virtually foolproof, except that it won't get him off the hook with all of the authorities. The Federal prosecutors will almost certainly be willing to let him walk on all of their money laundering charges in exchange for inside information on the cartels. It is the local and state police in Ohio that are the problem. They are still trying to tie him to Susan Parks' murder. That is why it is so important to make contact with Jorge Alda. He is the only one left who can link him to her death.

He has decided to employ one of his favorite negotiation tactics when it comes to handling his son — patience. He will simply wait him out. He knows that Jorge will eventually talk to him and they will settle the matter one way or the other. Meanwhile, he pours himself a glass of champagne and checks his email. There are three new messages.

The first one is from the cartel leadership, reminding him to attend a recently scheduled meeting in New York. He has already made plans for it and his personal jet is standing by for a flight later this afternoon. The second email is from Lara, letting him know that she talked to Jorge and that she relayed his message to him. There is nothing more that he can do there.

So, he moves on to the next item, which is something of a surprise. It is a note from Tommy Rollins, who wants to back out of a loan that he had offered him.

Walter agreed to a million-dollar interest free loan to help Tommy get back on his feet. The Feds had taken all of his cash in exchange for dropping money laundering charges against him. Walter thought the loan was the least he could do since Tommy kept his mouth shut about their mutual banking interests during his trial. This message is unexpected and potentially problematic because Tommy knows a great many of Walter's secrets. He is fond of Tommy and he's wondering if perhaps he should pay him a visit to discuss the matter in person. If he notices anything suspicious in Tommy's behavior, he will call in one of his mercenaries and make the problem go away.

He has another sip of champagne and calls a limousine service for a ride to the airport.

## CHAPTER 26

### July 15 2130 Hours • Miami, Florida

### Location: 767 First Class Cabin, Miami International Airport

Sam Dorsey and I are stowing our carry-on bags in the overhead bins for our flight to Rio de Janeiro. He smiles at me broadly.

"Devin, how in the world did you score us a couple of spots in first class? Government employees like me almost never get to travel in this kind of luxury. I was expecting to ride in one of those sardine-can seats back in coach."

"It's a nine-hour night flight to Rio Sam and we'll get in there early tomorrow morning. These chairs open up into beds so we can sleep most of the way and wake up bright-eyed and bushy-tailed when the plane lands."

"I know that, but these seats had to cost you a couple of grand each. You're unemployed and I want to know how you paid for them."

"In a previous life, I robbed a bank, but you're the freaking FBI and you already know that. Let's move on and work up some sort of game plan for tomorrow."

"You're not going to tell me, are you?"

"No, I'm not. You'd better buckle up. They're getting ready to push the airplane away from the gate. We can finish this conversation once we get airborne."

A short time later, we reach our cruising altitude and the captain turns off the seatbelt sign. Sam and I resume our conversation.

I ask, "What have you got worked out for our meeting with the detective in Rio?"

"I set up a session with him for the day after tomorrow. That'll give you time to talk to some of your friends and maybe get a little background information on the guy."

"Good," I say. "How do you plan on handling the conversation?"

"I'm going to start with a few basic facts, feeding him a little bit at a time. If there are any language issues, I'll have you speak to him in Portuguese. We'll both try to get a read on his body language and, if I'm happy with that, I may give him some more information and see how it goes. We're on his turf and since he's holding most of the cards, I don't want to rush into things. How about you? What are you going to do after we arrive?"

"My first stop is going to be at the American Embassy. I have an old friend there, but I haven't told him the purpose of my visit. He keeps secrets because that's part of his job. He doesn't know that we're aware that one of his embassy cars was bombed or that the gun used to kill one of my pilots was found in the wreckage. I'm surprised the Rio detective passed that information on to you. Cops from different countries aren't usually that cooperative."

"I was surprised, too, Devin. He shared a couple of other things with me over the phone, but I'm not yet sure how they fit together with this case. My initial gut feeling is that this guy really wants to help us. I also got the sense that he wants to get this stuff off his plate as quickly as possible, but I have no idea why. Do you have any thoughts about this?"

"No, I don't. Where are we meeting the detective?"

"It's going to be in his boss' office at ten in the morning, which seems a little strange to me."

"Why is that?"

"The top cop in all of Rio meeting with us right away is a little unusual to me for a couple of reasons. First, stuff like this is almost always passed up to the big boss through a chain of command from a set of lower level subordinates. Normally, someone in his position would only get involved if there was something he thought his guys couldn't handle on their own. This fellow seems to want to jump in with both feet."

"I guess I don't see anything wrong with that, Sam. This case clearly has international implications for his department. Maybe he just wants to stay on top of things."

"That may be true, but there's something else that's bothering me. When I first set up the meeting with Detective Ruiz, he wanted to meet me alone outside of his office. When I called him back to tell him what hotel we were staying at, he told me the meeting had been moved to his boss' office. He said that he hadn't told anyone about the meeting and that his boss had come by personally to reschedule it. Then he jumped all over Ruiz for not keeping him in the loop. If Ruiz didn't tell his boss about the meeting, how the hell did he find out about it?"

"It sounds like office politics to me, Sam."

"I've been doing police work a long time, Devin. I don't

know what's really going on, but my sixth sense is screaming trouble."

"Well, it seems to me that we'll just have to ride it out and see where it goes if we're going to make any headway. Excuse me. I'm going to the restroom and change into my sweats."

He asks, "What for?"

"They are really great for sleeping on airplanes and I don't want to wake up with a wrinkled suit like the one you're going to have on when you get off the flight tomorrow morning."

"Damn it. I'll be sleeping in the seat next to you. You could have told me to bring some sweats, too, Devin."

"I probably should have, but you know how much I enjoy watching you suffer."

He is clearly irritated when he says, "Do you have any other handy travel tips that you'd like to pass along?"

"Yeah, I do Sam. Ask the flight attendant for some earplugs because I snore."

He makes an obscene gesture saying, "Screw you and the horse you rode in on!"

At the moment, sleep attire is the least of our troubles, because Walter Paris' telephone is ringing in a New York hotel.

"I'm sorry to bother you so late Walter, but you wanted me to give you an update on the progress of our investigation here in Rio."

"It's no trouble, Commissioner, thank you for calling. What's the latest on the shootings and Jorge Alda?"

"We're pretty sure that Alda has left town. We've been looking for him for several days and something would have turned up by now if he wasn't already gone."

Walter says, "Those are my thoughts, too. Is there anything else?"

"Yes, my chief of detectives, Duncan Ruiz, has a meeting with an FBI agent in a couple of days. The guy is flying in from the States tonight and he's bringing a translator with him."

"Why haven't I heard about this sooner?" Walter asks.

"I just found out about it myself because my detective scheduled the meeting and he didn't keep me in the loop. The only reason I knew about it was because I've had his office and home phone bugged for weeks."

Paris asks, "Should we be worried about Detective Ruiz? It sounds to me like you don't trust him."

"No, he's just trying to be a good cop. I still have some leverage with Ruiz and I chewed his ass out pretty good. It won't happen again."

Walter says, "Good. If you can, get me the name of the FBI agent working the case. I'll see if I can get some information about him."

"Yes, sir, I'll call you back if there are any new developments. Goodnight."

# CHAPTER 27

July 16 1045 hours • Rio de Janeiro

Location: The Sheraton Grande Rio Hotel

SAM DORSEY AND I have just checked into our hotel room and he is admiring the view from the balcony window.

"Damn," he says. "First class airline tickets, our own limo driver, and now we've got a luxury suite with an ocean view in one of Rio's best hotels. I'm beginning to think that you really did rob a bank."

"Sam, I've decided to mix a little pleasure with our business on this trip. Don't be so stuffy, enjoy yourself. If you really think I robbed a bank, you can always arrest me."

He fakes a sneer saying, "You do know that the FBI has no jurisdiction here?"

"Now you're catching on, buddy. I set it up so the limo driver will give you a quick tour of the city starting with Sugar Loaf Mountain and then the statue of Christ the Redeemer in Corcovado. Then, he's going to take you to the beach for some more erotic sightseeing. I know that you think the limo and driver are an unnecessary expense, but there is method to my madness."

"How's that?" he asks.

"These days, Rio can be a dangerous place for the uninitiated. I know you can handle yourself, but you couldn't bring your service weapon through customs and we don't know what we're dealing with yet. The limo driver is a government trained security specialist. I've worked with the man before and you can trust him. He's armed and he knows the city. He'll keep us both out of trouble."

"And how will you be spending your day?"

"I'm going to have lunch with a friend. Afterwards, I'll try to meet with one of the street cops I used to know to see if I can get a little background on Detective Ruiz. Then, I'll treat you to a really nice dinner and we'll talk about everything over a nice glass of wine and some really great Brazilian jazz."

Sam grins and says, "See you at suppertime."

An hour later, a taxi drops me at a restaurant a few blocks from the American Embassy. My friend, Bill Marston, greets me at the entrance with a warm handshake.

"It's been too long, Devin. The last time I saw you was back when we were searching for Kate Holloway, the billionaire's daughter. I know you two were close. How'd that turn out after you got her home anyway?"

"She's doing fine, Bill. She pulled her life together and she has a thriving aviation law practice in Boston."

"Is she still married to Tommy Rollins?"

"No, they divorced a few months ago."

"I'm sorry to hear that. How's Tommy, anyway? He was always a hell of a lot of fun."

"He's one of the reasons I came to see you. Let's get a quiet table and I'll fill you in on the details."

Once seated, Bill and I begin our discussion in earnest.

"Bill, I'm down here for two reasons. One of them is business and the other is personal, but they are connected. Some of this stuff affects you, too. There's likely to be some blowback on the embassy, but you have my word that I'll keep your name out of it."

"Okay, what's going on?" he asks.

"You recently had one of your embassy vehicles blown up and that's related to why I came to see you."

I can see the expression on Bill's face shift to grim. I continue the conversation while my friend curses softly to himself under his breath.

"I'm helping an FBI agent who's investigating the incident because it's tied to the murder of a woman who used to work for me. The party, or parties, involved were also implicated in at least two murders here in Rio and one in Caracas. The FBI thinks that they may be coming after me or Tommy Rollins because I helped them with the investigation into one of the key players behind all of it. My gut sense of this is that it's going to get uglier before it gets better."

He shakes his head and says, "I knew something like this was going to happen, but I didn't expect to see an old friend in the middle of it."

"Look, I know you can't discuss confidential embassy business with me, but I'll tell you what I know and maybe some of that will be useful. If there is anything you'd be willing to throw my way, I'd appreciate it, because I'm poking around in the dark trying to sort it out."

He nods for me to continue.

"We have positive IDss on two of the shooters from DNA and fingerprints. Their files are classified as need-to-know under national security so we can't get pictures of them. We're pretty sure they are former CIA operatives freelancing as mercenaries, probably on the payroll of a guy named Walter Paris."

He says, "You mean the Wall Street star they used to call the "Boy Billionaire?"

"Yeah, that's the guy. He bought the airline I was working for and used it to move laundered drug money around for the cartels. A female pilot, who worked for me, found out about it and the FBI thinks he had her killed, although that's unclear at the moment. There were two other pilots who also worked for my company and they were killed here in Rio sometime in the last few days. The ballistics on the gun used to kill one of the pilots matched the weapon found in your blown up embassy car. It was military issue, leading us to suspect the 'mercs' that I mentioned earlier."

"Anything else?" he asks.

"Yes, we think someone high up in one of the agencies, FBI or CIA, is leaking information to Paris. So, be careful who you talk to about this."

Bill asks, "Do you have a guess as to where the leak is?"

"Personally, I think it's on the CIA side. Someone over there has been dragging their feet and stalling the investigation for months. On top of that, I think whoever that is may know the operative or operatives doing the shooting. Someone may also have leaked information about the meeting we're having with the Rio cops tomorrow."

Bill leans back in his chair to think and he's quiet for a long time. Rather than push things, I decide to wait for a response. The waiter brings our drinks and he has a sip before speaking.

"We've worked together on some dicey things in the past, Devin, but nothing quite like this. I need your word that you will keep me out of this, if you can."

"Done," I say.

"Several months ago, the CIA sent me an operative for safe keeping."

"Safe keeping?"

"Yes, the guy apparently refused some kind of questionable assignment and they sent him to me until they could figure out what to do with him. He was good with languages and a whiz with electronics and computers. So, we found a place for him. One day, an embassy guest tries to manhandle one of the escorts we sometimes use to entertain embassy visitors. The guest pulls a knife on her and our man gets between them and disarms the guy. He handles the whole business discreetly and with great care and discretion. To tell you the truth, I really liked the guy, he was a class act."

I say, "So, why do the FBI and the local cops think he went nuts killing people?"

"I don't think he did, Devin. There's a guy named Davenport and he's an upper level CIA executive. He works with someone we both know, Gil Pepperdine over at DEA. His agency works a joint drug task force down here chasing drug traffickers."

"So, Pepperdine knows the guy that the DEA sent you?"

"Could be, but that's uncertain. What I do know is that Davenport called me and asked for the escort's address and phone number. The next thing I know, one of the embassy cars blows up in front of her house and she goes missing. I'm pretty sure he was behind it."

"What happened to the girl?"

"I don't know. No one found a body. My best guess is that the man you're looking for got the woman out in time. He had a thing for her and she might be with him."

"You got a picture of this guy?" I ask.

"Yes, and I have one of the girl too, but you don't know where you got them."

"My lips are sealed."

Bill shows me a picture of the lady on his cellphone.

"Handsome woman," I say.

"She is that. You can see why our guy might have fallen for her."

I say, "A man on the run traveling with a hooker is a little unusual for a hired gun, don't you think? It seems to me that he would be more apt to leave the woman to save his own skin."

"Normally, I'd agree with you, but I once saw them in a Rio restaurant together and they looked happy. I'm pretty sure this is a lot more than a one-night stand. Here's a picture of the guy."

I'm completely stunned when he shows me the photograph. This is the faceless man from my prescient dream and it's completely unnerving.

"Are you alright, Devin? Do you know this guy?"

I don't think it wise to share my night visions with Bill and I alter my response.

"I've seen this guy somewhere before, but I just can't remember where."

Bill says, "He used the name Hamilton while he was working here at the embassy. I doubt that is his real name because it almost never is with these guys. What's the name of the cop who's looking into this?"

"His name is Duncan Ruiz and I'm assuming that he's the same fellow who dropped by to see you. I'm going to try and hook up with a couple of local cops we used to work with when we were doing missing persons for the embassy. Maybe, they can give me the lowdown on him."

Bill waves a hand and says, "I can save you the trouble. Do you remember Enrique Melgar? I used to call him Hank because that was the English translation of his name."

"Yes, what did he have to say about our man?"

"Apparently, he's a first rate cop, persistent, honest, and on top of that, everyone thinks he's a decent human being, too. I talked to three different people and they all gave me the same story. I feel bad that I had to hold out on him because it looks as though he's trying to do the right thing."

"That's a big help, Bill, because it means I won't have to run all over town asking questions that might get back to him."

"You need anything else?" he asks.

"Does the embassy still keep counter-intelligence gear around? I'd like to borrow a couple of items."

"You worried about phone taps and bugs?"

"Yeah, somebody was following us after our flight got in this morning. They were sloppy and Sam and I picked up on it right away. We got a license number, but I doubt it'll do us much good down here."

"Do you think it was Ruiz's men?"

"I don't know, but someone besides Ruiz knew we were comng and we didn't share that information with anyone else."

"Okays, let's go back to the embassy and I'll get you what you need."

# CHAPTER 28

## July 16 1430 Hours • Boston, Massachusetts

## Location: Top of the Hub Restaurant, Boylston Street

Tommy Rollins enters the restaurant atop the Prudential Building and strides toward the table. Walter Paris smiles to himself quietly because this is something that he has long admired about Tommy. The man always walks into a room as if he owns it. He extends his hand with a broad smile.

"Hello, Walter. It's nice to see you again."

"Next to see you too Tommy, have a seat. What would you like to drink?"

He nods to the waiter, "Maker's Mark, on the rocks, please."

Walter says, "I got your email turning down my loan offer. May I ask why?"

Tommy lies and says, "My ex-father-in-law and I owned some property together and we sold it. I made enough on the deal that I no longer need the loan."

"Ex-father-in-law?" Walter asks.

"Kate and I divorced some time ago. The tabloids had a field day with it. The headlines read: "Billionaire's Daughter Divorces Crooked Husband."

"I'm sorry to hear about that, Tommy. I always liked your wife, but I don't think she cared much for me."

Tommy says, "Well, it doesn't matter much now because we're done. Her father gave me the proceeds from the real estate deal to make sure that I stayed out of her life and didn't come back begging for money. I'm pretty much dog shit with the Holloway family."

Walter asks, "How about the police, have you heard anymore from them?"

"The state and local cops in Ohio squeezed me a couple times about Susan Parks' murder, but there was nothing I could tell them because I didn't know anything."

"How about the FBI and the IRS?"

"I haven't heard anything from the FBI. Once the IRS cleaned me out financially, they agreed in writing not to prosecute and let it go."

Walter says, "I heard from one of my sources that an FBI agent named Dorsey is in Rio nosing around with your buddy, Devin Ross. You know anything about that?"

"Devin and I aren't friends anymore and we haven't spoken in months. I don't know what's happening in Rio."

Walter sighs and says, "I'm sorry things went so badly for you, Tommy. I'm still willing to help you anyway I can, if you need it."

Tommy waves his arm casually saying, "I knew what the risks were before all of this stuff got started, Walter. Sometimes, you win big and sometimes, you lose big. Thanks again for your offer, but I'll be okay."

Tommy finishes his drink and excuses himself. Paris lingers to make a telephone call.

"Mr. Sullivan, this is Walter Paris. How long will it take you to wrap up your operation in Rio?"

"It shouldn't take more than another week to conclude our business here."

"Good, I may have another assignment for you."

"Do you want us to continue working on Plan B for taking care of your associates in Columbia and Caracas?"

"Yes, continue with what you are doing. I want to be certain that we can take out the cartel leadership, if it becomes necessary. How much time do you think you'll need before you can spare one or two of your best men for a few days?"

"If you need someone right away, I can hire a freelancer. Otherwise, it might take a couple of weeks."

"No need to hurry, Mr. Sullivan. I'd prefer to work with your men directly because they're pros and they don't screw up."

"Sir, may I ask the nature of the new assignment?"

"It may turn out to be nothing, but I just met with a former business associate and he could become a problem. If that happens, I may need your disposal services. I'll be in touch, if that becomes necessary."

"Yes, sir, we're only a phone call away if you need us."

Walter Paris ends the conversation and takes a sip of his drink. He sighs and says to himself, "It seems that I can't trust anybody these days. First it was Jorge and now maybe Tommy Rollins."

# CHAPTER 29

## July 17 1045 Hours • Rio de Janeiro

## Location:
## Police Colonel Wilbur Santiago's Office

There are four people in the office: myself, Sam Dorsey, Detective Duncan Ruiz and Colonel Santiago. After the formal introductions have been made, Sam Dorsey begins the conversation in English, directing his remarks to Ruiz.

"Sir," he says, "The FBI's investigation into this case has mostly stalled. Luis Marcos and Ruben Clemente were the primary witnesses against Walter Paris in the Susan Parks murder. As a result of their deaths, the only other person who may be able to help us is Jorge Alda. We believe he may be here in Rio and we'd like to offer our assistance in any way we can to help you find him."

Before Ruiz can respond, Santiago interrupts with, "You're telling me that you have no other way to connect Paris with the murder?"

Sam says, "That is correct."

At this point, I notice that Santiago is almost smiling to himself. I can also see that Duncan Ruiz has taken note of the subtle change in his boss' body language. Sam Dorsey once again addresses his remarks to detective Ruiz.

"As requested, I ran the ballistics on the gun that you found in the stolen American Embassy car explosion. It matches the one that was used to kill Luis Marcos in the first shooting at the hotel. I can tell you that it was a military issue weapon. You also sent me bullet fragments from the Ruben Clemente shooting. They were too badly damaged to tie to a specific weapon, but we identified those fragments as coming from military weaponry, too."

Ruiz nods and says, "Did you have any luck with the fingerprints or the DNA sample that I sent you?"

"Yes, we were able to positively identify two potential suspects."

Both Ruiz and his boss seem to be surprised. Santiago looks downright uncomfortable and I'm sure that Sam Dorsey has picked up on it, too.

Sam says, "Both men are former US military and we believe they are now working as mercenaries, possibly for Walter Paris. We are currently working on getting their photographs, but we are in the middle of an interagency jurisdictional conflict and it may be a while before we can get those pictures."

Duncan Ruiz smiles sardonically and says, "Sounds to me like somebody high up on your end is trying to keep a lid on this. They don't want the embarrassment of having one of their fair-haired boys caught up in an international scandal."

Sam is very direct, "I'm afraid that is exactly the case, sir."

Ruiz asks, "So, where do we go from here?"

Sam says, "I was hoping maybe you could tell us, because right now we're grasping at straws."

Santiago clears his throat and says, "At the risk of seeming inhospitable, I don't think there is much we can do to help you.

We're pretty sure that Jorge Alda has left the city, which would take him out of our jurisdiction. We've tried to run down his known associates, but other than the two men who were killed, we haven't had any luck."

I ask, "How about family members, maybe a mother, father or siblings?"

I already know that Jorge is an only child from my previous conversations with him. I just want to see if detective Ruiz has been doing his homework.

He says, "I've had my assistant working on that for several days, but Alda is a common name here in Rio. Counting the suburbs, there are more than eleven hundred people with that name. It's going to take a while. Another problem is that many people here don't have landlines. The trend has been to use cellphones because they are cheaper and you can pay as you go. It would help if I had a first name to narrow down the search."

Sam says, "I may be able to help you with that. When we arrested Jorge Alda, we also confiscated his cellphone. As I remember it, he placed several calls to numbers here in Rio. We were just beginning to look into that before I left. If you give me access to a computer, I can email my office and have them forward those numbers to you."

"That would be a big help, thank you."

Colonel Santiago abruptly ends the meeting with, "Agent Dorsey, if you'll permit me, I'll walk you down to our command center and get you set up online. Afterwards, I hope you gentlemen will allow me to buy you both lunch. Duncan, will you call Pierre's and get us a table?"

"You got it, boss."

While Ruiz is getting our lunch reservations, I'm busy writing a note to him on a piece of paper that I've pilfered from his boss' desk. I'm still writing when he finishes the call.

"What are you doing?" he asks.

I shift to Portuguese for my response, "I'm taking a chance and breaking with protocol. There are a few things here that I'd like you to take a look at when your boss is not around. I know that it's asking a lot from a stranger, but I think there are some things you should see privately."

"Why should I trust you?"

"You don't have to trust me. Do you know Enrique Melgar?"

"Yes, we came up through the ranks together. He is like my brother. The gringos down here call him Hank. Why should I call him?"

"Before you decide to share this information with your boss, call Hank and ask him about me. If you don't like what you hear, you can do whatever you want with this stuff and Sam and I will leave town. Is that fair enough for you?"

He nods in agreement and asks, "What have you got?"

"I've written most of it down for you, but here's the short story. Jorge's mother's first name is Lara. There's also a license plate number for a car with a couple of guys in it that's been following Sam and me since we got here. Unless they are your people, you may want to look into it. There are also instructions on how to use some equipment that I'm about to give you."

I hand him a package and say, "Someone is leaking information on this end as well as ours. This is counter surveillance equipment and you may want to use it to check your telephones and apartment for listening devices. I've included some electronic bugs so you can do some listening of your own. There is also some software and other gear along with instructions for cloning someone's cell phone, if you want to track or listen to their calls without them knowing about it. Keep this between us and you have no idea where you got this stuff. If you want to know more, we'll meet you at Rudy's Club later this evening. Make sure you're not followed. If you decide not to come, Sam and I will leave and we won't bother you again. Your boss will be back soon. Have we got a deal?"

He extends his hand and says, "Agreed."

Ruiz places the devices and my notes into his briefcase. A few minutes later, his boss returns with Sam Dorsey and we all go out to lunch. The food is excellent and, not surprisingly, very little is discussed about the case. Soon, Sam and I are in our limo headed back to the hotel.

"How'd it go with Ruiz?" he asks.

"I left him a trail of bread crumbs just like you asked me to."

"Do you think he'll show tonight?" he asks.

I say, "If he's the cop everyone says he is, he'll be there. What was your take on the meeting today, Sam?"

"I think that both men know more than they are letting on, Santiago more so than Ruiz. Did you notice the change in his body language when he learned that we don't have enough to go after Walter Paris?"

"I did and Ruiz noticed, too."

"So, what's our next move?" he asks.

"There's not much we can do until we see if Ruiz meets with us tonight."

Sam gestures over his shoulder towards the car that has been following us and says, "What do you want to do about our friends back there?"

Our driver, Ben, offers a suggestion.

"You want me to ditch those guys?" he asks.

I say, "No. That would only let them know we're on to them, Ben. Why don't you take us over to Joatinga Beach? It's only about twenty-five kilometers from here and it's far less crowded than Copacabana. I can go for a swim and I know a place over there where you and Sam can get some boards to ride the surf. The guys following us can sit around in the hot sun and watch us have a good time. How does that sound?"

Ben reaches over the back of the seat and high-fives me.

I grin at Sam and say, "Ben grew up on the water and he's a talented surfer. You are also pretty good on a board, Sam. High school surfing champ in Santa Monica, right?"

"Do I want to know how you found that out," he asks?

"I have a confidential informant and I'm not at liberty to divuge her identity."

"You've been talking to my wife."

"Yes I have. She said that you've been working too hard and to make sure that you had a good time. You've got a winner there, Sam. Liz is just looking out for you. I sent her a dozen roses in your name. You should call her later to make sure she got them."

"Thank you. I've been gone a lot working this case and I haven't spent as much time with her as I should. I need to take her on a little vacation when we get back."

A moment later, we're on our way to Joatinga Beach.

Police Colonel Wilbur Santiago is on the telephone giving Walter Paris the details of our meeting.

# CHAPTER 30

## July 17 1515 Hours • Somewhere North of New York City

## Location: Walter Paris' Private Jet

Wilbur Santiago says, "They don't have much, Walter. Agent Dorsey and Devin Ross are down here on a fishing expedition, pure and simple. They do have the identities of a couple of shooters, but the CIA won't release their names or pictures. Even if they do get them, I don't think they'll be able to tie them to you."

"That's good to know, Wil. Is there anything else I should be worried about?"

"No, I think that covers it. If something comes up later on, you'll be my first call."

Walter thanks him and hangs up the air phone. He's pleased because he can update his cartel associates at their meeting later today. They've been pressing him for more information on the investigation. His pilot puts on the seatbelt sign and begins a descent into LaGuardia Airport. The aircraft touches down at five-fifteen and a limousine whisks him into the city. This quarterly gathering is scheduled at the Waldorf and several of his cartel associates greet him when he enters the conference room.

To the untrained eye, this would appear to be nothing more than a group of corporate executives getting together for a strategy session over drinks and dinner. To law enforcement people who know the players, they are some of the most dangerous and vile people in the criminal world. They routinely sanction money laundering, drug trafficking, torture, murder, and other forms of violence anywhere they think it necessary.

This evening, Walter, and one of his assistants, will use a Power Point presentation with video clips and still slides to update the cartel members on the status of their financial empire. They are quite pleased because he has made them all a lot of money. Walter is happy, too, until one of his friends pulls him aside for a private conversation.

Martin Roah says, "Some of our brethren are still concerned about the Keystone Airlines debacle and Jorge Alda."

Walter asks, "Exactly what are they worried about?"

"They want Jorge dead and they're wondering why it hasn't happened yet."

Walter says, "They needn't be concerned because I've taken care of it."

"If that's true, why are FBI agent, Sam Dorsey, and his friend, Devin Ross, in Rio talking to the police about the case? Jorge Alda is still on the run and you don't know where he is."

Walter is momentarily puzzled because he just got that same information a short time ago. He soon realizes that his associates must also have a connection with the police colonel and that he has leaked the information to them. The cartel leadership has probably been monitoring his personal activities for months and that is not a good thing. It would be unwise to hide the truth.

"Martin, give me a month and I promise I'll have this wrapped up."

His friend presses a finger into his chest and says, "You have exactly thirty days or we'll take care of it, and I do mean all of it."

Martin Roah smiles menacingly and walks away to join his cronies. Despite the efficiency of the room's air conditioning system, Walter Paris begins to sweat. He knows the cartel will kill him if he doesn't make the problem go away. There are literally billions of dollars at stake here. The long-time friendships he has so carefully cultivated will not save him if the police get to Jorge before he does. He politely excuses himself and returns to his room. His first telephone call is to a man in Rio de Janeiro.

"Mr. Sullivan, this is Walter Paris."

Sullivan says, "Two calls in one day, things must be heating up."

"They are heating up. How soon can your men put Plan B in place?"

"We're almost ready, two or three days tops."

"Good, most of the cartel leadership will be returning home after this meeting. I'll be able to give you the exact locations of most of them in a few days and we'll get things rolling. I've wired eleven million dollars to your offshore bank as requested. That should be more than enough to pay your men and give yourself a hefty bonus. Is that satisfactory?"

Sullivan is almost giddy because this is nearly twice the amount they had originally agreed upon.

He says, "That is more that generous, sir. Thank you. Will there be anything else?"

"Yes, when this job is done, I may have one last assignment for you involving someone that you know. After that, you and I will have no further contact with each other. Is that clear?"

Sullivan says, "Crystal clear, sir."

Walter hangs up and sits on the edge of the bed. The next part of his plan is particularly diabolical. It involves Jorge's mother, Lara. He places a second call to Rio de Janeiro to another of his operatives known only as "Cooper."

"Mr. Cooper," he says, "I would like your men to pick up Lara Alda exactly as I specified in the text message I sent you a few days ago. Take her to the agreed upon location and hold her there until you hear from me. She is not to be harmed in any way."

"Consider it done, sir."

"One more thing, Mr. Cooper — make certain that you get her cellphone when you pick her up."

"We'll take care of it."

Walter hangs up and stretches out on the bed to stare at the ceiling. He is jet-lagged and very tired when he drifts into a restless sleep. Visions of a trip to Rio de Janeiro and Lara flood his memory and dreams. Sam Dorsey and I are also in Rio, but we are not welcome in Walter's sleepy musings.

# CHAPTER 31

## July 17 1835 Hours • Rio de Janeiro

## Location: The Sheraton Grande Rio Hotel

"I WANT YOU TO DITCH the white shirt and dark suit tonight, Sam."

"I don't have much else to wear, Devin. It's kind of the FBI uniform."

I point to the closet and say, "There's a casual shirt and a light-weight sport jacket in the closet that should fit you. I hope you don't mind, but I picked them up earlier today while you were out."

Sam shakes his head and says, "I can only assume that you're trying to help an old white guy blend in with the locals."

"That's part of it, but I also got you a change of clothes to hide this."

I give Sam a small box with a pistol in it.

I say, "It's a forty caliber Klock-23 with two loaded clips and another fifty rounds, which I doubt we'll ever need. I believe that is currently the standard FBI issue, is it not?"

"It is," he says. "And, you even got the right holster. I was feeling a little naked without it. Are you expecting trouble at the club?"

"No, but we're not using the limo tonight because I want to ditch anybody who might be following us. We'll slip out the back and catch a cab a few blocks away from the hotel just to make sure. Rudy's Club is safe enough, but it's on the edge of a rough neighborhood and the cabbie will have to drive through the favela to take us there."

"Are you packing heat, too?"

"Yeah, I've got a nine-millimeter Browning. It was standard issue when I worked at the embassy. I figured we should both carry weapons that we're comfortable with."

Sam says, "I don't think detective Ruiz would be pleased if he knew we were armed."

"Then we just won't tell him. Better change so we can get going. The club is on the other side of town and it'll take about forty minutes to get over there in traffic."

Ten minutes later, we exit the side entrance of the hotel and walk a few blocks to catch a cab. We're soon on our way to Rudy's Nightclub. We pass the favelas on the way and Sam points out the window to a bleary-eyed kid wearing headphones slumped against a trash can shooting up. He's lost in a sea of music and heroin.

"I saw some beautiful things in Rio when Ben took me on the tour yesterday, and, out of curiosity, I asked him to drive me by the slums or the favelas as you call them. The ghettos back in the States don't hold a candle to the filth and complete loss of hope that lives here. I've never seen so many damaged children. That kid can't be more than fourteen or fifteen, same age as my kids. I feel the urge to help him in some way, but I don't speak the language and I doubt if a few kind words will make any difference."

"Wave at him, Sam, and give him a smile."

"Do you really think that will help anything?"

"There are hundreds of languages in the world and a smile speaks them all. Sometimes, that is all that we can offer a lost soul."

He waves at the young man and the kid smiles and waves back.

"You seem to have more than a casual interest in this, Sam."

"I do. A couple of years ago, I was part of a task force looking into some people who were harvesting human organs illegally and selling them to hospitals in the States. There were cops here in Rio working with some local doctors to make it happen. The police were killing orphans from the favelas. Sometimes, they killed kids two and three years old, letting the doctors remove the organs and sell them. They split the profits. We caught the people doing the buying in the States, but we couldn't prove they knew where the organs were coming from. It was an ugly business and it has always stayed with me."

I say, "I remember that because *Sixty Minutes* did a piece on it. You'll be glad to know that detective Ruiz was one of the Rio cops who tried to stop it. For his trouble, some of his colleagues threatened his family, shot at him, and it cost him more than one promotion over the course of his career."

"He sounds like a man we can do business with, if he shows up. There's nothing in this for him except trouble. What makes you so sure he'll be there?"

"I'm not sure, but he's our last shot at making something happen. If he can't help us in some way, the case is pretty much over."

Our taxi driver pulls up in front of the club and I tip him handsomely, asking if he'll pick us up in a couple of hours. He agrees, and Sam and I enter the building. My friend is immediately awestruck by the hostess who greets us at the front door. He's even more impressed when an exquisite looking enchantress takes our drink order.

"Devin, I don't think I've ever seen so many beautiful women in one place. Men must come here in droves just to gawk."

"They don't come here for the women, Sam. It's the music and food, that's the real draw."

Sam and I enjoy a marvelous meal and some wine. The music is superb and we just can't help but sway a little to the soothing bossa nova rhythms. Nearly an hour passes and there is no sign of the detective. Sam is thoroughly discouraged and ready to leave when Ruiz enters the room out of breath and approaches our table.

"My apologies, gentlemen. There were some men trying to follow me and I had to give them a bit of a runaround before coming here. It would not sit well with some of my colleagues if they knew I was meeting with you."

He takes a seat next to Sam, orders a drink, and directs his next comments to me.

"I spoke with Enrique Melgar, the cop you once did missing persons work with a few years ago. He had good things to say. You were more than just an embassy translator. You worked for the DEA as a pilot and you're skilled with firearms and hand-to-hand combat. You also had a shootout in the jungle with some drug traffickers in Venezuela, which you barely survived."

Sam starts to speak, but Ruiz raises a hand and interrupts him before he utters a word.

"Agent Dorsey, you don't know it, but your boss and I once worked together on a smuggling case a few years back. I called him and he had good things to say about you, too. You're risking your career coming down here on your own time to see me, because someone high up in the bureaucracy wants to keep a lid on it. We could waste a lot of time playing 'Get-To-Know-You,' feeding each other little bits of information. I think we should cut to the chase and get it done. I'll give you everything I've got, if you give me all of your stuff."

Dorsey says, "That works for me."

Sam pushes the entire case file across the table to Ruiz and commences a detailed discussion covering every aspect of the case, including a picture of the man known as Richard Hamilton. Ruiz reciprocates with some relevant facts of his own and he throws out some other things that surprise us both.

He says, "Thanks for letting me use the counter-intelligence gear. Someone has bugged both my home telephone and my cell. There were listening devices in my kitchen and bedroom, too. I also ran the license plate on the car that you thought was following you. It turns out they were my own people, probably sent by my boss."

Sam asks, "So, you think Santiago may be involved in this in some way?"

Ruiz says, "I think it probable because he insisted that I talk to a complete stranger about this case. I was offered money to do it, which I refused. I fed the guy just enough of half-truths to leave me alone. So, like you, I'm on pretty thin ice with the higher-ups. The sad thing is that, from what I can see, we still don't have enough solid evidence to arrest anyone."

Sam responds with, "Yeah, Walter Paris has covered his tracks pretty well."

Ruiz is slightly hesitant before saying, "Maybe not, because I have a couple of things that may help. First, I recorded the call my boss had me make to the stranger. If it is Walter Paris, would either of you recognize his voice?"

I say, "I used to work for the guy and I could tell you if it's him or not."

The detective plays the tape and I easily identify the man as Paris.

"There is one more thing," he says, "The man you know as Richard Hamilton broke into my apartment while I was sleeping and he left me another tape. Apparently, he drugged Jorge Alda and got him to talk about Walter Paris' operation. I made a copy for you, but you probably won't be able to use it in court because he drugged the guy."

After listening to part of the tape, Sam asks, "What do you make of this guy Hamilton and the woman traveling with him?"

"Your guess is as good as mine, but as I'm sure you've guessed, I know the woman. I interviewed her about the first murder and I busted her once for prostitution. I let her go on the prostitution charge and we sort of became friends after that. I know she worked at the American Embassy from time to time and your guy, Marston, sandbagged me when I asked him about her."

We talk for another hour or so before ending the meeting. We let the detective know that we'll be staying in town for sa few more days for a little mini vacation. He admonishes us to be careful and excuses himself. Sam and I pay our bill and go searching for a cab, because the guy who dropped us off is a no-show. The club hostess directs us to a taxicab stand a couple of blocks away.

We're about half way to the taxi-pickup, when I notice a jeep cruising next to us with four kids in it giving us the eye. Sam sees it, too, and places a hand on his weapon. Two more kids on a motor scooter pull up on the sidewalk behind us, brandishing machetes and demanding money. The jeep swerves in front us effectively, blocking our path. Some kids jump out holding knives. One of them has a small pistol, probably a twenty-two, which he's holding casually in his left hand. Sam and I are back-to-back.

I say to him, "These are just a bunch of punk kids looking for a quick score. They think we're a couple of hapless tourists. What do you want to do?"

He says, "You speak the language. Tell them we're policemen and we'll shoot them if they don't leave."

Sam flashes his FBI badge and I shout in Portuguese, "We're cops and we'll kill you if you don't walk away!"

One of kids yells back in Portuguese, "No way, Gringo!"

Without a moment's hesitation, Sam draws his weapon and fires two shots into the Jeep's radiator. A third shot shatters the car's headlight. The kid with the twenty-two drops it to the ground and the boys with the knives takeoff running. I pull my weapon and point it directly at the two remaining boys standing next to the scooter. They are defiant until I fire two shots, one taking out the headlight on the scooter. They, too, beat a hasty retreat down an alley.

Sam holsters his weapon with a grin and says, "Damn, that felt good. You're a little rusty, Devin. It took you two shots to take out the headlight on that scooter."

"Well, I'm not the freaking FBI, Sam. Besides, if you hadn't shot up their radiator, we could have used that Jeep to drive back to the hotel. So, you get to pay for the cab!"

Sam picks up the twenty-two pistol and unloads it. He breaks the firing pin against the curb and throws the gun into the sewer. He's chuckling out loud to himself as we walk another block to the taxi stand and catch a ride back to the Sheraton.

# CHAPTER 32

July 18  1015 Hours  •  Rio de Janeiro

Location: Sheraton Grande Rio Hotel

SAM DORSEY AND I are having a late breakfast in the hotel restaurant. We're both exhausted from last night's run-in with the street gang. We're experiencing a kind of delayed stress syndrome. The playful banter that we exchanged right after the gunfire has given way to thinking about how bad things could have been if we'd really had to shoot one of those kids. Neither of us wants to dwell on it, so we elect to talk about the case as a diversion.

I ask, "So, what's your take on detective Ruiz and the stuff he gave us last night?"

"I think he's genuine, Devin. He really put himself out there for us and he appears to be everything your friend says he is. That tape that Richard Hamilton made when he drugged Jorge Alda confirmed a lot of what we suspected about Walter Paris, but it would never hold up in court. It may give us some other leads to run down. But overall, I think Ruiz is right. We still don't have enough to arrest anybody. I'm really sorry you went to all the trouble to fly us down here. But, I have to admit, I've enjoyed getting away from the office. I just wish Liz was here because she could use a break too."

A woman approaches Sam's chair from behind and says, "She is here, you old fart!"

Sam turns and stares at his wife in complete disbelief. A moment later, they embrace and she kisses him.

I tease them mercilessly, "Hey, get a room!"

Liz comes over and gives me a hug saying, "He would never have done this if you hadn't made him think the trip was strictly for business. Thank you."

Sam says, "I'm sensing a conspiracy here."

"Absolutely, Devin and I set this up before the two of you left and he made arrangements for me to catch a flight last night. You're taking some time off whether you want to or not."

"Sam," I say, "You helped me out of a tight spot a few months ago and you trusted me when you had no reason to do so. I wanted to do something to say thanks. I've taken care of the hotel and the limo for another week. I'll move my stuff out of our room after we finish breakfast."

"And where are you going?" he asks.

"I'm moving down the hall to give you and Liz some privacy. I'm taking a vacation, too, and I'm going to show you the Rio de Janeiro that I know. We're going to have a great time."

Across town, detective Ruiz is having a conversation with his assistant, Daniel Montoya.

"Danny, did you have any luck running down Lara Alda?"

"Yes, once you gave me a first name, it was pretty easy to find an address. Where'd you get that information anyway?"

"It was Devin Ross, the fellow who was with the FBI agent yesterday."

Montoya asks, "I'm curious, why do you want me to keep this from the rest of the guys working the case?"

"I'll fill you in on that later, but right now, I think we should take a ride over to the woman's house and talk to her."

"Don't you think we should call first?"

"No, I don't want to take a chance that she might disappear on us. Let's get going."

They arrive at her home a little after twelve and ring the doorbell. Lara peers through the peephole, but she does not open the door. Detective Ruiz holds his credentials and badge up to the viewport and announces himself.

"We are with the Rio police department and it's important that we speak to you about your son. He's in danger and we need to protect him. If you're in there, please open the door."

Ruiz and Montoya can hear multiple locks clicking when Lara opens the door and waves them to a seat in the living area.

"What do you want?" she asks.

"Your son is wanted by the American FBI in conjunction with a murder case. Two of his friends, Ruben Clemente and Luis Marcos, were also involved, and they were killed just a few days ago."

Lara is visibly upset when she says, "I know Luis and his mother. She must be devastated."

Detective Ruiz says, "I'm sorry for your loss and I can't imagine how you must feel. I don't wish to seem insensitive, but we think the men who did this are also after your son. Do you know where we can find him?"

"No, we had an argument and he's not speaking to me."

"Was the argument about his troubles with the police?"

"No, it was a family matter and I'm not going to talk about it."

"Do you have a telephone contact for your son?"

"He just got a new cellphone and he won't give me the number. He did send me a text message letting me know that he was okay, but I accidentally deleted the number from the call log."

The detective sighs and says, "May I see your phone, please?"

She reluctantly gives him the phone. He casually slips one hand into his pocket and presses a button on a device concealed there. Lara's phone is instantly cloned and he hands it back to her after glancing at the caller log. Then he addresses his assistant.

"It doesn't look like there is much here that we can use, Danny."

They talk with Lara for another twenty-minutes and it's clear that she isn't going to divulge any more information about her son. Ruiz does not disclose the fact that he knows about her relationship with Walter Paris or that he knows that Walter is Jorge's father. When the conversation ends, he hands her his business card, along with a request to call him if Jorge contacts her. As Ruiz and Montoya leave Lara's home, there are two men with military haircuts sitting in a car half a block away. One of them is on the phone with Walter Paris.

He says, "Sir, it looks as though a couple of cops just paid Lara Alda a visit. Do you still want us to pick her up?"

"Yes, but wait until you're sure the police are gone and that nobody sees you. Take her to the place designated in my previous text message and keep her there until I arrive. I'm flying to Rio tonight to handle the rest of this personally. I'll see you tomorrow morning."

Walter Paris hangs up and summons a limousine for a ride to the airport. Detective Ruiz and Danny Montoya are unaware of the conversation that has just taken place between Paris and his Brazilian operatives. But, Ruiz's keen eye has just observed something that may be useful.

When they return to their vehicle, he says, "Danny, did you notice those guys sitting in the car across from Lara Alda's place?"

"No, I missed that."

Ruiz says, "Well, we're going to follow them discreetly and see where that takes us."

Fifteen minutes pass and the two men enter and exit Lara Alda's apartment with the woman in tow. She seems to be going with the men willingly, so the policemen don't intervene. About an hour later, they arrive at a condominium on the other side town. Ruiz speaks to his assistant.

"Danny, I want you to stay here and keep an eye on things. We'll take turns watching the place and I'll relieve you in a couple of hours. I'm going to catch a cab back to the office. I'll get a second car and bring you something to eat."

# Chapter 33

## July 19  0930 Hours  •  Rio de Janeiro

### Location: Antonio Carlos Jobim International Airport.

Walter Paris' overnight flight to Rio de Janeiro arrives at nine-thirty in the morning. He leaves the airplane and enters a waiting car where he places a telephone call to the men who picked up Lara Alda the previous day. The man, known only as "Cooper," answers.

"Good morning, sir. We've secured Ms. Alda and her cellphone. We're holding her at the location that you specified in our last communication. I might add that she is less than pleased with the arrangement."

"Thank you, Mr. Cooper. Please inform Ms. Alda that I will be there personally in a couple of hours to explain the situation."

"Will do and see you soon, sir."

Walter hangs up and directs his driver to a computer store on the other side of town. A small, odd-looking fellow, wearing glasses, exits the building and joins him in the back seat of the limousine. Walter hands him an envelope with some cash in it and details the task at hand.

"I need you to retrieve a number from an incoming call to a cellphone that may have been erased. Is that possible?"

The man replies, "Even if it's been deleted, I may be able to retrieve it from residual memory. It shouldn't take more than a few minutes, unless the phone is damaged."

Paris nods and their driver begins the trek across town. Forty-five minutes later, they arrive at a modest condominium in quiet neighborhood. It is one of three safe houses that Walter owns in Rio. He exits the vehicle quickly and goes into the building. Lara Alda explodes as soon as he enters the room and pokes a finger into his chest.

"Why the hell did you have these men bring me here? I don't care how much money you have, it doesn't give you the right to do this!"

Walter coolly raises a hand and nods to his men saying, "Mr. Cooper, would you and your associates give me a few moments alone with Ms. Alda?"

After they have gone, Lara steps in front of Walter, ready to launch a steady stream of expletives. She hesitates because she can see that he is in no mood for another outburst. He solemnly points to a nearby chair and angrily utters a single word.

"Sit!"

This is a side of Walter Paris that Lara has never seen before. The quiet gentleman that she has always known has suddenly vanished, becoming something else, something quite scary. He slides his chair directly in front of her and begins a very concise monologue.

"Lara, I am a criminal, a wealthy one, but a criminal nonetheless. I have done terrible things to acquire money and to protect myself. I'm prepared to do even more terrible things, if it becomes necessary. I am by nature, a selfish man, mostly looking after my own interests. But you and Jorge are the only things I've ever really loved. If I hadn't brought you here, it is very likely the cartels would have killed you, or at the very least, tortured you to find out where Jorge is hiding. I couldn't let that happen. I'm willing to kill people if that's what it takes to keep you safe. I have thirty days to fix this problem. If I don't act quickly, the cartels will kill all of us. Do you understand?"

Lara is overwhelmed, but her street instincts, honed during her years growing up in the worst slums in Rio, kick in instantly.

"Alright," she says, "What do you want me to do?"

"I need to use your telephone to get a message to Jorge."

"You can have it, but the police dropped by my place yesterday and they couldn't get anything out of it because I accidently deleted the call log."

He gestures toward the window and says, "I have a man outside who can take care of that. Will you help me?"

Lara nods and gives him the phone. Twenty minutes later, the electronics technician that Walter brought with him has retrieved the number from the deleted call log. Walter removes a card from his shirt pocket with a note for Jorge written on it. He takes the phone and taps the message into it.

It reads: "Jorge, the cartels have placed a price on your head. They will torture your mother and kill her if you don't talk to me. They've already killed your friends, Luis and Ruben, and they forced me to send men after you. I've called them off because I have a way to fix this. You have no reason to trust me and I don't blame you. All I'm asking for is a five-minute conversation. If you don't like what you hear, you can walk away and we'll all take our chances with the cartels. Text this number to let me know what you want to do. For now, your mother is safe with me. I'll wait forty-eight hours. After that, I'll take whatever steps are necessary to protect myself. — Walter."

He hits the send key and puts the phone into his pocket. He does not show Lara the message, even though she pressures him to look at it.

"What did you say to him?" she asks.

"I had to say some harsh things, but that's not important, Lara. What is important is that he contacts me in the next two days so we can put a stop to this. Right now, all we can do is wait and hope that he calls us."

Across town, detective Ruiz is hoping that Jorge Alda will call, too. He's been monitoring Lara's phone, using the surveillance equipment that I gave him a couple of days ago. He's debating whether or not to share this information with his assistant, Danny Montoya. He trusts Danny, but he doesn't know if the young man's phones are bugged or if there are listening devices in his home. There is no way to check for these things without getting Danny's consent and letting him know what's happening. For now, he decides to keep this business to himself.

In Manaus, Jorge has received Walter Paris' message and he is far less than enthusiastic. He is concerned about his mother. Although he didn't say so in his text message, Jorge knows that Walter will hurt Lara to get what he wants if need be. Jorge will do whatever he can to help her, but he doesn't fancy dying, either. He will talk to Paris, but he's going to take his time deciding how to do it. If he's learned nothing else from Walter, it is how to be patient. Perhaps a long walk along the river will clear his head and give him some ideas. He starts his motor scooter and begins a leisurely drive out of the city toward the shoreline and the jungle.

# CHAPTER 34

July 19 1015 Hours • Rio de Janeiro

Location: City Medical Examiner's Office

A DREARY-LOOKING MAN, wearing a lab coat, is eyeing a bundle of cash that a large unpleasant fellow has just placed on his desk. He has never seen this man before, but he has heard his voice on the telephone many times. A face-to-face visit is unusual. This guy is here in person to make a point and clearly he is not to be trifled with. This is not the first time that he has accepted money to make someone's problem go away. It is the first time that he has been paid so handsomely for it. Per the instructions he received earlier in the day, no names will be exchanged during this meeting.

"Yes sir, what can I do for you?"

"We have a different assignment for you this time. To get it done, we are paying several times your normal fee. In a few days, we will need your services at the scene of a shooting. We'll provide transportation and everything else you need to do the job."

"Usually, you're sending me to get rid of a body and now you're asking to help someone at a shooting?"

"That is correct. Here is a written plan of what we want you to do. Will you help us with it?"

The man in the lab coat almost laughs because for the kind of money they're paying, he doesn't really care what they want him to do. Besides, he knows they will kill him if he doesn't cooperate.

"I'll need a few days to rehearse my part in this, but yes, I'll help you."

"You have exactly three days to prepare. When you're ready, call us at this number. We'll also need you to block off one of your exam rooms for a few hours and you'll need to set that up, too. We'll give you the rest of the details later."

The coroner quickly places the cash in his briefcase. The big man nods, exits the room, and gets into a car waiting outside. He directs the driver to an address in the theatre district. A short time later, they arrive at an auditorium's backstage door. A man leaves the building wearing a baseball cap and sunglasses. He joins the big fellow in the backseat of the car. The big man hands him an envelope full of cash.

He says, "This money is a retainer for your services. Block out your schedule for the next week and wait for our call. You'll receive additional payment when the job is done."

The man in the baseball cap agrees and leaves the vehicle.

His driver asks, "Where to now, boss?"

"There is an auto body shop a couple of miles from here. That's our next stop. Here's the address."

When they arrive, the man leaves the car and he is greeted at the building entrance by another sturdy-looking fellow sporting a military-style haircut and an automatic weapon. They exchange greetings and the man enters the building. The place looks like an army tactical briefing area. A familiar voice calls out to the man from across the room.

"Hey, Bobby, did you get everything taken care of?"

"We're all set, Sully, but I'll check on those guys every day, just to make sure everything is running smoothly. How's the rest of the operation coming along?"

"We're about ready to go and you're just in time for a quick run-through of the mission. Call the guy out front watching the door and we'll get to it."

When the two men return from the front of the building, Sullivan starts his briefing.

"Gentlemen, our assignment is to take out two civilians, Walter Paris and Jorge Alda. I've been directed to do the shooting personally and your job will be to provide me with cover while I take care of business. There may be a third party involved in the operation, a Rio cop, Wilbur Santiago. Shoot up his car if you have to, but don't kill him. He is one of us and he is not to be harmed. You've been provided with recent photographs of all the people involved in this operation."

One of the men asks, "Can we go out on location today? Even though we've done several practice sessions here in the warehouse, I'd like to do a few live run-throughs on site to make sure we cover all the bases."

"That's a good question, Fred, and the answer is yes. After we're done here, we'll all drive over there and take a look around to review our escape routes. Even though there will only be the five of us, we'll have two getaway vehicles. I don't want to leave anything to chance. We still have a few more days to rehearse things to make certain this goes off without a hitch."

"I know you don't like a lot of questions,s Sully, but why have we beefed up the doors on the escape cars. This looks like a pretty easy hit to me. The extra bullet-proofing on the cars seems a little over-the-top. Are you expecting more trouble than we've talked about?"

That's what Sully has always liked about Jenkins. He looks at everything and he's not afraid to ask questions if he spots a potential trouble spot in a plan.

"Jinx, the last job that I did for our employer didn't go as planned and I don't want any screw-ups on this one. We're dealing with some nasty people who work for the cartels and we have to get this right. If we screw up, we could all end up dead. It seemed prudent to take every precaution."

Jenkins nods and Sullivan continues the briefing. When he's finished, he takes one last walk through the warehouse inspecting the vehicles, weapons, and other equipment needed to complete the mission. Satisfied the escape vehicles are ready to go, he addresses his next comments to a man named Tompkins.

"You'll be driving the ambulance and it will be the most critical part of the operation. You and Jenkins will only have a few minutes to get in there, pick up Jorge Alda's body, and get out. I know this is risky, but there has to be proof that we got the job done."

Tompkins says, "We're on it, skipper. Consider it done."

Sullivan slaps him on the shoulder playfully and says, "Good man."

He steps outside and punches a number into his cellphone. A voice answers cryptically saying, "I assume you're calling to tell me that you're ready to go?"

"We're locked, loaded, and ready to roll on this end. All we need is the day and time that you want the operation to start."

"I'll have that for you in a couple of days Mr. Sullivan."

The call ends and Sullivan gets into a vehicle with his men. They'll drive to the site of the shooting and walk through the operation several times to make certain that it will go as planned. In distant Manaus, Jorge Alda has nearly decided how to set up a meeting with Walter Paris. His plan must be foolproof or he will die.

# CHAPTER 35

## July 19 1650 Hours • Brazil

## Locations: Manaus & Rio de Janeiro

IT IS LATE AFTERNOON and Jorge Alda is busy texting a message to his mother's cellphone to work out a deal with Walter Paris. He's tired of running and he wants to put an end to this. He knows that if he doesn't do it, Paris will hurt his mother. He does not want to give up the location of his safe house in Manaus, so he has tentatively set up a meeting with Walter in Rio. He'll call him with the details when he arrives there later this evening. Once the message is sent, Jorge shuts off his phone and boards his flight. After he takes a seat, he removes the battery as a precaution, but it's already too late for that. Detective Ruiz has seen the message that he sent to Walter because he cloned Lara's cellphone the previous day. The question the policeman is wrestling with now is how best to handle the situation.

Ruiz is not certain who all the players are in the current sequence of events and he's being cautious. He's reluctant to trust anyone on the police force with what he knows. If he does, it might get back to his boss, Wilbur Santiago, who appears to be involved in this in some way. That is why the phone is ringing in my hotel room.

The detective asks, "Is agent Dorsey still at the hotel with you?"

"No, his wife flew into town yesterday and he's taking a little vacation. They're on their way to Iguazu Falls and they won't be back for a couple of days. Is there anything I can do to help you?"

"Do you have time to meet me later today?"

"I was going to have dinner with a friend, but I can change the time if it's important."

He says, "I don't want to disrupt your plans and I'd be happy to meet you at the restaurant for a quick chat. I only need a few minutes and I don't want to do this over the telephone."

"Okay, I'll meet you around six."

I hang up and walk down to the hotel lobby where my longtime friend, Astrid Mendes, is waiting for me. When I arrive, I can't help but notice that nearly all of the men in the room are drooling, each one trying to catch a glimpse of her. Astrid is one of a kind and I call her the Brazilian bombshell. She is about five feet four inches tall, slightly buxom and she's been turning men's heads for years. Astrid likes men and she loves the attention.

I was with her once when we walked by a construction site. She was wearing a very short skirt which drew whistles and catcalls from every man on the job. Most women would have been offended or at least a little embarrassed. Those words are not in her vocabulary. She immediately hiked up her already short skirt another couple of inches and walked by the site again, this time blowing all the guys a kiss. They loved it. When I asked her why she did it, her response was, "If you got it, flaunt it. I'll be old and gray soon enough and it would be a damn shame to waste it."

She was born just outside of Rio, but she lives in Montreal. She's in town visiting her mother. By chance, we're staying at the same hotel and I bumped into her during breakfast this morning. She greets me with a warm hug and a very passionate kiss, intentionally putting on a show for anyone who may be watching. I love it and I can almost hear the other guys in the room groan. We've never been lovers, but we are very close friends from our days working together at the British Embassy in Caracas.

I say, "You always know how to make an entrance, Astrid."

She smiles and says, "Yes, I do. And now, you're the envy of every guy in here, thanks to me. That's going to cost you a very expensive dinner and lots of wine to pay me back."

We pop into a cab waiting outside the hotel and I let Astrid know that our dinner will be interrupted by a short meeting with detective Ruiz. He's waiting for us at the bar inside the restaurant. I introduce him to Astrid and she excuses herself so the policeman and I can talk. He, too, is taken by Astrid's physical beauty.

"Devin," he says, "That is a truly remarkable woman. How did you meet her?"

"She was my firearms and evasive driving instructor when I worked at the embassy in Caracas. She's a crack shot, a kickboxer, and she used to ride motocross events on the weekends with her dirt bike. She speaks five languages fluently and she's a really sharp businesswoman. She can hold her own against almost any man I know."

Ruiz's jaw drops, and, for a moment, he stares at me in disbelief.

He says, "You're kidding, right?"

"Nope, every word I've said is completely true."

"Well," he says, "We can discuss that some other time over drinks. Right now, I want to tell you about a lead I just got on Jorge Alda. Thanks to the surveillance equipment that you gave me, I was able to intercept a couple of text messages between Alda and Walter Paris. Jorge is setting up some sort of meeting with him in the next day or so. He said he'd call him with the details later tonight. I was going to follow Paris, hoping to get eyes on Jorge, and I was going to ask agent Dorsey to go with me as backup. My assistant is the only one on the force that I can trust with this and we're spread pretty thin. I don't want to do it alone and I was hoping agent Dorsey was available."

Without thinking I say, "I'll go with you. I know that I'm a civilian, but I used to live here and I know the city pretty well. I'd like to help you if I can."

"I know you've had some training with this stuff, but this could get a little dicey and you're not armed."

I gently pat the nine-millimeter pistol under my jacket and say, "I took care of that right after I got here. I've even got an embassy permit to carry it."

"Alright, but this is just a reconnaissance mission. There are some very powerful people involved here. I don't want to barge into anything until I know what's really going on. When I get more information, I'll call your cell and we can meet somewhere."

Before he leaves, detective Ruiz says, "There is one more thing. Lara Alda is a player in this now. A couple of muscle guys picked her up right after I paid her a visit yesterday. They didn't think I noticed them sitting outside and I had my assistant follow them after they left. They've got her in a condo across town. Danny Montoya is keeping an eye on the place and he says she okay. Walter Paris dropped by there this morning and he's camped out in the living room with Lara and a couple of his security people."

"You're thinking Paris is holding Jorge's mom as a way to get him to come in?"

"I'm pretty sure that's what's happening. We have to be very careful because I don't want the woman harmed. I was wondering if you could watch the place where Paris is holding Lara Alda for a couple of hours, so Danny Montoya and I can get some sleep. We've been spread pretty thin the last couple of days and we could both use a break."

"Sure, just give me the address and let Danny know I'll be dropping by to relieve him. Is there anything else?"

"No, that's it for now. I'll let you know if anything else comes up."

"Alright, I'll keep my cellphone handy. You can reach me any time after dinner."

Ruiz says goodbye and I return to our table and sit next to Astrid.

She is taken aback when I say, "You're not really here to visit your mother are you?"

"Damn it Devin. You take all of the fun out of a good con. How'd you know?"

"You weren't very careful when you tried to listen to my conversation with the detective. I'm surprised because in the old days, you would have been more subtle."

"It's hard to be subtle when there may be people trying to kill someone you love."

I wink at her and say, "I always knew that you had a thing

for me, but flying all the way to Rio is a little over the top, even for you."

"I like you, Devin, but you know damn well I'm here because I'm worried about Tommy. He's the one who brought me up to speed on the investigation and told me you were coming to Rio. I love him and you and I are going to make sure nothing happens to my stud muffin."

"Stud muffin?"

"Yeah, that's what I've taken to calling him these days. Kind of cute, don't you think?"

"I know that men and women who are involved romantically often have pet names for each other, but I don't think I'd string those two words together if I was talking about Tommy. It would be a trifle embarrassing in public."

She smiles devilishly and says, "I only call him that when we're in bed together. Besides, I'm sure that Harley has a nickname for you."

"Harley left me for her ex-husband a few days ago."

"I'm sure that her leaving hurt you, Devin, but I say good riddance. That foolish woman kept you dangling about her true feelings for months. You were unbelievably patient with her. The good news is that Kate will be thrilled to hear that she's gone. She's been in love with you for years and you and I both know that you feel the same way about her. The only reason that you two aren't together is because she met Tommy first."

Astrid has unintentionally struck a nerve and I don't know how to respond. She senses the change in my mood right away, but she refuses to let it go. She reaches across the table and squeezes my hand.

She says, "None of this makes sense to me, either. What is clear is that I belong with Tommy, and you should be with Kate. Apparently, the universe has a sense of humor, or it wouldn't have thrown the four of us together in the first place. You think too much, Devin. If I were you, I'd just sit back and enjoy the ride."

"Actions have consequences, Astrid. Kate has kids to consider and the notoriety that goes with the billion-dollar Holloway name has to be reckoned with too. My being involved with her would be front page headlines for every tabloid in the country. They'll make up ridiculous stuff about us, just to grab a headline. I couldn't do that to her kids or to Kate. Maybe it will work out down the road, but not right now."

Astrid sighs and says, "I'd have to agree with you there, but it seems like a terrible waste of time for people who care about each other as much as the two of you do. She even has a pet nickname for you. I'll tell you what it is, if you let me help with your investigation."

"Alright, you've got a deal. Here's what's going on so far."

I spend the next hour or so bringing Astrid up to speed on everything we've uncovered over dinner and wine. I know I can trust her with the information because we've done this kind of work together in the past.

She finishes one last sip of the Pinot and says, "Where do you think I can help you?"

"Actually, I'd like you to be my safety net and follow me around while I'm with the detective. You know how to be discreet and I don't know where this is going. I'd like someone watching my back that I can trust. Do you have access to a weapon?"

Astrid fakes a frown and says, "Shame on you, Devin. You know me better than that. I wouldn't dare travel the city alone unless I was packing. I've got a 'Nine' and a couple of extra clips in my bag."

"I figured you had a gun somewhere because that skirt is so damn tight there's no place else to hide it."

She flashes a wry smile and hikes her already short dress just a wee bit higher to reveal a second smaller pistol strapped to the inside of her thigh.

"A girl can't be too careful," she says.

I lean over to kiss her and say, "Now, that's the Astrid I know and love. Do you have your own wheels?"

"I've got a friend's car, but I can get a motorcycle if I need one."

"Good,s because your first assignment is to drop by the back door of the embassy and pick up a couple of AA-12 shotguns and some ammunition."

"You want automatic shotguns? Those damn things will shred metal like tissue paper. Are you expecting to fight a war or something?"

"No, but I think our detective friend may be underestimating the opposition and I don't want to get caught short if things get out of hand."

"Consider it done. I'll pick them up right after dinner. I even brought my stealthy black jumpsuit so I can follow the bad guys without being noticed."

"Speaking of bad guys, Detective Ruiz wants me to sit on the apartment where Walter Paris is holding Jorge Alda's mother for a couple of hours so he can get some rest. How about backing me up? If Paris leaves, I won't be able to follow him for very long because he'd probably recognize me. He's never seen you and he'd never expect an attractive woman to be tailing him on a motorcycle."

She says, "Alright, I can help you with that, Luscious."

"Luscious?"

"Yeah, that's what Kate calls you behind your back. It's been a private joke between the two of us for years. That's almost as much fun to say as Stud Muffin."

I'm slightly embarrassed, but it really is funny. Tonight, laughter is a good thing because tomorrow, Astrid and I will begin our surveillance of Walter Paris.

# CHAPTER 36

## July 20 1330 Hours • Fifty Kilometers Outside of Rio

## Location: Abrico Beach

WALTER PARIS' CAR pulls onto a side road offering a beautiful view of the ocean. The information that he received last night said to come here alone. Detective Ruiz showed me the intercepted text message and I sent Astrid ahead to the meeting place. She is hidden in a secure location, waiting for Paris to arrive. The detective has discreetly followed Paris to this location as well, but he is unaware of Astrid's presence. Jorge Alda doesn't trust Paris, which is why the older man has arrived at Abrico Beach without his usual entourage. He exits the car and locks the door. Jorge has directed him to this somewhat remote, but well-known beach.

Paris leaves the road and walks toward the surf where he is immediately uncomfortable. The Abrico is a naturist beach, and, although there are only a dozen or so people wandering about, most of them are naked. Paris is fully clothed and he feels terribly out of place. Jorge knows that Walter is ever the proper English gentleman and he has deliberately sent him here just to annoy him.

His cellphone rings and he is further directed to an outcropping of rocks where a boat is waiting. He removes his shoes and the vessel's operator helps him through the surf and onto the boat. Once aboard, he is searched for weapons and his cellphone is confiscated. Satisfied, the man steers the craft to their destination, a small island less than a half-mile offshore. The boat is very fast and it only takes a few minutes to reach the island.

They arrive at a quiet beach and Walter is deposited alone on an empty shoreline. A few minutes later, Jorge Alda seems to appear almost out of nowhere. Walter is annoyed, but another part of him admires the young man's resourcefulness for arranging their meeting in a place where there is virtually no possibility of a sniper taking a shot at him. Jorge shouts a command to the boat operator.

"Come back in an hour and return Mr. Paris to Abrico."

The man nods and casts off. Paris and Alda are alone, and for a long time, neither of them speaks. Jorge stares at Walter's face, trying to find some familial resemblance, but it somehow escapes him. Walter is the first to break the silence.

"You brought me here Jorge. Let's get down to business."

"Alright, you said you had a plan to get us out of trouble. Tell me about it."

Walter hands him a manila folder saying, "It's all in there. Take a few minutes to look it over and then we'll talk."

Jorge settles on a nearby rock and begins to read. He's distracted by the notion that this man is actually his father. It takes him nearly ten minutes to read through the material. He's not happy with the plan and he says so.

"It looks like I'm taking all the risk here."

"I didn't say it was foolproof. I just said it was the best I could come up with on short notice. We don't have a lot of time and if we don't do something quickly, we're both dead, maybe Lara, too. Neither of us wants that to happen."

"Why should I trust you, Walter? You tried to have me killed twice."

"Yes, I did try to kill you, but I called it off because this is a way for both of us to come out of this alive. The only reason I sent those men after you was because you wouldn't return my calls. If we'd spoken beforehand, it would never have happened."

Jorge says, "Do you really think the cartels are going to let us get away with this? They want me gone as much as you do. One little slip-up in this deal and I'm dead meat. On top of that, the cartel's men may catch up with us before we can pull this off. They own half the cops and politicians in Rio and they've got eyes and ears everywhere. It wouldn't surprise me if they already have a copy of your plan."

"That's a chance we'll have to take because there isn't time for anything else."

"What about my mother? You and I knew what we were getting into when we went to work for these people. She had nothing to do with this and she deserves better.

"I let her go right after you talked to me last night, but Lara may have to go into witness protection with you. That would take her away from everything she loves. She'll have to change her name, leave all of her friends, and maybe live in another country. She may want to stay here in Brazil, but I think that would be unwise. She only has a couple of days to think about it, but it's her call. I won't try to influence her decision either way."

"So, the plan is that I won't testify against you about Susan's murder and you walk on that charge. The Feds will put us into the witness protection program and we all get to live in some off-the-map place for the rest of our lives."

"Would you prefer a jail cell?"

"It means I'll have to give up my flying career and everything I know. Mom will probably have to leave Brazil and all of her friends. What do you get out of this? I can't imagine you living in Idaho or some such place for the rest of your life."

"Jorge, I've been famous for a long time, or maybe I should say infamous. I've been on the cover of Time Magazine and on the front page of the Wall Street Journal. It would be very hard for me to hide for very long without somebody recognizing me."

"If you don't go into witness protection with me and mom, what are you going to do? The cartels will come after you with a vengeance."

"I have a contingency plan for that. As for your giving up flying, it would only be professionally. I've set aside enough money for you to own an airplane and for you and your mother to live very comfortably for the rest of your lives. It's a lot easier to live in the middle of nowhere if you're a millionaire and that will be the case for both of you. I've already sent the money to your personal accounts. You can call and verify it if you like."

Jorge ponders the deal for a few moments before saying, "Alright, let's do it. The day after tomorrow, I'll meet you in front of the theatre and turn myself in."

Walter is not surprised by his response because there really is no other choice. However, he is very curious about something else.

"I'm surprised that you haven't asked me any questions about my being your father. Why is that?"

"I've been so busy running and trying to stay alive that there hasn't been time to think about anything else."

"Well, if you do have questions, now is the time, because after this is over, it is very unlikely that we will ever see each other again."

"There is nothing else that I want to know about you, Walter. You had a woman that I cared about killed. Shortly after that, you had two of my friends murdered, and subsequently, you tried to have me killed. After seeing what kind of man you really were, my plan was to take all of the money I'd saved and just disappear to some remote part of the world. I really never wanted to see you again. You made that impossible when you held my mother hostage and forced me to talk to you."

Paris stares at Jorge for a long time before speaking.

"I think you know that I could never hurt your mother and that those things I said on the telephone were just idle threats to get you to talk to me."

"That may be true, but my mother would die for me and I would do the same for her. You would not do that for me nor would I do it for you."

"If that's the way you feel, why on earth did you agree to meet with me?"

"I did it because there is one thing that I've always trusted about you, Walter. Whenever you give your word to someone, you never renege on it. Even if it means life or death, you will honor a verbal commitment to the grave if necessary. Like it or not, it's part of who you are. I've seen you do it more than once. That's probably the only good thing left inside that rot-ten soul of yours. I've always respected you for it, but I despise you as a human being."

Walter is reeling and close to tears when he says, "So, now what?"

"In a few minutes, a boat will pick me up and take me away from here. In about an hour, the other boat will return and take you back to Abrico Beach. It's the only way I can be sure that your men won't follow me. I'll call you when I verify that the funds you promised have been transferred to my offshore accounts. After that, you and I are done. Goodbye, Walter."

Jorge walks away without another word leaving Paris alone with his thoughts. Astrid Mendes has watched these events transpire through a pair of high tech binoculars. She could not hear the conversation between the two men, but she easily recognized them as Jorge Alda and Walter Paris. She dials my number on her cellphone.

"Devin, I watched for Walter Paris just like you asked. He got on a boat and went out to a small island just offshore where he met with Jorge Alda. I recognized them from the pictures you gave me last night. What do you want me to do?"

"Is there any chance that you can follow Alda?"

"No. A high speed boat just picked him up and he's running down the coast like a bat out of hell. I can probably follow Paris when he comes back for his car."

"Okay, let's go with that. Just make certain he doesn't see you."

"Not to worry, I am a master sleuth. By the way, where the hell did you get these binoculars? Those guys were several hundred yards away and I could see them both clearly."

"Our mutual friend, Bill Marston, got them for me over at the embassy. They're kind of cool, huh?"

"Yeah, I'm watching a bunch of nudies down on the beach and it's like being a nurse at the doctor's office."

"I didn't know that you were a closet voyeur."

"I'm not, but this is just too damn much fun. The human body comes in all shapes and sizes. Right now, I'm looking at a fat guy who must weigh three hundred pounds. I believe the Latin term for this is "Tubis Buffalodis.""

I laugh out loud and say, "Well, don't enjoy yourself too much. I'll meet you for dinner tonight and we'll map out something for tomorrow."

"Okay, catch you later."

# CHAPTER 37

## July 20  1900 Hours  •  Rio de Janeiro

## Location: Restaurant, Sheraton Grande Hotel

ASTRID AND I ARE ENJOYING a glass of wine when I say, "So, how was your day at the beach? Did any good looking men show up or are you still hung up on the fat guy?"

"A couple of hot dudes came by later, but I had to follow Walter Paris and that wasn't much fun."

"Where'd he go?"

"He went back to his place and met up with a couple of his muscle guys. Detective Ruiz's assistant was watching Paris' condo, too, but he didn't see me. It looks like our buddy, Walter, is planning something, but I have no clue as to what that might be. You got any ideas?"

"It's just a wild guess, but I'd bet that he cut some sort of deal with Jorge not to testify against him in the Susan Parks' murder case."

"So, the Teflon King slips the noose again?"

"Could be, but we have no way of knowing for sure."

"Where's your FBI friend? I thought he was the reason you came down here in the first place. Shouldn't he be the one doing all of this leg work?"

"He's taking a short break with his wife, but he'll be back tomorrow morning. If anything important turns up, I'll give him a call. For now, we just have to wait and see what happens. I'm sure Detective Ruiz is doing the same thing."

Astrid says, "You really like Ruiz, don't you?"

"Yeah, I think he's a good cop in a bad place trying to do the right thing. If this business goes sideways and he gets caught snooping around, it could cost him his career. We know that his boss, Wilbur Santiago, is feeding information to Paris about the investigation and that he had me and Sam Dorsey followed when we first got here. Ruiz wants us to stay on the sidelines. That's why I didn't tell him that you saw Jorge Alda today. If nothing happens in the next couple of days, we'll pack it in and head back to the States. There is really nothing else we can do, but let's change the subject."

"Okay, what do you want to talk about?"

"What's happening between you and Tommy? Or maybe a better question would be, what's happening between you and Kate?"

"The short answer is that I stole her husband, and somehow she has forgiven me for it. God knows why, but she's still my closest friend."

I say, "Their marriage was in trouble long before you and Tommy hooked up. You just pushed the exit door open a little wider and he walked through it. Kate still loves him, but she knew it was time to let him go."

"It sounds like you've been talking to her."

"Yeah, she called me one night to vent."

She lets out a chortle saying smugly, "You two are as bad as me and Tommy. You've been dying to sleep with each other for years. You haven't consummated the act yet, but you will. I'm as sure about that as the sun coming up tomorrow morning."

I grin back at her to say, "Another good reason to go home in a couple of days."

Across town, Walter Paris is doing something that will alter our plans to leave Rio. It begins when he places a call to Detective Ruiz's boss, Wilbur Santiago. His voice is silky smooth when he speaks to the policeman.

"Good evening, Wil, I've called with some good news and to ask a favor of you."

"Hello, Walter. What do you need?"

"I've made contact with Jorge Alda and he's agreed to turn himself in. He'll only do it if I meet with him personally along with a police escort. He's worried the cartel will come after him and he wants a safety net. I'll have a couple of my men there to take him out, but I was wondering if you'd come along with some of your guys to make sure nothing goes wrong. It never hurts to have a little extra firepower."

Santiago is almost giddy when he replies, "I'll bring two of my best guys and we'll keep an eye on things for you."

"Thanks, Wil. I'll call you with a time and location as soon as Jorge gets back to me with that information."

Walter hangs up and turns to Sullivan, his most trusted operative, who has a question for his boss.

"I thought you said that Santiago was spying on you and working with the cartels behind your back. Why are you bringing him in on this?"

"We need a witness to see us kill Jorge and report back to the cartel. They won't believe I've killed him unless someone under their control confirms it. I'm pretty sure Santiago is on the telephone feeding this information to the cartel leadership."

Walter's assumption is correct. At that very moment, Santiago is talking to someone in Medellin, Colombia. Martin Roah, the man who threatened Walter at the cartel meeting in New York a few days earlier, takes the call.

He says, "Wil, I assume you've called to update us on Jorge Alda."

"Yes sir, he's turning himself in tomorrow. Paris says that his men will be there to kill him when he arrives. Walter asked me to bring a couple of men along for backup. Do you want us to take care of it?"

"No, don't intervene unless Walter fails to get the job done. I have given him a month to finish it and I want to honor that commitment."

Santiago says, "And if he doesn't get it done?"

"If that happens, I want you and your men to kill them both and there are to be no mistakes. Am I clear?"

"Yes, that is perfectly clear, sir."

"Good. Keep me posted if anything changes."

Santiago hangs up feeling elated and terrified all in the same moment. He knows the cartel will reward him handsomely if things go well. If they don't go well, he won't see his next birthday. He will bring two of his very best along to make sure there are no mistakes.

Walter Paris is having dinner in his residence, believing that his scheme will go smoothly, but his plan has a serious flaw. When Jorge Alda sent him a text confirming their meeting time and place, Detective Ruiz was able to intercept the message because he cloned the phone Walter is currently using. Because of that, he knows the exact location and time of Paris' meeting with Jorge. He's going to be there with Danny Montoya to arrest Alda and possibly turn him over to the FBI.

# CHAPTER 38

July 21 1100 Hours • Rio de Janeiro

Location: Sheraton Grande Hotel

I've slept late this morning because Astrid and I went out dancing last night and I didn't get back to the hotel until after midnight. It's eleven-thirty and I'm just stepping out of the shower when the telephone rings. It's Sam Dorsey.

"Morning Sam, how was your visit to Iguazu Falls?"

"It was fantastic, what an amazing place. Liz and I had a great time and I can't thank you enough."

"So, what are your plans for the rest of the week? I hope you'll take some time to enjoy the rest of the sights in Rio."

"I'd love to do that, but I just got a call from Detective Ruiz. Things are happening and he wants me in on it. Mind if I drop by your room to chat?"

"Sure, just give me a couple of minutes to get dressed."

Fifteen minutes later, there is a knock at the door and Sam joins me at a table on the balcony, wearing a broad smile.

He says, "We've had a stroke of luck. Detective Ruiz intercepted a text message between Walter Paris and Jorge Alda. They're meeting tonight and we have an exact location and time. Ruiz and his assistant want me to go along and arrest him. He thinks that my being there may make it easier to negotiate the politics with his boss when he finds out about it. What do you think?"

"I think you need to be damn careful, Sam. Walter Paris never leaves anything to chance. You can bet that he'll have some of his people there watching his back. They'll be well-armed and spring-loaded for trouble. If they think something is going wrong, this could very easily turn into a nasty shoot-out with you caught in the middle. On top of that, we're out of our element down here and we have no idea who else may be involved in this. I don't like it."

"I know this deal is a little sketchy, but if there is any chance of grabbing Alda, I have to take it. Ruiz gave me the okay to bring my weapon and there will be three of us; me, Ruiz and Daniel Montoya. They'll have shotguns as well as their side arms. That should be enough deterrence to ward off any serious trouble."

I'm still skeptical of his plan when I ask, "Do you want me to come with you?"

"No. You're a civilian and this is my job. You've helped me enough on this already, but there is something else you can do for me."

"What do you need?"

"I have a location and time for the meet, but I don't know the city. Would you drive me over there so that I can get a look at things and do a walk-through before I do the real thing tonight?"

"Sure, but let's grab a sandwich first, I'm starving."

The pickup point that Jorge Alda has chosen is in front of Teatro Municipal de Rio de Janeiro (The Municipal Theatre) in the center of the city. It is a beautiful structure completed in 1909, reflecting the architecture of a bygone era. It was completely restored in the 1970's with seating for approximately two thousand people. The interior of the building is pure elegance with polished granite walls and a red-carpeted marble staircase ascending to an exquisite upper mezzanine. The front of the structure features Greek-style pillars and a stone balcony overlooking the street. There are two domed rotunda-like structures on either side of the outside balcony, extending above the roofline of the building. The structure's name is etched in gold braided letters across the top front of the building. It is the city's much heralded symbol of old world class and charm.

There is a bus stop directly across the street, which is immediately adjacent to a large picturesque walking promenade, another tip of the hat to Rio's more decorous past. Sam Dorsey and I are casually strolling around the promenade. We're pretending to be tourists, carefully blending in with the crowd, all the while snapping pictures with our digital cameras. There is method to our madness because we will later use these photographs to plan tonight's encounter with Jorge Alda and Walter Paris. We dare not linger too long, if we are to avoid Walter Paris's men or others who may become players in the evening's festivities.

Later, we print the photos and spread them out on a table in my hotel room. Neither of us is comfortable with the layout of the promenade.

"I don't like it, Sam. There is nothing but wide-open space here and no place to duck for cover if things get ugly."

Sam says, "Detective Ruiz was thinking the same thing. His plan is to let Paris pick up Jorge and then stop them on a side street. That way, there will be less chance of a civilian getting injured if something goes wrong."

"Given just a cursory look at this setup, I can't say that I blame him for doing it this way. The promenade offers no protection if a firefight breaks out. All you've got to hide behind is that statute right there by the street. You're also vulnerable from those two streets on either side of the theatre. A couple of cars could come rushing down either side of the building and they'd be on top of you in a just a few seconds. It would be a good thing if you had a spotter on top of one of those buildings."

"Devin, you think like a cop. Where'd you learn all this stuff?"

"In another life, I used to set up security details for visiting dignitaries when I worked at the embassy."

"There isn't time for that and I haven't got the communication equipment for it."

"No problem Sam, I can have it for you in two or three hours. I know you don't want me involved in this, but I think I can get on top of one of those building and spot for you. I'd be out of sight and you'd have someone you can trust watching your back. I'll get you a wireless earwig so I can talk to you. Detective Ruiz won't even know I'm there."

"Alright, but you have to promise me that you'll stay out of it if things go sour."

"I'll stay out of it, but I've got to leave now if I'm going to get the equipment we need. You'd better get going, too. I'll meet you back here in a couple of hours."

As soon as Sam leaves, I place a call to my friend, Astrid Mendes.

"Hi Astrid. Are you up for a little action tonight? We got a lead on Jorge Alda. Sam Dorsey and Detective Ruiz are going to pick him up tonight. I thought maybe you and I could shadow them as backup. Interested?"

"They told us explicitly to stay out of this, Devin."

"I know, but Sam's wife would never forgive me if I let something happen to him. Besides, if they're really able to grab Alda, he can testify and put Walter Paris in jail. I know it's asking a lot, but are you in or not?"

"You know me, Devin. I'm always ready to rock and roll."

"Good, grab the AA-12 shotguns and that communications gear we picked up at the embassy the other day. I think we're going to need it. Meet me in my hotel room in about half an hour and I'll map things out for you before Agent Dorsey gets back. I don't want him to see you bring the stuff over to me."

"Sounds like you're expecting trouble or you wouldn't have me bringing all that firepower. Don't you think Ruiz and Dorsey can handle this?"

"They're good men Astrid, but I still think they are underestimating Walter Paris. There are only three of them and unless I miss my guess, Paris will have four or five well-trained mercs backing him up. He never leaves anything to chance and our guys will be outgunned unless we help them out. On top of that, I don't trust Ruiz's boss. He may be involved in this, too."

"Okay, I'll grab a few things and I'll see you in about half an hour."

When Astrid arrives, we quickly go over the layout of the meeting place.

I say, "I'll be on the balcony of the theatre. I'll have a clear view of the promenade, at least one of the side streets, and most of the main street in front of the building. I'll communicate with you and Dorsey through the headsets, which are all tuned to the same frequency. I checked the theatre schedule and there are no shows playing tonight."

"The place will be locked up, Devin. How are you going to get in?"

I grin and say, "You're going to pick the lock for me."

She says, "I'm starting not to like this plan already."

"I don't like it so much either, but it's all we've got."

She asks, "What's my part in all of this?"

"From my position on the balcony, I won't be able to see one of the side streets and I'd like you to sit on the corner of the promenade and watch that area for me."

"Okay, I'll bring my motorcycle, it'll be less intrusive."

"Be sure to wear your jumpsuit and helmet. I don't want anybody to recognize you. I'll wear a ski mask because we'll be in real trouble if we get caught."

Astrid says, "Maybe this will help if things get dicey."

She grins and hands me a police badge.

"I lifted this off a cop who wanted to buy me drinks the other night. I figured it might come in handy."

I say, "Okay, but let's get there a couple of hours before the meet. That will give you plenty of time to get me into the theatre."

"That sounds good to me. I'll meet you at the side entrance at eight-thirty."

Astrid leaves my hotel room and Sam Dorsey arrives a short time later. I give him the communications gear and one of the AA-12 automatic shotguns. He is not happy.

"Where the hell did you get this, Devin? This is military-grade weaponry that soldiers use to clear houses in Iraq and Afghanistan."

I say, "Don't ask, don't tell Sam. Just keep it in the duffle bag and don't take it out unless you need it."

He is hesitant at first, but he finally says, "Okay, let's do this."

# CHAPTER 39

## July 21 1945 Hours • Rio de Janeiro

## Location: Outside Balcony, Municipal Theatre

I'M STANDING ON THE OUTER BALCONY of Teatro Municipal, directly across the street from where Jorge Alda is to meet Walter Paris. As it turned out, we didn't have to pick the lock to get me into the theatre. An elderly uniformed security guard was making his rounds at the theatre when I arrived. I flashed the old man the Rio police badge that Astrid gave me earlier. He was very cooperative when I told him that I needed to watch the street for a possible drug deal on the promenade. He was happy to help and he escorted me upstairs to the balcony. I lied and told him I might need his help later in the evening. He seemed quite pleased that a Rio cop might be willing to let him in on the action. He'd wait for my call down in the main lobby.

Once situated, I call Astrid to test our headsets and microphones. She has hidden herself on the far side of the promenade. She's scanning the area with a pair of infrared binoculars.

I tease her with, "You all set there, killer?"

She replies, "Locked, loaded, and ready, boss!"

I say, "I love it when you talk dirty, Astrid."

She says, "I'm always aroused when I play with guns. Too bad Tommy isn't here. We could have a hell of a lot of fun waiting for these guys to show up."

My response is, "Don't get too riled up, baby. I'm hoping the evening will be more boring than watching paint dry. If there is any excitement, stay out of it. I don't want you to get hurt. We're only here to be eyes and ears for Sam Dorsey."

She asks, "What about Detective Ruiz and Danny Montoya?"

"They don't know we're here and I'd like to keep it that way."

"Then why did you have me bring the other AA-12 shotgun and all this ammunition?"

I say, "Best way I know to keep you safe, Astrid."

"Alright," she says, "I'll give you a call if I see anything unusual."

I resume my scan of the area in front of the theatre while I munch on a candy bar. There are only a few people down there milling around on the sidewalk. There is a small group of kids with a boom box break-dancing on the promenade trying to impress a couple of young girls who have accompanied them. Additionally, there are three or four skateboarders, a woman walking her dog, and a couple of street musicians playing their guitars. Two paramedics are sitting on a park bench next to their ambulance, taking a break. They're both eating sandwiches and apparently joking about something. I'm restless and more than a little uncomfortable. Surveillance is not my line of work, but Sam Dorsey is a friend and I need to watch his back.

Dorsey, Detective Ruiz and Danny Montoya arrive in an unmarked police car and park on a side street about an hour later. Montoya leaves the vehicle and takes up a position out of sight near the entrance to a building next to the theatre. Ruiz remains in the car with Sam and again admonishes him to stay put. Sam is wearing a tiny wireless headphone, secretly imbedded in his left ear. Although he can hear me, there is no way he can talk to me without Ruiz noticing. He does have a walkie-talkie so he can communicate with Ruiz and Montoya, if needed. This is not an ideal arrangement, but it is better than nothing at all. About twenty minutes before Jorge Alda is supposed to arrive, things begin to heat up. I get a call from Astrid. She has spotted something through her binoculars.

"Devin, a car just pulled up on the far side of the promenade. I can see three people in it and one of them is Ruiz's boss, Wilbur Santiago. I don't like it."

I don't like it either, but I tell her to keep an eye on them while I pass that information on to Sam Dorsey. I'm barely finished talking when Walter Paris arrives. He parks his car in the no parking zone directly in front of the theatre. He exits the vehicle and walks across the street to the promenade. Moments later, an armored truck drives by, very slowly. Walter nods to the driver as it passes. A second vehicle passes behind the truck with three men in it and Walter gives that car a subtle wave as well. Duncan Ruiz has also taken note of Paris' nod to the passing vehicles. From his position, Ruiz cannot see Santiago and the two cops that are with him at the other end of the promenade. Sam passes that information on to the detective, who is quite surprised and a little irritated.

Ruiz says, "Where the hell are you getting this stuff?"

Sam replies, "Let's just say I've got someone watching out for us."

Ruiz nods and keys the mike on his transceiver, passing that information on to his partner, Danny Montoya. From his position in the adjacent building, Montoya can now see Wilbur Santiago and the two men with him. He lets Ruiz know that he has them in sight. Ten minutes later, a man on a motorcycle swings by the front of the theatre, slowing down as he passes the promenade. On his second pass, he stops and gets off the bike. He removes his helmet and walks toward Paris. It's Jorge Alda.

He's about twenty feet from Paris when the car with three men in it speeds up over the curb, screeching to a stop directly in front of him. A big man jumps out and fires two shots into Alda's chest, sending him to the ground. He then turns and shoots Walter Paris twice, hitting him in the leg and shoulder. Paris drops to one knee and he watches helplessly as the man fires two more shots into Jorge Alda's body. Seeing what's happened, Danny Montoya immediately begins firing his shotgun at the man who shot Alda. Two more men immediately jump out of the car and begin firing at Montoya with automatic weapons, effectively pinning him behind one of the building pillars. There is complete chaos as a full-fledged gunfight erupts on the promenade. Civilians are running everywhere, looking for cover to avoid being hit in the crossfire. One man is struck in the back and goes down instantly. The two paramedics take cover behind their ambulance. One of the skateboarders is hit and the others speed off as quickly as possible.

The men firing at Danny Montoya are moving quickly to get into a better position to shoot him. Seeing this, Sam Dorsey says, "I'm getting into this whether you want me to or not."

Ruiz nods his okay, and Sam pulls the military shotgun from the duffle bag. He leaves the car and begins firing at the men shooting at Montoya. He hits one of them, sending him to the ground. Ruiz guns the motor on his police car and drives between the shooters, providing temporary cover for Montoya. His quick action gives the young policeman time to get away from the heaviest gunfire. Ruiz rolls out of the car and he and Montoya use the vehicle as a barricade between themselves and the shooters. Even with Sam Dorsey's help, the two policemen are still heavily outgunned. I begin firing at the shooters from my position on the theatre balcony across the street, but at this distance, my nine millimeter pistol isn't very effective.

With Sam Dorsey supporting them, Ruiz and Montoya are able to hold their own against the shooters. That works until an armored truck pulls up onto the promenade. The windows on the vehicle have been modified, allowing the men inside to shoot out of them. The armor plating on the side of the truck makes them nearly immune to gunfire. The vehicle is acting like a tank and it is moving in behind Sam Dorsey. He's so busy firing at the other shooters that he doesn't see it. I yell at him through my headset to let him know what's happening. He sees the truck approaching, but there is nothing he can do to stop them. I start firing at the truck from the balcony, but the bullets just bounce off the armor plating. Sam is caught in the middle and there is nothing I can do to help him.

The truck is nearly on top of him when a motorcycle pulls up behind it. The helmeted rider jumps off the bike and begins firing an automatic shotgun at the truck. It's Astrid and the military projectiles she's using slice through the side of the truck like butter. The driver swerves away from Sam and speeds toward the other shooters, who jump inside. The armored truck takes off like a shot, knocking over a street lamp as it barrels down the road. All but two of the shooters get away. One lies dead on the street and the other is sitting on the ground a few feet away from him. He is badly wounded. When he sees Detective Ruiz and Montoya approaching him with shotguns at the ready, he drops his weapon and surrenders. The whole business has transpired in less than three minutes, but it seems like an eternity.

I exit the balcony and run down the stairs inside the theatre. I yell at the security guard to call an ambulance. I'm barely out of the building when I see an emergency vehicle pull up. The paramedics hop out and begin treating the shooting victims. I take a quick glance across the street to make sure that Sam is okay and he gives me a thumbs-up. Astrid drives her motorcycle to the side entrance of the theatre to pick me up. I get on the back and we speed off into the darkness. Wilbur Santiago has watched the carnage from the far end of the promenade.

He turns to his driver and says, "I've seen enough, let's get the hell out of here."

In front of the theatre, Detective Ruiz, Sam Dorsey and Danny Montoya cautiously assess the damage. Ruiz and Montoya approach the wounded shooter and place him in handcuffs. Sam Dorsey checks the other downed shooter for a pulse, but the man is already dead. He glances over at Jorge Alda. He has apparently survived the shooting, but it doesn't look good. There is blood everywhere, and even at this distance, he can see part of Alda's intestines and stomach pouring onto the sidewalk. The paramedics quickly place him onto a stretcher and load him into the ambulance. Another med tech helps the wounded Walter Paris into the same ambulance and they speed off to the hospital. Minutes later, several police units arrive and begin to seal off the area.

The promenade is an absolute catastrophe. Not counting Jorge Alda and Walter Paris, three people have been wounded. Two others, including one of the shooters, are dead. Once the scene is secured with police tape, Detective Ruiz, Danny Montoya, and FBI Agent Dorsey begin collecting evidence and taking photographs of the area. There are shell casings and blood spatter everywhere. It's going to be a long night.

# CHAPTER 40

## July 22 1045 Hours • Rio de Janeiro

## Location: Sheraton Grande Hotel

ASTRID AND I ARE DINING in the hotel restaurant. We're both reeling from last night's events, but she's hiding it better than I am. My hand is trembling slightly when I lift the decanter to pour us some more orange juice.

She says, "It looks like you could use a little vodka with your morning juice."

My reply is, "You're probably right, but getting shot at was not how I wanted the evening to go. How come you're so relaxed about it?"

"Part of me actually got a rush out of it. The problem I have now is that I'm feeling a surge of sexual energy and Tommy's not here to help me work it off."

I laugh out loud because this is vintage Astrid. We've known each other a long time and there is something very soothing about sharing a chuckle with an old friend. Our reverie is only temporary because Sam Dorsey has entered the room and he is making his way to our table. Detective Ruiz is with him and I'm guessing the scowl on his face is meant for us.

Ruiz points an accusing finger directly at me saying, "I thought I told you to stay out of this."

I smile back at him and say, "Stay out of what? I have no idea what you're talking about."

"Oh," he says, "You mean you weren't the guy on the theatre balcony talking to Sam in his headset. The ski mask was a nice touch, but I know it was you."

"Detective, Astrid and I were out all evening having dinner and drinks with friends. Just ask her."

He turns his gaze toward Astrid, who is now standing beside him. She playfully slides her arm into his saying. "Good morning Duncan, it's nice to see you again. Why don't you and Sam join us for breakfast? I heard that you had a rough night."

Ruiz is beginning to thaw when he says, "Damn it, you were there, too! The motorcycle helmet and the jumpsuit couldn't disguise that body of yours. What I'd like to know is where in the world did you get that military shotgun? It's illegal for civilians to have them in this country and I should arrest you for it."

She turns on some tongue-in-cheek charm saying, "Look at me, Duncan, I'm a lover not a killer. I wouldn't know one end of an AA-12 automatic shotgun from the other. How could you think such a thing of me?"

Ruiz relents with a smile saying, "You know, I guess I was mistaken in all the excitement last night."

She kisses him on the cheek saying, "See, I knew there was a logical explanation for those errant thoughts of yours."

Now, we're all laughing and both men sit down to give us more details about the shootout.

Detective Ruiz says, "Thanks guys, you saved our lives last night, but please, don't ever do anything like that again. I'm going to have one hell of a time explaining what happened."

I ask, "What's the status of Jorge Alda and Walter Paris? I saw them both go down, but Astrid and I had to get out of there quickly so no one else would see us. I have no idea if either of them made it."

Ruiz says, "Alda's injuries were too severe. He died on the way to the hospital. I gave Sam the pictures from the morgue earlier this morning. Paris was hit in the arm and the leg, but he'll be fine. His security people met the ambulance at the emergency room and carted him off to a private medical facility before the ER docs really had a chance to look at him. We're not exactly sure where he is at the moment. We've got people watching his private jet to make sure he doesn't leave the country without talking to us. The truth is, we can't arrest him for anything because we can't prove he's committed a crime.

"What about the civilians who were there?"

"We have one dead and several more wounded. The good news is that Sam hit one of the shooters. We've got him locked in a medical detention facility for murder. He's not talking and I doubt that he ever will."

"What's going to happen to him?"

"I'd love to see him executed, but we don't have the death penalty here in Brazil. The best we can hope for is life in prison."

I say, "Your boss was there last night, Duncan. How does he figure into this? Why didn't he help you when the shooting started?"

Ruiz says, "My best guess is that he was checking up on Walter Paris. I bugged his phone with the equipment that you loaned me and I intercepted a couple of calls to Martin Roah this morning. Roah is an upper level lieutenant for the

Rojas Cartel in Colombia. My boss called and told him that Jorge Alda is dead and that Walter Paris was wounded. The guy sounded relieved, but it seemed to me that he was also upset about something else. I have no idea what that might have been."

Sam asks, "Where does this leave you, Duncan? Your boss can't be too thrilled about the shootout and all of the publicity. You didn't tell him that you were tracking Walter Paris and he'll probably make you pay for it."

"He chewed me out pretty good, Sam, but he can only take this so far. He was on scene at the shootout with two other cops and they didn't help us. Danny Montoya saw them there, too. If word of that gets out, he'll lose all of his credibility with the other cops on the force. I let him know that there were multiple witnesses who saw him last night. Once I pointed that out to him, he dropped the matter and let me go."

Sam Dorsey and Detective Ruiz are exhausted, but the previous evening's excitement has given them ravenous appetites. They are both throwing down breakfast as if it's the Last Supper. When we've all finished eating, I ask another question.

"What about Richard Hamilton? Have your people been able to get anymore as to his whereabouts?"

The detective says, "No, but we're pretty sure he's left the country and we have no idea where he's going."

Sam Dorsey is completely disillusioned when he says, "I should never have come to Rio, Duncan. I got a bunch of people shot up and Walter Paris got away again!"

Ruiz tries to console him saying, "This isn't your fault, Sam. We did the best we could under the circumstances. This is on those mercenaries who started the firefight, not us!"

There is nothing left to say, and, after an extended period of silence, Duncan Ruiz is ready to leave. He stands and shakes Sam Dorsey's hand.

"We both deserve better than this, Sam, and I'm truly sorry that you didn't get your man. I promise that I'll keep digging into this. Something will come up that we can use to get Paris. When that happens, you'll be my first call."

We say our goodbyes and when the detective leaves, I speak to Sam Dorsey.

"You didn't have much to say, Sam. I know that look. What's bothering you?"

"I don't know what it is, Devin, but something about this just isn't squaring up with me. It's all just a little too neat for my taste."

"Do you think Ruiz is holding something back?"

"No, he's a class act and I think he did everything he could to help us. I just feel like I'm missing something."

"Maybe a trip to the beach will help you sort it out. Why don't you and Liz stay in Rio a little longer and relax? There's no hurry to rush home now. Astrid and I will show you the sights and we can all fly home together at the end of the week. It'll be my treat."

"That's probably not a bad idea. I'm going to catch a lot of heat because of my involvement in the shootout. None of this was officially sanctioned by my boss. They may force me to retire or bounce me out of the Bureau altogether."

I grin and say, "Sounds like another reason to hang around for a few more days."

"You're probably right, Devin, but let me talk to my wife first. She was pretty upset about the shooting last night and she may not want to stay."

Sam did manage to talk Liz into staying until the end of the week and the four of us had a marvelous time together. We catch a late night flight back to the States and I'm sitting next to him as he stares out the airplane window into the darkness of the Amazon jungle below. Something is still troubling him.

I ask, "Have you figured it out yet?"

He says, "I'm not sure, but I found this at the crime scene next to where Jorge Alda was shot. I didn't share it with Detective Ruiz. Do you have any idea what it is?"

He gives me a small tube-like capsule with a tiny, almost invisible, wire protruding from it. Except for its very small size, it reminds me of the explosive charges that we use on airplane-engine fire extinguishers. They're called squibs. The chemicals used to fight in-flight fires are stored inside a pressurized bottle next to the engine. When a fire is detected, the pilot pulls a handle inside the cockpit, which detonates the squib, releasing the chemicals to extinguish the flames.

I'm immediately concerned because smaller versions of these devices are used to simulate gunshot wounds in the movies. The actor being shot wears one of these things under his shirt strapped to a packet of fake blood. Another actor points a gun at him firing a blank cartridge. In the same instant, a radio signal is sent to the squib causing it to explode. The charge rips a hole in the actor's clothing sending fake blood everywhere. The actor being shot is also wearing a protective pad between the squib and his skin so he won't be injured. To the untrained eye, the entire sequence appears to be a real gunshot wound. I think that we may have all been duped by a fake shooting and I relay my theory to Sam.

He says angrily, "If you're right, Devin, Walter Paris has just pulled another fast one on us."

That is exactly what has happened, and at this very moment, Paris is on the telephone selling the rest of his story to the cartel leadership.

# CHAPTER 41

## July 24  2130 Hours  •  Rio de Janeiro

## Location: A Private Medical Facility

Martin Roah asks, "Where the hell are you, Walter? I've been trying to reach you for a couple of days."

He replies angrily, "Thanks to you, I'm in the freaking hospital with bullet holes in my shoulder and leg. Damn it, Martin! You gave me your word that you would let me take care of Jorge Alda. Instead, you send some of your guys to kill both of us."

"You have to believe me. We had nothing to do with it. Someone hit us, too! They killed two of the cartel leaders and they blew up my house. I barely got out alive. Right now, we have no idea what's going on. Our best guess is that it was some kind of secret military strike ordered by the government, maybe DEA or CIA. We've got people digging into it, but it may be some time before we figure out who did it. You and I need to get together face-to-face and talk about this."

"Why the hell should I trust you, Martin?"

Roah says, "Because we've been friends for years. On top of that, the reality is that we are both men of our word. If we make a deal, that's the way it is, period."

Paris says, "Well your reality check just bounced with me big time! I'm out and I don't want to have anything to do with you."

"Look, think this through for a couple of weeks and take some time to heal up. Give me a call and we'll talk about this again. Maybe we'll have some answers by then. Can we at least agree on that?"

Paris pauses for effect before saying, "Alright, I'll give you a call when I'm feeling better."

He ends the call and lies back onto the bed smiling. He's just pulled off the perfect crime. It had cost him millions, but it was worth every penny. Jorge Alda wasn't dead. Walter's team faked the shootings on the promenade with special effects borrowed from the movies. They used tiny explosive charges and fake blood. The paramedics, having lunch next to their ambulance on the promenade, were actually his people. They loaded Jorge's body onto a stretcher and placed him into the ambulance. Then, they helped Walter, who also appeared to be wounded, into the same vehicle and hustled them off before the police got a good look at either of them. When they got to the hospital, his team met them with another ambulance and whisked them off before the ER doctors had a chance to look at them. They drove them to a secure area where a special effects makeup artist made it look like Jorge had been shot several times, including a fake bullet wound to his head. Walter's men had previously bribed the coroner to take pictures of his body lying on a slab in the morgue. Those pictures were emailed to detective Ruiz and his boss. Walter had even taken the gruesome precaution of allowing a surgeon to cut into his own body, creating quite convincing wounds to his shoulder and leg. His plan had nearly backfired when Ruiz and his assistant starting shooting at his men, but it had worked beautifully otherwise.

Jorge Alda was aboard a government jet on its way to Washington. The US Attorney handling the case, agreed to put Jorge and his mother into the witness protection program. He would not have to testify against Walter about the Susan Parks murder. State and local authorities in Ohio had also agreed not to pursue the matter. In exchange, Walter would quietly supply the government with inside information on cartel activity. After a suitable period of time, Walter could take his billions and walk away.

It was actually his men who were responsible for killing part of the cartel leadership. They also blew up Martin Roah's home, making it look as though it was the work of some clandestine government agency. The cartel would never know that he had orchestrated all of it. He would meet with Roah and the remaining cartel members in a few weeks to talk things over. They'd kiss and make up, and Walter would resume his life as if nothing had happened.

There were still a couple of loose ends that he wants to tidy up. Wilbur Santiago is one of them. For several years, Walter believed that Santiago was working for him exclusively. Now, it is clear that he also works for the cartel, supplying them with crucial information about his activities. He despises disloyalty and he'll make Santiago pay for it, but not today. He'll wait a few months and Wilbur Santiago will have an unfortunate accident. He does not want to arouse suspicion amongst his colleagues. He will have to plan his death very carefully.

The last item on his to-do-list is Tommy Rollins. His relationship with Tommy has left him in a quandary. He likes him, because throughout his trial, he kept his mouth shut, never once revealing their financial relationship or money laundering activities. He risked going to jail for Walter and he refused to give him up to the authorities. That kind of loyalty deserves to be rewarded and that was why Walter offered him the interest-free million-dollar loan to help him get back on his feet. He accepted initially and then turned down his offer, claiming that he got the money from another source. That is what is troubling him. He's wondering if he's cut some sort of deal with the Feds, which might end up exposing their connection later on. Perhaps, it would be better if Mr. Rollins simply went away altogether. Either way, there is no hurry. He'll take a couple of months to think about it and then make a decision.

# CHAPTER 42

## September 23 1435 Hours

## Location:
## Eastbound 17,500 Feet, Northern Arizona

THE SKY IS CONSTIPATED and it hasn't rained in this part of the country for nearly two months. The clouds have come out to play and there is thunder and lightning dancing in the distance, but the desperately needed moisture is still playing hide and seek. The earth is a parched southwest brown and barren. Surface temperatures are nearing one hundred and eleven degrees Fahrenheit. The intense sunlight beating against the landscape is pushing atmospheric turbulence to great heights, making for a bumpy flight across northern Arizona.

As a flight instructor, I'm occasionally asked to do checkouts in the PC-12 airplane because I've been through the requisite school at Flight Safety, an internationally recognized flight training company. Additionally, I have several hundred hours flying and training pilots in this particular aircraft at Keystone Airlines, my former employer. I'm doing a ride-along for a new Pilatus pilot. His insurance company has insisted that he fly with me for a few hours before they will underwrite the policy on his recently purchased three-and-a-half million dollar airplane. Given the value of the aircraft, I can't say that

I blame them, but this is one of those rare cases in which the extra training really isn't necessary. The pilot sitting next to me is atypical of the kind of person who so often buys this kind of aircraft.

The usual candidate is quite often an inexperienced pilot whose personal wealth has allowed him to purchase a machine that is well beyond his actual flying abilities. That is not the case with my current flying partner. He's a former regional airline captain who has made a lot of money developing a computerized aircraft routing program. It has saved several of the major airlines millions by allowing them to move their vast fleet of aircraft from one place to another far more efficiently than has ever been possible in the past. His innovation has made him rich and he's rewarded himself with a new airplane. I haven't touched the flight controls once since we left the ground in San Diego.

I say, "Dave, I'm surprised that your insurance company asked me to ride along with you. Given your previous airline experience, this should have been a slam dunk."

"They didn't ask me to do extra training, I requested it. You can teach me stuff about the airplane that isn't in the book and I want to do this right. I figured a coast-to-coast flight would be a good place to start."

David Ferguson has expertly demonstrated his skills as an experienced pilot, which gives me time to think about other things. Specifically, I'm considering the events of the last two months. It has not been a happy time. First, Walter Paris has managed to walk away from trouble again. He's done terrible things yet, he always seems to get away with it. My FBI friend, Sam Dorsey, was reprimanded for his participation in the shootout in Rio, despite saving the lives of Duncan Ruiz and his assistant, Danny Montoya. He was nearly forced into early retirement. Worse yet, we both think Jorge Alda is alive and in the witness protection program. We have no hard proof of this, but Sam's contacts at the Justice Department strongly hinted that it had happened. It appears that those responsible for killing my former employees will go unpunished.

There is still no word as to the whereabouts of the man known as Richard Hamilton or his traveling partner, Belle. They seem to have just vanished. The FBI has officially closed the investigation and Sam Dorsey has been assigned to another case with a formal written notice to leave the Walter Paris business alone. When I returned from Rio de Janeiro, I stopped in New York to see my friend, Gil Pepperdine, over at the DEA. I gave him a copy of a taped conversation between his associate Bob Davenport and my friend Bill Marston at the US Embassy. He knows that Davenport ordered the hit on Hamilton's girlfriend Belle, but he too has been instructed to stay out of the matter by those well above his pay grade. I am angry and appalled by how many government agencies are willing to sweep a young woman's murder under the rug.

Although I've had a couple of job offers, I'm still mostly unemployed. For now, I'm content to spend my time ferrying airplanes and taking on instructional jobs like this one. My trip with David Ferguson will last another day with an overnight stop in Denver, where he'll visit some friends. Tomorrow, he's agreed to drop me off in Erie, Pennsylvania before proceeding on home to New Jersey. My truck is parked at the airport and that will give me a chance to visit some of the people I used to work with in my previous job.

After landing in Denver, Dave and I enjoy a fine meal at the home of one of his close friends. We leave early the next morning, arriving at the Erie airport at one fifteen in the afternoon, thanks to a fifty-knot tailwind. We say our goodbyes and I take a few minutes to drop by the Keystone Airlines flight office to say hello to a couple of friends. They've promoted Jim Ryan to director of operations and he's sitting at my old desk when I knock on the office door. Always good-natured, he greets me with a friendly handshake and a broad smile.

"Come on in Devin, long time no see."

"I don't want to linger too long Jimmy. I'm not on the company owner's nice-to-see-you list."

He says, "I just don't understand it. You saved his company and he screwed you over without even a thank you."

"That's water over the dam. Is there anything new happening around here?"

"No, we're still hauling boxes for FedEx and UPS. Oh, there is one thing that should make you feel better. I fired the boss' nephew the other day."

"What happened?"

"He came to work after he had a few drinks at the local pub. The idiot wore his uniform into the bar and another patron saw him climb into one of our airplanes to fly a trip. He called the FAA and they called me. I met his flight with the Feds when he got back. He refused a breathalyzer test and they revoked his license. Bruno couldn't save the kid this time and I fired him on the spot."

I say, "I guess the good news is that he didn't hurt anybody or crash an airplane. Is there anything else happening?"

"Not much, but another FBI agent dropped by a week or

so ago asking more questions about our murdered employee. I was surprised because I thought they'd wrapped that stuff up months ago."

It's a surprise to me, too, because Sam Dorsey told me the case had been formally closed. This new information will require a phone call to see why it has suddenly been reopened. Jim and I chat for a few more moments before I head for home. During the drive, I'm puzzled by the FBI's renewed interest in the Parks' murder case. I am even more puzzled by the police cruiser sitting in front of my cabin when I pull into the driveway. Mitchell Parrish, the local police chief, gives me a friendly wave as I approach the house. Brooks Falls is a small town and I've known Parrish since kindergarten. He's a good friend.

"Hi, Devin, I was hoping you'd show up. We had a little excitement. Someone broke into your place. He scared the hell out of your girlfriend, but she's okay."

I'm completely bewildered for a couple of reasons. First, learning that someone has ransacked your home is always disturbing. My personal space has been violated, leaving me feeling quite vulnerable. Second, I haven't had a girlfriend since Harley left almost three months ago. I'm completely stunned when she rounds the corner of the building looking very pregnant.

The Chief says, "I was on duty when the call came in and I recognized your address right away. I used to come out here and fish with you and your dad when we were kids, remember?"

"I remember. Was anything taken?"

He says, "Not that I could tell, but you can let me know later after you have a chance to look the place over."

"Thanks for taking personal interest in this, Mitch. I really appreciate it. Is there anything else that I should know?"

"No, I'm pretty much done here. She got a look at the guy and I'll put his description out over the police network. That way, there'll be some other cops in the area on the lookout for him. This looks like a simple B-and-E to me, unless you can think of a more specific reason for someone wanting to break into your place."

"I don't have anything of any real value inside."

"Okay, I'll check with some of the other cabin owners on the lake to see if any of them were hit. Otherwise, there's not much else that I can do."

I shake the policeman's hand and he departs leaving Harley and me to stare at each other.

I ask, "Are you ok?"

"Yeah, I'm fine. I apologize for coming by like this, but I was dropping off a box with some of Susan Parks' belongings in it. She was my roommate for a short time and she left a few of her things at my place. I know that you sometimes keep in touch with her mother and I was hoping you'd return them to her. It's mostly personal stuff, high school and college yearbooks, family photos, and some jewelry. I'm sure her mom would like to have them."

I nod and say, "I'll take care of it."

I'm avoiding the most obvious question. Harley's pregnancy is the proverbial six-hundred pound gorilla sitting between us and we're both pretending it isn't there. After a lengthy period of silence she says, "I should be going."

I'm standing in the driveway next to her Jeep when she approaches me. I reach down and take her hand as she opens the door on the driver's side of the car. She stops long enough to give me a hug and I can feel the tears running down the side of her face. As she pulls away, I gently place a hand on her tummy.

"Is there anything we need to talk about?" I ask.

Her voice is barely above a whisper when she says, "No."

A moment later, she's gone and I'm feeling empty.

# CHAPTER 43

## September 24  1845 Hours

## Location: Brooks Falls, Cambridge Lake

I've prepared an Asian spaghetti salad for supper consisting of noodles, chopped cabbage, sliced red peppers, scallions, grilled chicken and a spicy peanut sauce. It's one of my favorites, but the evening meal is somehow less than enjoyable. I'm tired and the day's events have left me feeling unsettled. I'm staring out at the lake trying to make sense of it. Despite the cheerless nature of recent proceedings, I am, for reasons completely unknown to me, laughing out loud. Through some odd epiphany, I realize that I have been attempting to make sense of insanity. From time to time, my life seems to erupt into chaos and confusion. During those storied moments, the hard and fast linear rules of Aristotelian logic, which I tend to lean on, simply do not apply. A good stiff drink is often a far better solution. So is a phone call from an old friend. Sam Dorsey's voice is a cheerful presence on an evening that is far less than perfect. I'm still laughing when I pick up the telephone.

He says, "You're certainly in a good mood."

"No, not really, it's just that, so far, it's been a pretty bizarre day."

He asks, "You want to talk about it?"

"Why not, I've heard that confession is good for the soul?"

I quickly tell him everything that's happened and soon, he too is laughing out loud.

"Devin, I'm an FBI agent chasing bad guys all the time and my life is damn boring compared to yours. Sometimes, you remind me of that cartoon character, Charlie Brown, from the Peanuts comic strip. You'll be thrilled to know that I've only called to throw another log on that raging bonfire you've got going over there."

"So, either you're telling me that the Great Pumpkin and Santa Claus are just fairy tales or you're going to be like Lucy, snatching the football away just before I try to kick a field goal."

"That's pretty much the case. I got a call from our friend, Duncan Ruiz, down in Rio. I thought I'd pass on a few things that might be of interest."

"I thought the Bureau slapped your hands and told you to stay out of things."

"I'm like you, Devin. Once I get something stuck in my craw, I won't let it go until I figure it out. I'm pissed and I want to find a way to nail Walter Paris as badly as you do. We're in this together and I'm not letting up until I get some answers."

"Okay, what have you got?"

"Ruiz's boss, Wilbur Santiago, is dead, an apparent heart attack. At least that was the coroner's official finding."

I say, "But, Detective Ruiz thought otherwise."

"Yeah, he did. He has suspected the coroner of shady dealings for some time and he had another doctor run a toxicology test on a sample of Santiago's blood. He was cleverly poisoned, making it appear as though he had a heart attack. Ruiz thinks Walter Paris had something to do with it."

"I think so, too. It was probably payback because Santiago was spying on Paris for the cartels. Walter hates disloyalty."

Sam says, "There's more news. Ruiz got a lead on Richard Hamilton or whoever the hell he's pretending to be this week. He figured out how he and Belle got out of Rio when he had all of those cops looking for him. He took a cruise ship. Ruiz's men were looking for him in all the usual places — the airport, train, and bus stations etc. No one was expecting him to take a slow boat to China."

"China?"

"Sorry, that was just my clumsy attempt to use a clever figure of speech. He caught a twenty-eight-day cruise touring a bunch of cities along the South American coast and the Caribbean Islands. Here's the kicker, the cruise ended in Miami. Near as we can tell, he's back in the States."

"How did Ruiz figure it out?"

"For security, the cruise lines take pictures of everybody that gets onboard their ships. He had a hunch and called them. Hamilton and Belle were disguised as an older couple, but Ruiz has known the woman for a long time and he recognized her."

I'm thinking out loud when I say, "Why would a guy on the run from two or three different government agencies come back to a place where nearly everybody is looking for him?"

"Your guess is as good as mine and I'm as baffled by this as you are."

"I have a question for you, Sam. How come you didn't tell me that the FBI has reopened the Susan Parks case?"

"As far as I know, we haven't. They could have done it without telling me, because right now, I'm persona-non-grata at the Bureau. What makes you think we're digging into it again?"

"I was at the Keystone Airline flight office earlier today saying hi to a couple of friends. One of them said that an FBI agent had stopped by asking about the case two weeks ago. I thought maybe it was one of your guys."

"I don't think so. Did he get the agent's name?"

"I didn't ask, Sam. With all the heat that you caught over this thing, I didn't want to ruffle anybody's feathers and get you into any more trouble."

"I appreciate that, but let me look into this and call you back in a few days."

"Okay, but don't get burned on my account."

I hang up and settle into a chair near a window overlooking the lake. It's peaceful here and I can feel my eyes getting heavy. I'm nearly asleep when the telephone rings again. It's Harley and as always, she gets directly to the point.

"Hello, Devin, I'm calling because I owe you an explanation for my behavior today. I left without saying much and I'm sure you have some questions."

"There were a couple of things that crossed my mind."

"Let me answer the most obvious questions first. Yes, I'm pregnant, and no, it isn't your baby. I was involved with my ex-husband while you and I were together. I was too embarrassed to tell you that earlier today and I'm truly sorry."

There is no simple way to ease into this conversation and I am quiet for a very long time while I try to think of something to say. Harley finally breaks the silence.

"Are you still there?"

"I'm listening, Harley, but I honestly don't know what you want from me."

"You don't have to say anything. I just didn't want you to go around thinking that you might be a father. It sounds like you have enough on your plate without worrying about me. Have you found another job?"

"Nothing full-time yet, but honestly, I haven't been looking that hard. I've been ferrying airplanes all over the country and checking out new pilots for the Pilatus Aircraft Company. They've been paying me very well and there's been no need to work full-time."

"Good, I'm glad you landed on your feet, no pun intended."

"Harley, I know it's none of my business, but didn't you once tell me that you preferred not to have children?"

"That was true until I got pregnant. Something marvelous happens when you become a mom. My whole attitude changed about everything. I've become very protective of the life growing inside me. I can't explain it, but somehow, it seems right and I feel terrific."

"What does Mike think about all of this?"

"He's thrilled because he's always wanted children. I was the one who didn't want to be a mother. It's one of the things that broke up our marriage."

I say, "Well, I wish you both the best."

"Thank you. I know it wasn't easy for you to say that. You've always been more gracious than I deserve. I'm sorry I made such a mess of things. I should go now."

"Before you do, I have an odd question for you. What did the guy who broke into my house look like?"

"It's really hard to say because he was wearing glasses and a baseball cap. He was dressed like a kid, striped polo shirt, shorts, and high-dollar sneakers. The strange thing is that I'm pretty sure he was older, maybe in his forties. He was fit and very polite, a complete gentleman really."

"What do you mean?"

"I was scared to death when I walked in on him. He had a gun, but he put it away almost immediately and he tried to calm me down. What was really strange was when he saw that I was pregnant. He smiled and he asked me when I was due. It actually seemed to please him that I was going to be a mom. He tied me to a chair, but I was able to get free in a few minutes. It was almost as if he wanted me to get away."

"Did you notice anything else?"

"Not much except that this guy was smooth. There was never any wasted motion or energy. He knew exactly what he was doing. This fellow was a pro trying to look like an amateur. He was about six feet tall with short brown hair. I don't think he was there to take your stuff. I think he was looking for something specific, but I have no idea what it was. I told all of this to the policeman, but he seemed to think it was a straight ahead robbery. The police chief is your friend. Didn't you talk to him before he left?"

"I didn't go into any details with the police because it didn't seem important at the time. I wanted to make sure you were okay first. I'll dig into it a little more later on."

"Do you think the break-in is related to the FBI investigation of Keystone Airlines?"

"I have no idea, but it's probably good that you're not involved in this anymore. I'm sorry things didn't work out for us, but you were right when you said goodbye a couple of months ago. Some things just aren't meant to be. I have to go, but I hope you have a good life, Harley."

"You deserve happiness, too, Devin. I hope you find it. Goodbye."

The line goes dead and I don't know what to think or how I should feel. I was surprised by how much I still cared for Harley. Another part of me is relieved to be free of such an unstable relationship. After a few minutes of silence, my psyche regroups enough to think about other things. Harley's comments about the burglar and the FBI's visit to Keystone Airlines have stirred something in the back of my mind. I'm not sure how or why, but I feel as though these events are connected in some way. It's as though I have some important pieces to a puzzle, but I'm not yet sure how they fit together. I have sip of wine and slide further down into my Barcalounger, once again staring at the lake, looking for answers. They would come two weeks later in the form of an urgent telephone call.

# CHAPTER 44

## October 8  1435 Hours

## Location: Rapid City, South Dakota

I'M GAZING OFF INTO THE DISTANCE at Mount Rushmore, one of this country's most easily recognizable landmarks. I've visited many of our national parks, but this is a first. I've wanted to come here ever since seeing Cary Grant and Eva Marie Saint climb down the face of it in the Hitchcock movie, North by Northwest. I'm here in Rapid City doing an insurance checkout for a new Pilatus pilot. It is not going nearly as well as the one I did for another fellow a few weeks ago. The airplane's owner is not a strong pilot. Fortunately, he knows it and he's hired me as his aerial babysitter.

The trip began in Chicago with an intended final destination of Salt Lake City. We've stopped here at my suggestion because the owner had a late night and he's very tired. His flying was sloppy and I corrected a couple of serious navigation errors, one of which would have had us landing at the wrong airport, if I hadn't pointed it out to him. He's currently taking a nap in the pilot lounge. His family was riding with us. I've rented a car and driven them to the monument to relieve their boredom while daddy gets some much needed sleep. I excuse myself and enter the snack bar to grab a quick sandwich and a Coke. My cellphone rings before I've taken the first bite. The call is from my friend, Astrid Mendes. She's worried and angry all in the same breath.

"Hi, Astrid. What's wrong?"

"Someone tried to kill Tommy last night. He's got some cuts and bruises, but he's going to be okay. The doctors are going to let him go home tomorrow."

"What happened?"

"I'm in Montreal, so I haven't got the whole story yet. Apparently, he was getting some cash from an ATM machine and someone tried to mug him. He fought the guy off with the help of some stranger passing by. I'm catching a flight to Boston in a couple of hours and I'll let you know more when I get there. Where are you now?"

"I'm in South Dakota on my way to Salt Lake City. I won't get in until late tonight, but I'll catch a flight into Boston first thing tomorrow morning. Where are you staying?"

"I don't know yet, but I'll figure that out once I get into town."

"Okay, give me a ring on my cellphone and I'll meet you after my flight gets in tomorrow."

The call ends and my party and I linger in Rapid City for another hour and a half before departing for Utah. The next day, I catch a flight to Boston, arriving late in the afternoon. I stop my rental car in front of Tommy's Brookline home at four-thirty. There are two large gentlemen standing on his front porch, eyeing me suspiciously as I approach the house. I suspect they are armed and I'm relieved when Tommy's ex-wife, Katherine, steps outside and lets them know that I'm a friend. She greets me with an overly sensuous kiss and an extended hug before we enter the house.

Tommy's been released from the hospital and he's resting in a comfortable chair in the living room. He has a small bruise under his eye and his left arm and hand are bandaged. Otherwise, he appears none the worse for wear. He stands to shake my hand, but he loses his balance and I have to catch him. He winces and moans out loud when I slide an arm around his waist and help him back into the chair. Apparently, his injuries are more serious than I first thought.

A worried Katherine says, "I've got to pick up the kids. They went to a movie with Astrid, but I'll bring them around to see Tommy later."

She kisses us both and leaves. Tommy tells me what happened.

"Last night, I dropped by an ATM machine to get some cash and this big guy comes rushing up to me out of nowhere and stabs me in the chest a couple of times before I know what's happening. I was wearing a Kevlar vest and it saved my life. The guy was a pro, but he wasn't expecting me to fight back. The karate training we had as kids kicked in and I was able to fend him off. I was holding my own against him when I reached for the gun on my hip. The damn thing got caught on the holster. About that time, a second man jumps from a car and fires two shots at me. The vest stops the bullets, but the impact breaks two of my ribs."

"This doesn't sound like a random street mugging, Tommy. Those guys wanted you dead."

"I thought I was dead, but another guy steps in and fires a couple of rounds at the man who shot me. I finally get my gun out and the guy with the knife takes off running towards his car. He helps his buddy in and they speed off. I was lying on the sidewalk, too dazed to get a license plate number. I was bleeding badly and I thought I was a goner, but this stranger helps me up and somehow gets me back to my car. Samantha is sitting behind the wheel screaming in shock."

"Sam was there?" I ask.

"Yeah, she saw the whole thing and it scared her half to death. That's why Astrid took her to the movies with David. They all needed a break to unwind."

I'm livid, not just because Tommy's been hurt, but I'm even angrier because his daughter had to see it. This is my extended family and I desperately want somebody to find the people who did this. Tommy continues his story.

"The passerby puts me in the car and gets Sam calmed down enough to drive me to the ER. The docs wheel me inside and the guy who saved me disappears without a word. I never got a chance to thank him. I was able to describe the men who attacked me, but I was in so much pain that I couldn't give them much about the fellow who helped me."

"Was there any surveillance footage from the scene for them to look at?"

"They hope that they can get something from the ATM camera, but it might take a couple of days."

My head is buzzing when I say, "Hold that thought, Tommy. I've got something I want you to look at. I'll be right back."

I don't know why, but our conversation has triggered a peculiar thought. I retrieve my laptop computer from the car and return to the house. I want Tommy to see a photograph that I have on file.

I point to the picture and ask, "Is this one of the guys who attacked you?"

"No, that's not either one of them, but it's possible he might have been the guy who helped me. I was too banged up to get a good look at him. Who is he?"

"I don't know, but I've got a sneaking suspicion that he's been dogging both of us. I need to check on a couple of things first to confirm it. What's your WIFI access code? I want to email this photo to a couple of people to see if I'm right. It may take a little while for them to get back to me."

Tommy says, "Good, while you're waiting for them to call back, we'll have time for a couple of drinks. I'm somewhat indisposed, so I hope you don't mind fetching the libation. There's cold beer in the fridge and I'll have one of those. I know that you prefer wine and there's a bottle of red in the cupboard if you want some."

I return with our drinks to find Tommy chattering away on the telephone. I'm distracted because I think I've found another piece of the puzzle. I'm reluctant to say anything to my friend, but things are beginning to take shape. Although I think I know what's happening, I need to have my email messages returned before I can be sure. I also want to have a conversation with Tommy's daughter, Samantha. Her description of the Good Samaritan may be of some help. I just have to wait until she returns from the movies.

# CHAPTER 45

## October 9  2030 Hours

## Location:
## Brookline, Massachusetts, Tommy Rollins' Home

OUR MOTLEY LITTLE GROUP has just consumed a couple of large pizzas. Astrid and Katherine have returned from the movies with Tommy's kids, Samantha and David. We've all been laughing and kibitzing with each other for the last hour. I'm standing in the kitchen doorway taking it all in. I love all of these people and it just doesn't get any better than this. Katherine moves in behind me and slides her arms around my waist.

"Thanks for coming, Devin. I always feel better when you're around."

I squeeze her hands and say, "I know you're worried, Kate. I wish I had something comforting to say, but right now, I can't think of anything. How are the kids coping with the situation?"

"They're each handling it in their own way, but I think they're okay. David is quite mature for his age and he's taken a very pragmatic approach to the whole business. My son is a lot like you. He only speaks when he has something worth saying, but when he does, he makes every word count. My daughter, on the other hand, is quite talkative and as a teenager, she speaks fluent sarcasm. She's been busting my chops all day. How did she seem when you spoke to her earlier?"

"She's scared, Kate. She almost lost her dad last night and she saw the whole thing. I'm pretty sure she's still in shock because something like that has got to be just terrifying. She's trying to hide it with bravado and that's also why she's been giving you a bad time."

She says, "I've got counseling sessions set up for both of them later this week. Was she of any help when you asked her for more details about the mugging?"

"Yes, she did have some information that was useful. She was able to identify a man in a photograph that I showed her."

"So, you have a lead on one of the guys who jumped Tommy?"

"No, Samantha recognized the guy who rescued him."

"Do you know who he is?"

"Not yet, but I'll have a better idea when I get a response to some emails that I sent out earlier today. I think that one or both of the people that I sent messages to may have had contact with that same fellow."

Katherine's mood turns serious when she says, "You don't think this was a random mugging do you?"

I say, "You don't think it is either. That's why you've got all of that private security hanging around the front of the house."

She places her hands on her hips and says emphatically, "I had to do something. Tommy's broke and he can't afford it. The kids stay with him most of the time and I want to make damn sure they're safe. I'm loaded and the extra money I spent for security seemed like a really good idea!"

"Take it easy, Kate. I'm on your side. I think it was a smart move."

She says, "You think Walter Paris had something to do with this, don't you?"

"Yes, but let's not bring that up in front of Astrid and the kids. Let them enjoy the rest of the evening."

"I know that look, Devin. You've got something else on your mind. Come on, spill it."

"Maybe later, Kate, but now is not a good time."

"Alright, but I'm going to hold you to that."

What I'm not sharing with Katherine is Tommy's plan to deal with Walter Paris. In their anger, he and Astrid have concocted a misguided scheme to kill him. Astrid is a well-trained weapons expert and shooting Mr. Paris from a considerable distance would not be a difficult task for her. Tommy knows where Paris will be in a couple of months and they think they can bump him off when he visits his Block Island home over the coming holidays. They had mapped out the whole thing, including surveillance, weaponry, and escape routes. They asked me to help them. I want to see Paris gone as badly as they do, but this would be murder and I just couldn't go along with it. I've argued with them both privately, pointing out that they would never be able to live with themselves if they ever did something like this. I still don't know if I was able to talk them out of it and it's troubling me. I'm trying to think of a way to diffuse the situation when Katherine interrupts my musings with a question.

"Where are you staying tonight?" she asks.

"I'll get a room at the Parker House downtown."

"Don't bother," she says, "If you give me a ride home, you can crash in my back bedroom. The kids use it when they're at my place. They're staying here with Astrid and Tommy tonight. I'm leaving them my car because the police took Tommy's

Audi, hoping to find some evidence to help them with their investigation."

"Thanks, I'll take you up on that."

By ten o'clock, everyone is tired. Katherine and I say goodbye and I drive her back to her place in Cambridge. On the way, the conversation turns personal.

"Kate, it's been several months since your divorce. Are you dating anyone yet?"

She says, "It's hard when you have kids. Besides, you have to kiss a lot of frogs to meet a prince and I'm not getting in that line. I was sort of hoping you might be available now that Harley's out of the picture. You know that I've been lusting after you for years."

I laugh and say, "Isn't lust one of the seven deadly sins?"

She chuckles saying coyly, "Seven sins is only one for each day of the week and it hardly seems like enough to me."

This kind of verbal banter is something Kate and I have been doing for years and I have missed it. We have been emotionally and intellectually drawn to each other since the beginning of our friendship. She was dating Tommy at the time or I would have scooped her up in a heartbeat. We very nearly had an affair once, but out of respect for their marriage and the potential adverse effect on her children, we didn't let that happened. Times have changed and I can feel myself being drawn to her when I stop the car in front of her home. She leans in to kiss me passionately and I let it happen willingly.

Once inside, I unpack and check my phone for messages. I've received two texts from the people I emailed pictures to earlier. The first one is from my former girlfriend, Harley Jensen. She recognized Tommy's rescuer as the man in the photo that I sent her. The other message is from Jim Ryan over at Keystone Airlines. He has identified that same fellow as the man who dropped by his office posing as an FBI agent. Katherine notices a change in my demeanor after I read the texts.

"I take it the messages have confirmed your suspicions?" she asks.

"I think so. I've got one more thing that I want to check on, but it can wait. I'm tired and I'm going to bed."

"Would you mind some company?" she asks.

"You and I have talked about this before, Kate. We've both thought about taking things to the next level for a long time, but this is really bad timing."

She hugs me saying, "This isn't about sex, Devin. I'm stressed out and I don't want to sleep alone tonight. I promise to behave myself."

I nod in agreement and we retire to the bedroom. Katherine snuggles close to me and falls asleep quickly. I'm pondering what to do next, or whether I should do anything at all. For some reason, Tommy has a guardian angel that seems to know a lot more about what's going on than I do. I'd like to meet my friend's benefactor because I think we have a common interest. Unfortunately, I have no way to contact him. I needn't have worried, because two weeks later, he found me.

# CHAPTER 46

## October 22 1900 Hours

## Location: Brooks Falls, Pennsylvania, Cambridge Lake

I'VE JUST RETURNED TO MY CABIN after ferrying a Pilatus PC-12 aircraft from Zurich back to the States. I'm hungry and jet-lagged as I settle into my Barcalounger and turn on the television. The Boston Celtics are playing the Cleveland Cavaliers and it looks to be a good game. I picked up a couple of chorizo burritos from a nearby Mexican restaurant and I intend to wash them down with a glass of red wine. Once my tummy is satisfied, I snuggle into a blanket and dose off in the chair with the TV blaring. I'm sleeping soundly and I don't notice the man with a gun when he enters the room and turns off the television. One wouldn't think that silence should wake you, but some inner sense is telling me that something is wrong. My uninvited guest is wearing a ski mask and he is sitting in a chair directly in front me as I rub the sleep from my eyes.

He speaks very casually saying, "I'm sorry to disturb your nap, but I'm a little pressed for time and we need to talk."

I'm wide awake when I say, "If you really want to talk, I'd feel a lot better if you put that gun away."

He says, "I don't want to shoot you. I just want to talk."

I smile and say, "I don't want to shoot you either. So, why don't we both put our guns down?"

I remove the blanket with my left hand to reveal a nine-millimeter pistol pointed directly at him. We are both silent because armed standoffs are never a good thing. I am the first to relent.

"We have to start somewhere so, why don't I go first?"

I place my weapon on the floor next to my chair. After a slight hesitation, he does the same while posing an intriguing question.

"Why would you trust a masked stranger not to shoot you?"

I say, "If a man with your skills really wanted me gone, I'd already be dead."

"Still, you took a chance and I'd like to know why."

"I took the risk because I think I know who you are and what you're looking for."

He says, "I doubt that, but why don't you humor me."

"Alright, here's the short story. You once worked at the American Embassy in Rio using the name Richard Hamilton. You're on the run from the police and a couple of other government agencies. You're traveling with a woman named Belle, and you used another fake ID to get the two of you on a cruise ship to Miami a couple of months ago. You disguised yourselves as an elderly couple traveling under the name Johnston to get through customs and onto the ship. Two weeks ago, you saved my friend Tommy's life when a couple of guys tried to kill him in front of an ATM machine in Boston. You knew where to find Tommy because you got his address from my Rolodex when you broke into my place a few weeks ago. You were hoping to get the information you needed from Tommy, but there's too much security around him now. So, you came back here, hoping to get what you need from me. Does that about cover it?"

My masked friend lets out a sigh saying, "What are you, some kind of cop?"

"No, I'm just an interested party."

"Okay, what is it that you think I'm looking for?"

I say, "It's not a thing that you're looking for, it's a person and his name is Walter Paris."

"What makes you think I'm looking for him?"

"Unless I miss my guess, your real name is Morgan Parks. Susan Parks was your daughter and Walter Paris is responsible for her death. You want payback and I don't blame you. Susan was a friend, and I want to see him pay for it, too."

The man removes his mask and I can see that his features match photographs that I'd previously emailed to my colleagues for identification.

He's completely exhausted when he asks, "How did you know?"

"I didn't know for sure until I found your picture in some of Susan's personal belongings. My former girlfriend was her roommate for a short time and she dropped off some of her stuff, hoping I'd return it to her mom. You walked in on her when she brought the box by my place and it scared the hell out her."

"I'm really sorry about that. She's a lovely woman and she appears to be pregnant. I hope the baby is okay."

"We're not together anymore, but let's stay on task. I didn't know who you really were until last week. There was a family photo in the box that my girlfriend dropped off and I recognized you right away. I had two other sources confirm it. You used a fake FBI ID to talk to some people at Keystone Airlines and one of them recognized your picture after I emailed it to him. My girlfriend also recognized you when I showed her your picture after you broke into my place. I haven't told anyone who you are because we have a common interest."

He says, "Yeah, we both want Paris."

"That's true. The difference is that you want him dead and I'd be happy to see him rot in jail for the rest of his life."

He says, "You and I both know that's not going to happen. Paris is far too smart for that and he's already beat the cops half a dozen times. On top of that, the Feds are protecting him. I've been trying to track him down for months, but he's got homes all over the world. He's never in one place for more than a couple of weeks at a time, which makes it nearly impossible to find him. So, why don't you just tell me where he is and I'll make the problem go away."

"I don't know where he is, and neither does my friend, Tommy."

He says angrily, "Then what the hell good are you?"

"I don't know where he is right now, but I know exactly where he'll be in a couple of months. I'm thirsty, let's have a drink and talk about it."

He picks up his gun angrily saying, "I don't have time for this."

I say, "As I see it, you don't have time for very much of anything these days. The CIA, DEA, Rio cops, maybe the FBI, and probably Walter Paris are all looking for you. Unless you're very careful, one of those entities is going to catch up with you. Besides, you have a traveling companion that you want to keep safe. You're worried about Belle and it's interfering with your judgement. You really need to think this through."

He holsters the weapon and joins me in the kitchen. I offer him a beer, but he declines.

"I don't drink alcohol anymore, but I'll take a soft drink if you've got one."

I hand him a Coke saying, "I was briefly employed by the same secret agency that you once worked for and I left them for pretty much the same reasons that you did. They wanted me to do things that were unconscionable and I said no. You think that you want to kill Paris, but for the last couple of months, you've gone out of your way not to kill people. You spared Jorge Alda's life when you drugged him and you didn't hurt detective Ruiz when you broke into his apartment. You saved my friend Tommy's life, and you didn't hurt Harley when you tried to sneak in here a few weeks ago. Tonight, you could have easily killed me, but you put your gun down and now we're having a drink together. I suspect that you've killed before, but for some reason you stopped. I'd like to know what's changed. If you answer that question for me, I'll tell you where to find Walter Paris."

"It was Belle," he says, "She asked me not to hurt anyone, including Walter Paris. She said there would always be people like that in the world and that I should let somebody else get him. We argued about it and I lied to her, saying that I'd leave him alone. I can't let this go because there are only a handful of people out there who are good enough to get him. I'm one of them."

I say, "Alright, he's going to be on Block Island this coming New Year's Eve. He meets a few of his cartel friends there every year to lay out plans for the coming months. They'll have some pretty good security people with them, but I'm sure a man of your talents can find a way around them."

He shakes his head and looks at me incredulously saying, "Your conscience doesn't bother you, knowing that I mean to kill him?"

"Mr. Parks, my conscience isn't the issue here, yours is. You're risking a future with someone you love for revenge. Real love is a rare thing sir. Most of us spend a lifetime looking for it. Forget about Walter Paris. You're very resourceful, so take Belle and go somewhere where you can make a good life together."

"I can't do that because I think Paris knows who I am. He will come after me, Belle, and maybe even my ex-wife. I won't let that happen."

"I know that, which is why I won't get in your way."

"Okay," he says, "What can you tell me about Block Island? I've never been there."

"It's about fourteen miles off the coast of mainland Rhode Island. It's also only about thirteen miles from Montauk Point on Long Island, New York. Those two places are probable escape routes, because there are only two ways to get on or off the island — by air or by boat. It has a population of just over a thousand people. It's a close knit community and everybody knows everybody. It would be hard for a stranger to wander around there for very long without someone noticing. For that reason, you'll have to plan some kind of night operation. You'll probably need a single-engine airplane with the registration number blocked out to make this work. There's one located at the Plymouth, Massachusetts Airport in hangar number six. Here are the keys for the hangar and the airplane. I know you're a pilot and that you got a commercial license before you became a Navy Seal."

My guest is completely dumbfounded when he says, "You're a lot more than just a casual bystander in this. Who the hell are you really and where did you get all of that information about Block Island so quickly? You couldn't possibly have known that I was coming here or what I might be planning."

I smile back saying, "No, I didn't know you were coming here. It's like I said earlier, I'm just an interested third party. Anyway, I've got a map of the island that you can have, along with Walter Paris' address. I've marked its location on the map. And with that, I think I've said enough. The rest is up to you. Good luck."

"How do I know that I can trust you?"

I say, "Because I could have told the FBI who you really are and what you're planning. They'd be all over this if they knew about it. A few minutes ago, we decided not to shoot each other and that implies to me that we can trust each other."

He lets out a deep sigh and takes the information and the map that I've provided. He says goodbye and leaves without another word. I would never see the man again. I didn't tell him that I took the plans to kill Walter Paris away from my friend, Tommy. He knew about Walter Paris' place on Block Island because he'd visited him there a couple of times. He also knew about his annual meeting with the cartel members because Walter had casually mentioned it to him once. Tommy and Astrid very nearly carried out their plan. It took a lot of drinks and the threat of exposing them to the police to keep them from going through with it. Now, it was someone else's decision to make, and, although it bothered me a little, I didn't plan on losing any sleep over it.

# CHAPTER 47

### December 31  2315 Hours

### Location: Block Island, Rhode Island

The man known as Richard Hamilton is standing a hundred yards away from Walter Paris' home with a detonator around his neck. He quietly rigged the home with explosives two weeks ago and he's toying with the notion of pushing the button. He's watching Paris through an infrared sniper's scope attached to a fearsome looking rifle. He is reluctant to detonate the blast because the other men in the room have done him no harm. He thought perhaps it would be easier to shoot Paris through the window and avoid any collateral damage. Paris is entertaining four members of the drug cartel and they are the only people in the house. These are bad men and it was once part of his job to eliminate bad people. He can't understand why it is that he's having so much trouble deciding to do this. He knows he doesn't have much time to pull it off and still get away with it. In his frustration, he did not notice the man standing behind him with a shotgun.

A familiar voice says, "Don't move, Ricky. I'd hate to kill a friend."

Hamilton turns around to see his former Navy Seal partner, Sullivan, aiming squarely at his stomach.

"Hello, Sully, I figured you'd be around here somewhere, but I was hoping to get this done before you found me."

Sullivan smiles and says, "I picked you up on the infrared sensors just after you got here. I figured you'd show up when I found the explosives that you set at the house a few days ago. I left them in place because you'd know that we were on to you if I removed them."

Hamilton asks, "So, you're working for Paris again?"

He says, "Well sort of. He figured you'd come looking for him. He hired me for this because I'm one of the few people who know what you really look like. You spent so many years walking around in disguise that I don't think even you know who you really are anymore. Why do you want to take this guy out anyway? He never told me why you were looking for him."

"He had my daughter killed and I couldn't let that go."

"Then why didn't you just do it? You've had more than enough time to shoot him or push that button and blow him up."

"I promised someone I care about that I'd stop killing and this was bothering me. I hesitated and now I'm going to pay for it. Where are the rest of your men? I saw a couple of them earlier."

"Once I saw it was you, Ricky, I told them to take a hike so that I could take care of this personally. I only had two other guys with me and they are boarding a helicopter just down the road."

"Why haven't you killed me yet? The Sully I used to know would have blown my head off without flinching."

"I have two reasons. First, despite our differences, Navy Seals don't kill each other. You could've blown up my car when I tried to kill your girlfriend back in Rio, but you didn't, and I owe you for that. Second, I don't like that son-of-a-bitch Paris either."

Sullivan lowers the shotgun saying, "Do what you have to do Ricky."

"No, I'm done killing people."

Sullivan says, "I sold my soul to the devil a long time ago, but I've always admired your ethics. Paris will have me killed if he finds out that I let you go. Give me the gun and the detonator and I'll take care of it. You got a way off this rock?"

"Yeah. How about you, Sully?"

"You know me. I always have a way out. I'll give you thirty minutes before I blow the place. Now, get the hell out of here."

He relinquishes his weapon and the detonator and he thanks his friend. Hamilton has one last question for Sullivan before leaving the island.

"Sully," he says, "What's your real name? They gave us all fictitious identities when we worked for the Agency to protect our families. We'll never see each other again and I'd like to know who you really are before you go."

Sullivan says, "It's Stevens, Paul Stevens, what's yours?"

He extends his hand and says "My name is Parks, Morgan Parks. It's nice to meet you, Paul."

They give each other a quick wave and both men disappear into the woods. A small single-engine plane lifts off Block Island twenty minutes later. Its pilot looks over his shoulder and watches Walter Paris' home disappear in an enormous explosion. Richard Hamilton is very much relieved. He lands at the Plymouth Airport unnoticed and returns the airplane to the hangar. He gets into his car and drives into the city as if nothing has happened.

# CHAPTER 48

## January 3 1830 Hours

## Location: Brooks Falls, Pennsylvania, Cambridge Lake

I CAN HEAR A CAR pull into my driveway. It is equipped with a set of government plates and my friend, Sam Dorsey, exits the vehicle looking a trifle disgruntled. It's snowing and I don't know if he's unhappy about the weather or if there's something else on his mind. He wipes his feet on the doormat and I invite him in.

"Hello, Sam. You're the last person I expected to see on such a miserable day. What brings you by?"

"You know damn well why I'm here. Someone blew up Walter Paris and a few of his cartel buddies a couple of days ago. I'm guessing that you know who did it."

"That's news to me. When and where did all of this happen?"

"It was at Paris' house on Block Island, a little after midnight on New Year's Day."

"Well, it sure as hell wasn't me. I was having drinks with you and Liz."

"Yes, but I have a sneaking suspicion that you know something about it."

"I have no idea what's going on. What makes you think that I do?"

"Well, my sneaky little friend, you've been keeping me in the dark about a few things, not the least of which was the visit you received from Richard Hamilton. I did some checking and I interviewed a couple of people at Keystone Airlines. I showed them a picture of Hamilton and they identified him. He went by there impersonating an FBI agent asking about you. They gave him your address and I'm pretty sure he came to see you."

"Nobody named Hamilton came to see me, Sam."

He says, "And I suppose it wasn't Hamilton who saved your friend Tommy's life when someone tried to kill him in Boston. The cops up there sent me the ATM surveillance footage and Hamilton was the one who drove the bad guys off. I'm guessing that Walter Paris sent those men after Tommy. I'm thinking that maybe Tommy was looking for a little revenge and he used some of his ex-wife's money to pay for a hit squad. He has contacts with people who could do a job like this. Tell me if I'm getting warm."

"Tommy had nothing to do with it, Sam. He was in Hong Kong flying a trip when it happened. I know that because he called me on New Year's Day to wish me well."

Sam is completely frustrated when he says, "I worked on this case for months, and then the Bureau locks me out when things get interesting. I didn't come here to give you a bad time. I just want to know what's going on."

"Sit down, Sam and I'll tell you what I know. I owe you that much. It's a long story, so how about I get you a drink before we start."

He nods and an hour and three beers later, he's heard most of it. I've saved the best part for last.

Sam says, "I followed everything you've told me, but I still can't see why Hamilton went after Walter Paris."

"The answer to that question is in the box over there in the corner. Take a look at the family photograph sitting on top."

He examines the picture for a few seconds, but he doesn't make the connection until I point it out to him.

"It's an old photo, Sam, but I'm sure you can see the family resemblance."

"Jesus, this guy was Susan Parks' father. No wonder he went after Paris."

"Yeah, but he didn't kill him, Sam. It was an inside job. One of Walter's own men took him out. Kind of ironic, don't you think?"

"And how do you know that?"

"A little birdie told me and I'm not at liberty to divulge a name. I would appreciate it if you pass some of this on to Detective Ruiz down in Rio. And please, let him know that his friend Belle is okay."

Sam says, "I'm glad I wasn't involved in this, Devin. The cop in me wouldn't have let Hamilton go after Paris, but I'm glad it's over and I really don't care who did it. There are no winners in this thing."

"Yeah," I say, "It's a lot like that old Rolling Stones song."

He laughs out loud, and, almost on cue, we both mouth the lyrics to "You Can't Always Get What You Want."

We talk for another hour before he heads for home. I'm left to ponder what has happened on a very cold January night. Jorge Alda and his mother, Lara, are likely living in some remote town as part of the witness protection program. Walter Paris was vaporized in an enormous flash of fire and smoke and they will never see him again. In December, Bob Davenport retired from the CIA and there were no repercussions for his part in the attempted murder of Belle or his association with Walter Paris. The drug cartels lost some key players in the Block Island explosion, but I have no doubt that their organization will recover and that it will soon be business as usual. Sam Dorsey and Duncan Ruiz are both good cops who tried to do the right thing and the bureaucracy cut them out of the loop when they got too close to a truth the higher-ups wanted to bury.

Finally, there's the matter of Richard Hamilton, aka Morgan Parks. He's lost a daughter to murder and I can't even begin to imagine what that has done to him. He served his country and he tried to do the right thing, too. For his trouble, he is now a man without a home and a knight without honor who should have been dubbed a hero. I hope that he can find peace in some far off place because he's earned it. He sent me a message telling me that Belle was pregnant. He went on about how much he looked forward to getting a chance to be a father again. I can only wish them well in my mind because there was no return address.

It's all quite depressing and I feel terrible. The first few weeks after Christmas are always a little disconcerting. The weather is usually less than agreeable, and after the holidays end, there's always a letdown because the joy of the season seems to evaporate. I throw another log on the fire and curl up in the Barcalounger for a short nap. I do not hear the knocking on the front door. I only waken from my slumber when the telephone rings.

"Wake up sleepy head and open the damn door. It's freezing out here."

It's Katherine and she's waving her cellphone at me through the window. There's a whoosh of bitterly cold air when she enters the room.

"What the hell are you doing here?" I ask.

"I was in a blue funk. Tommy took Astrid and the kids skiing. Astrid told me that they're getting married next week in Aspen. I figured it would happen eventually, but I didn't think it would be this soon. For obvious reasons, I'm not going to the wedding. It's awkward because my kids will be there and I won't. I'm also depressed because the holidays are over and I was hoping that you could cheer me up."

"What did you have in mind?"

"Well, as you so correctly pointed out a long time ago, a full-blown public romance is clearly out of the question for any number of very sound reasons. I was sort of hoping we could maybe discreetly do the friends-with-benefits thing every now and then and see how it goes."

"You drove all the way from Boston in a raging snowstorm to tell me that?"

"Actually, I was in Pittsburgh handling a legal case and I rented a car. It still took me half the day to get here in this weather."

"How did you know that I'd even be home?"

"I called your mom before I left and she said you were out here all by yourself. I took a chance that you wouldn't go out in this nasty weather and here I am."

I smile and say, "Well, we'd better get you out of those wet clothes and into bed."

"I'm not sleepy, Devin."

"I'm not either, but I'm sure we'll think of something. Just don't call me Luscious."

"You've been talking to Astrid," she says.

"Yes, she let the cat out of the bag when we were in Rio. But please, I'd rather keep that pet name you have for me just between us."

She kisses me and says, "Well, Luscious, does this mean what I think it means?"

"I think it does. We've put this off for far too long, Kate. It's time that we did something about it. Besides, it's far too cold outside for either of us to be sleeping alone."

The End

## OTHER NOVELS BY DALE BOYD

– CONNECT ONLINE –

Visit the Author @daleboyd.net

Purchase e-books and paperbacks
See photo gallery
Check out Author's blog